AF431091

Improper Queen

Taylor Westwood

Copyright © 2023 by Taylor Westwood

All rights reserved.

No portion of this book may be reproduced in any form without written permission from the publisher or author, except as permitted by U.S. copyright law.

Contents

Chapter One

Lady Liana Monroe sat in the stifling carriage contemplating just how much her life took an unexpected, yet not entirely unwanted, turn. She imagined a simple life with a husband she could tolerate while practicing her magic in secret. Instead, she fell in love with the King of Triaedian and her secretly powerful magic became known to all the key players in this game of power among the royals and elite.

She'd woken peacefully in Damien's bed late in the morning of this warm summer day. And after the difficult night she survived - the magic it required to help Cass birth her baby girl, her resulting panic and magic-fueled race through the woods, and the mercenary holding a knife to her throat – Liana had been more than happy to wake with Damien's comforting arms, and spicy scent enveloping her.

He said he loved her last night. Confessed many things that set her soul aflame with joy.

She had been over the moon at his confessions because she was terrified by the fact that, despite her better judgment, and despite her conviction to stay guarded, she loved him just as deeply. He may have relayed some harsh truths as well. Including her own bias towards all men and her stubbornness to accept everything she truly yearned for but never dreamed of having. That had been most difficult of all to hear because he had been right. Damien offered her everything she ever wanted, and she was too stuck in her own mind to accept him.

Never did she think she'd find love in this kingdom ruled by males. Nor did she think she'd find a male that would cherish her for the being she was, not the power contained within her. Damien loved Liana not because of the unique magic she possessed, but because of who she was.

On an entirely unexpected and unwelcome observation, he said that he suspected her lady's maid - the only woman that showed her the proper love of a mother, who protected her secrets since she was a child, who helped cultivate her magic instead of scolding her for it - was stealing her memories. Liana couldn't believe it, refused to believe it. Phillipa would never steal her memories, nor could she when that kind of magic was far more advanced than a servant should know.

Liana looked to her lady's maid sitting opposite her in the carriage. Phillipa insisted on caring for her and escorting her home after Damien sent word to her parents last night that she was safe and staying at the castle. There was no doubt in Liana's mind that Phillipa loved her, would do everything in her power to protect her, which is why she doubted herself in thinking Phillipa wouldn't steal her memories.

There remained the undoubtedly gaping hole in Liana's memory from when she was a child though. It was this hole that she believed this intrinsic and all-consuming fear of anyone discovering her magic stemmed from. Something clearly happened, and Phillipa was her only lead. She couldn't face it though. Couldn't face it if it was true. If Phillipa took her memories, Liana wasn't sure how she would deal with that.

She knew the woman would have only done it to protect her, to keep her safe from whatever happened, but she was nineteen now, almost twenty in a couple months. Whatever happened, Phillipa should have told her about it by now. She was old enough to know. Old enough to know the trauma that plagued her soul so greatly that her magic forced her to flee the safety of her home for places unknown.

For years she lived in fear. Lived with this nagging whisper of danger lurking around every corner that kept her on edge and hiding her magic from everyone. To think Phillipa held all the answers to this mysterious terror gutted Liana. She didn't want to think of the woman that was more of a mother to her than Lady Monroe as one that hid something so vital from her. And to do it in such an invasive way, to steal her memories, that was unforgivable in mage culture. It was forbidden to use mind magic to take away someone's memories. The punishment for it being death.

Liana forced her eyes toward the older woman. She had aged quite a bit in the past few years, but still held the youthful plumpness to her cheeks. Brown hair grayed at the temples which was twisted into a simple updo. Lines crinkled at the corners of her eyes which Liana watched grow over the years the more the woman laughed at her antics or narrowed her eyes with each glare. She did so more often for the latter. Liana always got herself into less-than-ideal situations that Phillipa didn't agree with but nevertheless, went along with simply to protect her.

It became more difficult to reconcile the woman she knew so well, the one that kissed every scrape and bruise, to the woman that possibly stole her memories. Phillipa was not the type to perform such an unfathomable act. Then again, she would do anything to protect Liana, even protect her from herself as Damien pointed out.

Sensing her stare, Phillipa looked to Liana. "Everything all right, dear?"

Liana rolled her lips inward, not yet ready to confront her, and nodded.

"What happened last night when you ran out after the babe was born?"

Liana didn't want to talk about that either, but it seemed a far less stressful topic. She shrugged and went back to staring out the window, her bare feet pulled up on the bench beside her, leaving the sturdy boots so at odds with her delicate gown on the floor. "I panicked and ran. After my power dwindled, Damien was able to track me. He brought me back to the castle." Purposefully leaving out the bit about the mercenary holding a dagger to her throat, Liana spared the woman the extra worry.

Feeling sweat drip down the hollow of her back, Liana whipped up a breeze to pass through the carriage. Both ladies sighed in relief.

"You seem to have recovered much quicker than the time by the lake," Phillipa pointed out.

"I didn't expend as much but it was still enough to drain me." That time by the lake Liana used so much magic that she was surprised she was still alive. She hadn't even known she was capable of such dramatic feats although she certainly thanked the gods considering it saved Charlotte's and Damien's lives.

"Gods bless," Phillipa praised. "Gods bless the king for finding you as well. I don't dare think of what could have happened to you out there all alone."

Liana glanced out the window to avoid the maid's gaze. When she retold her account of events last night, she left out the part where that mercenary caught up to her. Left out the part where he held a dagger to her throat. Left out how Damien nearly went as feral as a shifter and ripped the man's head off.

She'd heard of vampires devolving into their natural state. A fugue of pure animal instinct on the hunt, an alpha predator, virtually unkillable and with enhanced senses that nothing could outrun. She'd seen that creature last night. Saw Damien as strictly vampire, no trace of the human she so dearly loved left in him as he tore the mercenary's head off as if it were as easy as plucking a leaf from a tree.

The gore of it had her stomach turning once more and she took a few deep breaths to calm herself. To think Damien was capable of such brutal acts fit more with the persona she knew before meeting him. Rumors touted him as a ruthless king but in all her time spent with him, she found him to be kind and cunning. Last night showed her just how little she truly knew of the king, or how little he decided to show her.

"What has you thinking so hard, dear?" Phillipa questioned.

Liana smoothed out her features, relaxing her furrowed brows. "Phillipa, do you think I'm a fool for loving the king?"

Her maid startled. "Why ever would you think that? He is an honorable man and ruler to our kingdom."

Liana picked at her nails. "I hardly know him."

Phillipa scoffed. "You've spent nearly two months at his side. You should know him very well by now."

"But what if he is only showing me what I want to see? What if he is playing a role so that I will fall in love with him?"

Phillipa's face went red and her lips pursed before she sat forward to grab Liana's hands. A hand cupped her chin to force her to look into her maid's furious face. "I have watched you grow up, Liana and I have watched as you've done reckless and foolish things. But I will not let you make such an idiotic mistake again. That man loves you with every beat of his heart and wants to marry you. Stop being so suspicious. And while you're at it, stop thinking the worst of males, as I'm sure you've realized by now, that not all of them are power-hungry bastards."

It was on the tip of her tongue to lash out at her maid, to accuse her of making her this way, for taking her memories away and hiding the truth. Liana bit it back though. The last thing she wanted to do was hurt the one person she coveted the most in her family. Phillipa would be hurt if Liana said such things, she knew that much for sure.

Liana pulled out of her grip and sat back on the carriage seat and turned her flushed face into the breeze.

"Perhaps you are right. Damien said as much to me last night as well."

It had been difficult to hear when he spoke the truth. He had been playing a role to win her over, but only because she was so biased and damaged that she wouldn't have accepted him in his true form. Instead, he pretended to be the exact thing she despised, a man after her power, just so he could get close to her without her suspicions always getting between them. He presented himself in a lie just so he could get close enough to her to reveal the truth of his feelings because that was what she needed in that moment, and that was the most eye-opening act of love Liana could have ever imagined. He understood her from the moment they met and still pursued her in a way that she would be receptive.

She fidgeted with her dress as she thought about what that also implied. His love made her heart soar, but the truth of how he had to go about revealing it said more about her character than she cared to admit. Was she truly so biased and prejudiced when in fact, she prided herself on being the exact opposite? She held so tightly to her belief that males think themselves superior to women that she nearly missed out on her chance at happiness.

In truth, she did judge the high-society males as a whole. At least the mage males to be certain and she never encountered the vampires or shifters much to know them. The majority of the high-society mage males were stuck in the ways of the old when women were used as nothing more than property to be bartered. But surely not all mage males were alike, just as she was unlike the other high society females.

Damien spouted a lot of truth to her last night, and she worried that she had only scratched the surface of what it all meant for her and the future.

Phillipa moved beside her on the bench and took her hands more gently. "Sweetheart, this world has been rough on you. It is only natural that you are guarded, as you should still be, but not with the male that has offered his heart to you. Let yourself be happy."

She nodded. Her heart knew she wanted Damien, but her head and her magic kept telling her not to trust anyone. "I will try to be happy, Phillipa," she said on a sigh. "I will try." And that was the best she could offer at that moment.

Phillipa nodded, patting her hand in comfort. She paused, feeling the sharp sting of Liana's new ring. "This is quite a beautiful piece."

Liana gazed at the sparkling emerald Damien gifted her as an engagement gift. "It is. I am not used to its weight yet."

"He certainly favors you in emeralds. This will match nicely with the necklace he gifted you for the ball. In fact," Phillipa said, looking more closely at the ring, turning and twisting it upon Liana's finger. "The gold is the same, as is the design. I wonder if he acquired them at the same time."

Liana thought the ring looked similar to the necklace, although she did not compare since it had been stashed away for safekeeping in her father's safe. The ring sparkled in the sunlight streaming through the carriage window and she wondered if Damien did buy them together. He said last night that he loved her since the night they met, and that he planned on marrying her from the very beginning. There was something far more special knowing he bought the ring with love in mind rather than obligation.

A smile bloomed on her lips as a blush singed her cheeks. She loved the idea of him loving her. It was all she secretly wanted. Far more than her privacy and to practice magic, she wanted true love. Someone to love her unconditionally. A love that would not imprison her, nor suffocate her desires but encourage and support all that she wanted. Damien was that someone and if she would finally let herself believe that, she'd be happy.

"Oh, my dear. I'm so excited for you." Phillipa gushed, seeing Liana's radiant smile.

"Damien told me this morning that he will announce our engagement at the end-of-season ball."

Phillipa smiled as Liana reminisced of her dreamy morning.

When she woke in his arms earlier, she'd never felt so safe. She'd laid still as she basked in the warmth of him cuddled behind her. Took her time soaking in the feel of his muscular arm holding her so tightly as if she might run away. The scent of his herbed soap that was so uniquely him and perfect. His chest rose and fell evenly, moving her body with it. In that moment, she didn't want to move. She didn't want to face the reality of the day and break the serenity she found with this man.

He did wake eventually though. His arm had tightened around her, and he buried his face in her neck to breathe her in deeply before kissing the skin just below her ear. Even now, she shivered remembering his lips on her. That vampire knew exactly how to rile her and sometimes, when he riled her in that way, she didn't mind it at all.

Neither of them were eager to leave bed this morning, which is when they started discussing what they didn't want to do today. Top of the list for her was facing the world. Top of the list for him was letting her go. She found it all incredibly sweet, until he said that he would have his scribe start drafting letters to tell the kingdom of their engagement after the official announcement. He had to calm her down after that because it brought back her fears... new fears of becoming queen and being the center of attention.

Liana looked to her maid. Despite the suspicion and unanswered questions, Liana felt she could trust Phillipa especially since she needed her the most right now. "You will move with me to the castle when I am married, won't you?"

"Of course, my dear. I go wherever you go," Phillipa implored.

Relief filled her stiff limbs. Her future hung dauntingly before her, but she knew that with Damien and Phillipa at her side, she'd be able to bear it all.

Chapter Two

No one questioned her when she returned home, although Charlotte and Hannah did linger around her bedroom while they all either read or knitted in silence. They didn't talk about last night, nor did they say anything which was quite a rarity for them both. Liana found it oddly relaxing to be near them. Normally she'd hide in her room or on her balcony. Now though, their presence soothed rather than irritated.

Her peace didn't last long though considering they had yet another dinner to attend tonight.

The Monroe sisters stood side by side, Liana in the middle as always, in the foyer of Lord Dietrich's home while the men shook hands. Their father greeted their host first, followed by William.

"It is a pleasure to host you and your family tonight, Lord Monroe."

"We are most appreciative of the invitation," her father replied.

Lord Dietrich gave the youngest boys a quick nod hello before bowing to the ladies. He went a step further and took Hannah's hand to place a gentle kiss upon it.

Hannah blushed prettily.

"Always a pleasure to see you, Lady Hannah."

"Same to you, my Lord."

Liana envied the way her sister's lilting voice sounded so effortless and soft. She knew the other ladies admired that, and the male mages absolutely admired it. But, she supposed she didn't need to be jealous anymore. Her male was not a mage and he seemed to like her just as well.

"Let us all move to the den," Lord Dietrich guided, never letting go of Hannah's hand.

Sat in their respective seats, the servants arrived with the plated food.

Liana's mind strayed to her private morning with Damien, the stolen touches and brief kisses an unmarried mage female was not allowed to experience. She loved the way she felt in his arms, as if she were special and treasured.

"Lady Liana?" Lord Dietrich questioned which had Liana's mind spinning.

"I apologize, my Lord, what did you ask?"

He gave an indulgent chuckle. "I asked how your courtship with the King was progressing."

She blushed thinking about their king. "Quite well, Lord Dietrich, thank you for asking." Thankfully, the rest of her family kept quiet about the engagement as they were asked to do. Liana didn't think her mother capable of keeping such a juicy secret, however, Damien asked specifically that no one breathed a word of it yet.

"I do wish you the best of luck. It would be a mighty triumph for the mage community to have a mage claim a royal seat for the first time in all of Triaedian's history."

Liana's heart skipped several beats. She had not thought of it that way before, had not entertained the idea that she would be the first mage to sit on the throne of Triaedian. If she weren't nervous already, she'd just found a new thing to worry about. The pressure and expectation of that title was too much to bear right now.

Clearing her throat, she gave a polite smile. "It would be an honor to represent the mage community if the King decides to choose me for his bride." That was the farthest thing from the truth though for Liana despised most of the mage community, the males anyway, and the gossip-mongers.

"Yes, what an accomplishment that would be," Lord Dietrich reiterated.

Liana covered her sneer by sipping on her glass of wine, because of course marrying a kind and loving man was something to be worshiped as political gain instead of a sacred union between two souls. Liana couldn't help but wonder when it all went wrong for the mage. The shifters and vampires outgrew the ideal of patriarchy generations ago. While she was sure there were still power-hungry politicians, their females were at least valued equally among the males. Most of their marriages were founded on true bonds rather than societal expectations.

She glanced at Charlotte across the table. Her eldest sister sat primly upon her chair while she took delicate bites of the tender roast. Primed to the very marrow in her bones, Charlotte was everything a mage male could ask for; intelligent but quiet, beautiful, proper, and came from a powerful family. Hannah was quite the same but far more delicate.

It saddened her to no end to look at her suppressed sisters. Hannah didn't seem to notice as she stared glossy-eyed at Lord Dietrich, convinced she loved the man. Charlotte, with her cunning mind hid her intelligence behind lowered eyes.

All three Monroe sisters were expected to marry for gain. Liana could only pray to the goddesses for thanks that she found someone beyond that.

She didn't pay much attention to the conversation so when Lord Dietrich stood, she looked around, confusion marring her brow. He held his glass up and looked toward Hannah.

"My dearest Hannah. You are beautiful beyond words and the sweetest girl I've ever met. Your father has granted me the honor to claim your hand in marriage. You will do me the greatest honor by becoming my wife."

Tears sprang into Hannah's eyes. "It is such an honor to hear, Lord Dietrich. I eagerly await our nuptials."

He lifted his glass into the air, a broad smile across his face. "You've made me incredibly happy."

Liana could only think that at least Dietrich's proposal was a bit more heart-felt compared to Ranville's for Charlotte, not that the female is asked her opinion on the matter and is simply expected to accept. Liana had been unconscious at the time of Ranville's proposal, but her sisters told her that Ranville asked their father for her hand in marriage then told Charlotte they were betrothed once she'd recovered from being shot in the chest with an arrow. Her eldest sister deserved far better than Ranville even if Charlotte had pursued him from the beginning.

Lady Monroe cheered and clapped her hands together as tears fell down her face. "Oh, how wonderful! My youngest daughter is getting married, to a Lord no less!"

Everyone raised their glasses in cheers to the couple.

After dinner, drinks were served in the sitting room and conversation was consumed with talks of their wedding. Lady Monroe became far too preoccupied guessing at what everyone else would be doing for their ceremonies because the wedding season would be upon them as soon as the courting season officially came to an end in a week. One more ball and the torture would end. Until next year at least.

Yet, a new and worse form of torture would ensue where the ladies would gossip endlessly about wedding decor, wedding guests, wedding attire, and anything else wedding related. Different instrument, same tune, she thought.

By the end of the night, Liana itched to get home and out of the formal gown then curl up in bed with a novel. And when she finally did just that, she stared at the emerald upon her finger, fire dancing in the exquisite cut.

Simply thinking of Damien had her heart flipping in her chest. She craved to feel his arms around her once more like how they slept the previous night.

She jumped out of bed and ripped a small piece of parchment before writing a short message. With a simple spell, the parchment disappeared, going directly to Damien. She jumped back into bed, a smile permanently etched there and her mind unwilling to focus on her novel. When he slipped through her balcony door a few minutes later, she wasn't all that surprised either.

Sitting up, she raised a brow and cast a silencing spell around her room. "You shouldn't be in my bedroom, Your Majesty." A smirk kicked up the side of his mouth. They both found it amusing when she teased him with his title.

"And you shouldn't leave your door unlocked," he countered as he swaggered up to her bed. He sat on the edge, bringing their faces far too close. She drank in his features as if it had been months since they'd last seen each other.

"I didn't mean for you to come here with that letter," she admitted.

"You said you'd dream of being in my arms tonight. I told you I'd do whatever it takes to make your dreams a reality."

She chuckled derisively. "I don't recall those words ever passing your lips before. Besides, that was far too romantic to have come out of your mouth."

He smirked, a challenge glinting in his eyes. "I am the most romantic vampire alive."

"No, you're just the only one powerful enough to force people to believe that."

"I cannot force you to do anything, my tempting vixen." He leaned in as if to kiss her but held back.

An odd sense of pride filled her at his restraint and teasing. He did this for her. He was hers to love and indulge in. "True, my king. But *you* will do whatever *I* say."

His nose brushed against hers as he tilted his head. "Anything, my queen."

She pressed her lips to his in a tender kiss. She kept it chaste then shifted so he could lay beside her on the narrow bed while she stayed beneath the thin sheet. He stretched his long body beside hers on his back and she snuggled into his side, her head resting on his chest.

With a contented sigh, her mind finally quieted and her eyes drifted closed.

"How was the rest of your day?" he asked, his voice quiet.

"We went to dinner at Lord Dietrich's. He is now engaged to Hannah."

"That is happy news. Why do you sound so forlorn?"

"I am not forlorn. Perhaps unenthusiastic is a better description." She breathed deeply, his familiar scent calming her even more. "I want Hannah to be happy but she is marrying as she always expected to."

"Did she say she was unhappy with her fiancé?" His fingers trailed back and forth along her arm.

"No. She seemed like a fool in love."

"Are you not a fool in love?" he challenged.

Tilting her head up, she opened her eyes to glare at him. "I am no fool." She said nothing about the love part. She told him last night that she loved him, but that was a topic she'd yet to mull over and truly understand. If being in love felt like it did in this moment with him, to feel cherished in his arms and that every word she said mattered, then she was in it deeply.

He raised a questioning brow. "Then why do you say it as if anyone that is in love is a fool? Why are you skeptical that she is not happy?"

"Because she is falling right into what is expected of her. She is marrying a Lord on the mage council and will be pregnant in no time."

He chuckled at her dramatics then sighed, getting serious once more. "As truthful as that may be, who is to say Hannah is not happy with everything? Perhaps she loves the lord and is content with her life." Liana huffed in annoyance at his logic. "Not everyone is as rebellious as you, Liana. Most just want to create a stable and safe life, and those of us in the upper classes are privileged enough to seek out wealth as well. Hannah is creating her safe and wealthy life which is what will make her happy."

Liana lifted herself up on one arm to look at him, the other arm resting over his chest. "You mean to tell me that these mage females deluded themselves into thinking that they want a life shackled to a man without any say in how things are done?"

He frowned. "You are so harsh sometimes, my little mage," he observed, the nickname taking a bit of the sting out of his observation. "All I am attempting to say is that they know the way of this world, the way of mage culture, and in order to have a decent life, they create whatever happiness they can. For most, that means an easy life where food and security are guaranteed, like with Hannah and Dietrich. He will provide for her the life she was always taught to expect."

Liana stared at this intelligent vampire. She couldn't say he was wrong in his observations, but she wouldn't say he was exactly right either. She was raised in the same household with the same ideals, yet here she lay with a vampire for a groom.

"I see your point, but that would never be me. I would never delude myself into thinking I would have been happy with Keeper Olivier even if he were the safe and stable choice."

Damien smirked. "I nearly forgot about him. What ever came of your courtship?"

Liana rolled her eyes. "He never spoke to me again after the afternoon tea by the lake. I believe he might have sent a letter to my father to rescind his offer of courting."

"Better for him anyway, he didn't stand a chance against me."

Liana snorted. "He was the only option before you forced me to accept your proposal."

That damn cocky brow of his rose once more. "Did we not agree just minutes ago that I cannot force you to do anything? You accepted of your own free will because of how enamored you were with me."

She rolled her lips to hide her smile. "Hardly. The thought of being Queen of Triaedian was too good to pass up."

His laugh shook the entire bed before he rolled them onto their sides and wrapped his arms around her. "You are many things Liana, but greedy for the throne is certainly not one of them."

Sighing, she buried her face in his chest once more, her arms curled against him. "Not at all. If it means keeping you for the rest of my life however, then I'll take the job."

Damien kissed the top of her head. "I'm yours, my love, with or without the crown."

Liana smiled, her entire body relaxed. "Will you stay until I fall asleep?"

"Of course, my little mage."

Chapter Three

Chatter in the ballroom of Sancta Valles Castle boasted of lively conversations and too much wine. The energy in the room felt less of desperation this time and more of resignation, at least for some, while others boasted excitement. It was far louder than the previous ball as well, likely due to the celebrations of many marriage announcements. There would be one major announcement tonight as well.

There had been some speculation over the past week that the king had narrowed his decision down to the vampire female or the mage considering he hadn't been seen with the shifter girl in weeks. He hadn't exactly been seen with Yvonne, the vampire female, either, but the gossip didn't pay much attention to facts.

At her mother's insistence, Liana dressed in her finest white silk gown with silver beaded accents along the bust and trim of the skirts. Phillipa constructed her hair into an elegant updo with jewels fastened into the ringlets and braids. She stood nervously with her parents in the ballroom they were all becoming familiar with. Hannah and Charlotte were off with their fiancés, showing off their matches to the rest of the elite mage community. Wesley disappeared early on, no doubt indulging in too much wine with his old mage school friends.

Carlisle and William snuck off the moment they arrived, not that Lady Monroe paid them much attention as she was so focused on Liana. She knew of her betrothal yet still worried, over what, Liana didn't much care. Probably about putting on a proper show for all to see when Damien officially announced their engagement. All of the castle servants knew at this point considering all the wedding preparations that were already underway. It was a miracle they hadn't let the news slip to the rest of Triaedian yet.

She sighed as she searched for Damien once more in the crowded ballroom. They'd already been here an hour. If he didn't show up soon, she'd send a tracking spell after him and hide with him wherever he was in this massive castle. After the last ball, when he left her waiting all night, she would curse him to the gods if he did so again, especially since it was his idea to officially announce their engagement tonight. She'd just as soon not tell anyone and elope.

"She looks rather proud for someone that did not get engaged. And what style of dress is that?" Her mother's voice snapped her out of her distress. Liana followed her mother's gaze to find Yvonne. The tall vampire wore a gorgeous navy gown that complimented her light skin and blonde hair but was very out of fashion from what the other ladies wore. Made of Chimerion silk that was as smooth as glass and shimmered with every breath, her gown was elegant yet much thinner and lighter than the norm.

"I quite admire her gown. I wish mine were similar," Liana admitted without hesitation. It looked so light and airy compared to the heavy gossamer of her own.

Lady Monroe didn't mince her gasp which had a passing couple startled so much that they stopped. Liana's jaw nearly dropped when she realized it was Keeper Olivier with a young girl on his arm. The man had been the furthest thing from her mind in these past weeks but she had to admit that he looked rather refreshed compared to the last time she saw him at tea. It likely had to do with the pretty young girl on his arm. Liana knew of her, of course. It was Miss Marie Vankirk from the temple. Her father was the priest for all the upper class mage in Sancta Valles. Despite the age gap, they seemed quite a good match for each other.

"Liana, do not say such things aloud. You know those vampires can hear everything." Lady Monroe attempted to whisper her misgivings but that was not something her voice was capable of.

Barely refrained from rolling her eyes, Liana grabbed a goblet of wine from a passing servant to gulp it down. "I'm going for a walk." She had to get out of there before the stares and whispers suffocated her.

Before she could even take a step, she felt him. Magic stirred beneath her skin alerting her to his presence even though she couldn't see him. It felt... happy. It was an odd thing to feel from her magic. She couldn't quite understand it considering all she ever felt when around people was fear and worry. The hairs on the back of her neck stood on end then his hand was at her elbow and his breath brushed against her ear.

"Walk with me," he whispered.

Liana let him lead her toward the dais, her mind so occupied with the extreme contentment of her magic that she did not notice the ballroom fall into a hush the farther they walked. Like an innocent child, her magic skipped with joy at his arrival and still tittered excitedly.

When he led her up onto the dais, all happiness fled while she stood in front of every elite member in Sancta Valles. A mixture of confused and concerned faces looked back at the pair. Liana watched as they caught sight of their linked hands, their countenances falling into shock.

"Good evening," Damien called to the room, his deep voice carrying over the crowd. "Thank you all for joining us this evening to celebrate the end of another successful courting season. May I congratulate you all on your matches and wish you long, peaceful and fruitful marriages. A toast," Damien offered, then a servant appeared with two goblets which Damien had to hand first to Liana because it seemed as though she forgot how to move, let alone breathe.

There would be no going back now. The entirety of Triaedian would know of their engagement by the end of the night after the mages sent messages to every corner of their kingdom.

Damien held his goblet aloft, his other hand still in a death grip with Liana's. "To all the happy couples."

Liana thought it might have been more apt to leave out the happy part, considering some people weren't entirely pleased with their matches, but she chugged down her wine anyway.

"And for my closing remarks on this season, I must say it was a surprise. When I offered to host this season, I held no ambitions to seek a wife." He looked back at her, mischief in his eyes. A bit of magic slipped out to zap his hand in a bit of warning. He merely smirked and held on tighter. "And then I met the lovely Lady Liana Monroe and knew I must participate this year. There are so many beautiful and elegant young women in our wonderful kingdom and I courted three of the finest. In the end though, only one stole my heart."

Liana attempted to keep the scowl off her face when she looked at Damien. She truly wondered who stood beside her because the king she knew would never declare such sappy sentiments to his people. Her fiancé smiled at the crowd.

"Allow me to introduce my fiancé, your future queen, Lady Liana Monroe."

Hardly anyone breathed, the room entirely silent and still except for Lady Monroe who examined everyone's reactions.

A few jaws dropped, still disbelieving.

Palms sweating, Liana felt her magic reacting in kind, preparing to protect her, to aid her in escape or whatever else she needed to relieve her of these nerves.

Someone stepped forward out of the corner of her eye and an invisible shield immediately went around her and Damien. He glanced at her, feeling the shift of magic in the air.

"I've got you," he whispered.

"Cheers to the king and future queen!" Damien's father called to the room, walking further into her line of sight. Relaxing, she released the shield and gulped more wine. A polite round of applause sounded through the room before the orchestra started to play.

Damien walked her off the dais, a servant taking their goblets, onto the smooth gray stone and right into the dance. She followed his lead, her body functioning on memory alone.

"You are stunning, my love," he said, not bothering to lower his voice or request a privacy shield. Liana erected one with a frown.

"Why are you..."

He cut her off, "No shield. Drop it." His lips barely moved, a smirk plastered to his face. Hesitating, she inspected him closer, his behavior so unusual, and finally noticed the tension around his eyes. She dropped the shield, his shoulders dropping with it. Letting go of his hands, they spun around only to come right back together.

"And such an elegant dancer," he complimented.

Liana smiled in return sensing something off in the moment. Too focused on not tripping over the voluminous skirts of her dress in front of the entire ballroom, she couldn't puzzle it together. So, she kept up the charade of being a proper mage female in high-society and danced with a deferring tilt of her head toward Damien. Soon enough, more joined them in their dance until all the new couples twirled and stepped around them.

When the music trailed into the next dance, Damien pulled her close and tipped her chin up.

"Look at me, my love. I have no wish to stare at the top of your head for the rest of the evening."

"Oh, but what a pretty head it is," she retorted. "Phillipa put a lot of magic into this hair."

A genuine smile bloomed upon his lips. "I shall thank her for such a lovely view then."

The song called for them to switch partners for a series of steps. As they returned to each other, the moment their hands touched, her magic surged with joy once more. Liana couldn't help the smile it caused even if she found it so odd. If she had any doubts over Damien, they were becoming much harder to recall, especially in light of her magic's acceptance of him. Never had her magic felt so calm, or even at peace. It certainly had never been happy.

"You are radiant, my love. I must be good for you."

A laugh bubbled up her throat. "For the first time, my king, I cannot disagree with you."

His hand tightened upon hers in a brief flash of surprise. "No deprecating comment to follow?" That damned brow of his rose and all she wanted to do was kiss him.

They switched partners again, her magic dimming but still content.

Reaching for him once more, she nearly collapsed into his arms, begging to be held by him in a manner that would be uncouth for fiancés in the mage community.

"None at all. You make me happy," she admitted since he seemed uncaring of who heard their conversation.

Eyes softening, he held her close for the briefest of moments before spinning her out then back in. "I'm sorry to have missed the last ball. If a bit of dancing was all it took to make you see how much you adore me, I never would have missed it."

Laughing, Liana had forgotten and remained completely unaware of the attention they still held over the entire room. Even those dancing watched their exchange.

"So sure of yourself all the time, my king. It is quite adorable."

"Adorable is not a word often used to describe me." He accentuated his point with a frown which only had her smile widening.

"Truly? I do not see why. You are adorable."

His lips peeled back in displeasure. "I'd pummel anyone else for teasing me as such."

The poor shifter girl that switched partners with Liana just then looked terrified to be dancing with the king, especially after the comment she overheard. Liana gracefully stepped into the shifter male's awaiting hands for a sequence of steps.

"Good evening, Sir," she greeted.

He glanced nervously at his new bride. "Good evening, my Lady. I do hope you and the king are having a wonderful evening."

She beamed. "The best evening, thank you."

She returned to her king, still thoroughly entertained by it all. "I believe we left off on you making threats. So vicious and adorable you are, my king."

He raised a haughty brow. "You are going to ruin my entire reputation in a matter of minutes."

"Me? Surely not. I could never have the power to do such a thing."

Instead of laughing as she intended, his brows furrowed. He stopped moving, the dance forgotten. One hand reached up to tuck an unruly curl back behind her ear. "You have all the power, my love."

Liana stilled, staring into icy blue eyes. There was no teasing now and an uncomfortable sense of panic creeped up on her. She did not want all the power, no matter the situation. Stepping back to keep the distance between them proper, she gave him a quick curtsy.

"Thank you for the dances, Your Highness. Shall we retire for a moment to rest our feet?" She didn't want to stop dancing, but she did want this private conversation to stop being so public. The only thing she ever wanted was to be sequestered away in a private room with Damien where life could not interfere.

Damien slowly returned to his kingly self, his shoulders pulling back, face going blank, before holding out a hand to her. She took it, her magic happy once more despite her own turmoil while he led her toward a circular table where his parents sat.

Damien held her chair out for her to sit then claimed his own, all four of them on one-half of the table so that they faced the room, only servants and guards at their backs. A plate was set before Liana which she gratefully dug into.

"Such a lovely ball, Son," High Lady Evangeline commented.

"Yes, excellent job," High Lord Ramone added.

Liana felt the tense atmosphere but didn't dare comment further. Despite their light-hearted interlude while dancing, Liana knew there was something else going on tonight and as the night wore on, she noticed it far more.

They mingled and met with the entire ballroom by the end of the night. They suffered through endless, heartfelt yet completely false congratulations on their engagement from the mage and a range of sentiments from the vampires and shifters. The mage offered dramatic smiles and enthusiasm, especially toward Liana. The vampires seemed more upset by their union than most, perhaps because their own female vampire did not win the heart of their king. While the shifters seemed indifferent or disappointed but still polite.

Through it all, Damien responded just as she imagined his kingly-self would. He took everything in stride but didn't hold back on the hostility when he felt like giving it out to any that didn't offer their full support. Nor did he hold back on blunt truths when someone brought up topics of the kingdom. He didn't brush them off, merely dealt with it efficiently and directly before moving on. This was a side of him she hadn't fully experienced yet, not that it changed her mind at all, but it did shift some perspective. Even Eva and Ramone stood by their side giving off the same air of disdain and confidence.

It felt as though they were all putting on a show for the masses. And perhaps they were. Perhaps they always were. Royalty after all were constantly under the public eye, held to much higher standards, or at least, suffered more gossip than most. Any sign of weakness on their part would leave them open to threats and ridicule. It was no wonder that Damien acted the way he did tonight. It was his role as king.

That still left her wondering as to why he did not want her to have a shield up to hide

their conversation or why he spoke so freely of love and adoring her.

Nearing the end of the night, they bid goodnight to those that bothered to stop before leaving. She remained with Damien and his parents, her siblings and parents sitting at a table nearby, their matches already gone for the evening.

Finally, Liana erected a privacy shield once the last patron left.

She turned to Damien immediately. He slung off his crown, the heavy metal clanking noisily upon the wooden table and ripped his jacket off.

"I can feel your magic and your ire, Liana. I do not wish to get into this tonight." He let out a heavy sigh and collapsed into a chair, knocking back a goblet of wine. He motioned for a servant. "Blood," was all he said. The servant took the goblet and disappeared with vampiric speed.

"I am not angry, Damien. I am merely curious. And do not dismiss me as nothing more than a nuisance, not after tonight, not ever."

Sighing, he slumped in the chair. Combing his hands through his hair, he stood once more and pulled her into an embrace. "I am sorry, my love. I am exhausted and dreadfully thirsty. What are you curious about?"

After savoring his closeness, she stepped back to think more clearly. "It can wait. Clearly, you need rest more than I need answers."

"No, I am fine. What are your questions?"

She felt more of a burden than anything and refused to make herself more of one. She'd figure everything out on her own anyway.

"Nothing. We can talk tomorrow."

The servant returned with the goblet on a tray, filled with nearly black liquid inside. She knew it was blood. Even still, as he reached for it and gulped it down in three swallows, she did not look away.

"Completely renewed. Talk to me."

She huffed. "Seriously, Damien. We shall speak tomorrow. Have a good night."

His arms captured her, preventing her from leaving. "Tell me now or I shall sneak into your room tonight."

"That is not the deterrent you think it is. Now I will purposefully hold my tongue." She loved having him sneak into her bedroom and certainly wouldn't prevent him from doing so.

"The pair of you, I swear to the gods," Eva swore at them.

"Son, are you still a fledgling? Do you truly sneak into her bedroom?"

Damien smiled, unashamed. "Climb the trellis to her balcony and all."

Ramone held his taut stomach as he laughed. Eva glared at her husband then her son. "You keep that girl pure until the wedding, Damien. We don't need a scandal on our hands."

Liana buried her red face in his chest while he just laughed. "No need to worry, Mother, I know the rules."

She clucked her tongue. "Coming from the most notorious rule-breaker in the kingdom."

Ramone only laughed harder.

"Liana, what concerns you?" Damien asked, getting serious once more.

"What was tonight all about? Why did you prevent me from using a privacy shield? Why did you let everyone listen to your unneeded declarations of love and sappy sentiments?"

He raised that damned brow. "Sappy sentiments? Did you not enjoy them?"

Stepping back, she planted her hands on her hips. "I don't mind them, but only in private. I see how you are with your people, how you need to act as king which was at odds with how you treated me tonight."

He returned to his seat and slung one arm over the back. "Precisely the point. I wanted everyone to see that with you I am different. I wanted them to see that what we have is real, that we love each other, and it is not just some political plot."

She glanced at his parents, conscious of the fact that he spoke of love so freely, before claiming the seat across from him. "To what end though?"

"To garner more support for your union," Eva interjected.

Liana considered that. The pieces didn't fit though. She hated to admit it, hated that she wasn't as cunning as them. "How and why?"

Damien loosened the buttons at his wrist and began rolling up the sleeves. "We are the first public figures of different species to marry in Triaedian. There have been others, of course, but none quite so influential. Since the inception of Triaedian, the Ashwood line has only married other vampires. For me to deviate, it could be misconstrued in many ways. Most importantly as a move for power."

Her brows furrowed. "I still don't see," she admitted.

"The reason we still have separate councils in a kingdom that is supposed to be unified is

to keep the power balanced between all the species. Even though vampires rule as the monarchs of Triaedian, the other species still have power and influence. That is the only way our kingdom has stayed the somewhat peaceful nation it has been. By taking you, a mage, as my queen, it upsets the balance."

"So, you think the shifters will feel slighted? That they will have lost power?"

Damien shook his head. "Maybe, but the main concern is for the mage. That they will think this is a move to gain more power over them."

Liana opened her mouth to argue but snapped it closed as realization dawned. "They think you will control me and any influence I have over my father and the mage council to promote your agenda."

Damien nodded. "Precisely."

"But I am a female mage. They don't listen to a thing I say."

"Ah, but that is the point, my dear," Ramone started. "They didn't listen to anything you said before. But now you will carry the word of the king. Everyone will listen."

Liana sat back, her mind reeling. "The mage council will not entertain a word I say, even if they think I speak for the king. They would think of me as just a puppet." And it was those words that it truly sunk in. "And that is why our union is such a problem," she said aloud. "Because, instead of our union being of equal power and me fighting for mage interests, you would have control over me and the rest of the mage community, making you more powerful than ever before."

She slumped in her chair just as Damien had.

"However, they do not know you, my love, nor do they understand our relationship. You

would never allow me to use you like that."

Liana frowned at him. "I do not enjoy your teasing right now."

He leaned forward to take her hands in his. "It is only a bit of a jest because you know I am right. You'd never allow it, nor would I ever even entertain the idea." He kissed the back of her hand. "Now, please, do not let this ruin your night. I let them see the truth of our marriage, our love, and that is the end of it. Shall we retire to a billiards room for more drinks and entertainment or would you prefer I escort you home?"

Liana wanted to discuss things further, to puzzle out and plan how to react to such notions about their marriage. He clearly did not want to continue talking. She would fight him on it, but with his parents hovering and her family still lingering at their table, she let it drop. This way she'd have time to think on her own before approaching a conversation everyone else already understood. If there was one thing she hated more than pompous males, it was feeling unintelligent.

She stood, Damien rising with her. "I shall bid you farewell. I am quite tired, as I am sure my family is as well. We will make it home on our own, my king."

His eyes crinkled at the corners at her insinuation of leaving without his aid but he kept his smile in place before kissing her hand again, his lips falling close to the emerald ring he'd given her. "Goodnight then, my love."

Liana ushered her family out, her mind already replaying every moment of their night, analyzing every gesture and word spoken that she could recall. There was far more espionage than she anticipated, far more than she thought herself capable of dealing with. She'd have to catch up quickly if she was going to survive in Damien's world and still keep her independence.

Chapter Four

Liana fidgeted nervously with the emerald upon her finger as Phillipa dressed her in one of her favorite worship gowns. The bright lilac satin complemented the chestnut curls cascading down her back which Phillipa twisted into her hair last night. Half of the curls were pulled back at her temples and twisted into a bun then secured with a lace bow which matched the ruffled lace lining the high neckline and tickled her throat with each breath. Luckily the sleeves on this gown were short and the petticoats kept to a minimum which kept her from suffocating beneath their weight. The lace continued down the center of the bodice to her waist before the sleek skirt draped over her legs. Her favorite detail was the lace lining the bottom edge of the skirt which the seamstress fashioned in a new design straight from the shores of Chimerion which featured a scalloped pattern. Liana loved it.

"The other servants said the whole city is talking about your engagement," Phillipa commented as she helped Liana into her silver slippers.

Liana groaned even as her eyes landed on the decorative poster on her bed which held the official announcement of her engagement to the king. Apparently, it arrived before dawn, hand delivered to all the important families in the city while others were plastered around the city for all to see.

"That was the last thing I needed to hear this morning, Phillipa."

"Oh hush. You knew you couldn't keep it a secret forever. He announced it at the ball last night."

Liana wished they could have at least tried to keep it quiet. But that would have been impossible considering Damien was the king and everyone loved to gossip.

She caught herself on the negative thought and corrected herself in an attempt to be less judgmental as Damien and Phillipa accused her of being. *Most* everyone in high society loved to gossip.

"Are you prepared to face the chatter at worship today?"

Liana sighed and pulled on the delicate lace gloves to match her ensemble then slid her ring back on over the fabric. "I am as ready as can be."

"Don't you take any mind of what they say. Remember that the king loves you and that is all that counts."

Liana nodded as she observed her maid fussing with her gown. She still hadn't found the courage to ask Phillipa about the memories locked away in her mind in the past few days since returning from the castle. In part, she was too scared about what horrors she may reveal. Another part of her didn't want to even believe that her most trusted confidant had been lying to her for years. She was being a coward. She knew that. Yet that fact didn't sway her into acting.

Her bedroom door swung open, Lady Monroe bustling in. "Oh, my dear, you look lovely," Lady Monroe gushed. Hustling over, her mother put an arm around her shoulders to lead her out the door. "I knew this gown would be the right choice for today. All eyes will be on you after the king's announcement. Oh," Lady Monroe squealed before taking Liana's hand in her own. "Your ring is impossible to miss against the white of your gloves. How wonderful, dear. Excellent thinking."

Liana simply smiled at her mother. The gloves went with the gown. She had no ulterior motive in wearing them, although the emerald did seem to sparkle the slightest bit more.

"Come now, the others are waiting for us." Lady Monroe dragged her downstairs to where the rest of her family waited. Charlotte and Hannah in their finest worship gowns as well while the boys all wore their most elaborate coats and boots.

"Everyone must be on their best behavior today. All eyes will be on us after the announcement of your sister's engagement," Lady Monroe instructed the siblings.

"Yes, Hannah must be so excited," Liana interjected facetiously.

Lady Monroe huffed. "We are very excited for Hannah, but you know very well I was talking about you, Liana. Now, we don't want to embarrass the King. You all represent the extended family of the crown and must act as such."

"That means, keep your fingers out of your nose, Carlisle," Liana teased.

Her younger brother stuck his tongue out at her.

"Honestly, Liana, you are going to be queen. Can you not behave for even a moment?" Lady Monroe complained.

"I was merely trying to help, Mama," Liana replied innocently. No one bought her act.

Charlotte laced her arm through Liana's. "Come, sister. Let us walk to the temple," she suggested, then quieter said, "Before Mother finds a way to punish us all for that mouth of yours."

Liana chuckled. "Carlisle is so fun to rile though."

"Perhaps, but Mother is not, and I do not have the energy to deal with her hysterics today."

Liana's lips rolled in as she tried to stifle her laughter.

As they stepped onto the street, Hannah joined on Liana's other side, and she walked arm in arm with her sisters. Before they made it a few steps, two guards fell into place a few paces ahead of them. Liana looked back to find two more trailing the family. She couldn't tell if they were mage, vampire or shifter but they were most definitely Damien's soldiers with their black uniforms and gold insignia.

He hadn't mentioned adding security and there was little to do about it now. After everything that happened in the past few weeks with the rebels, and that mercenary the other night, she was glad for the extra guards.

Once they entered the temple, the guards stayed with them which meant they were mage because only mage were allowed during their worship time. The four guards split up, one sitting directly behind Liana while the others stood around the temple.

Just as before the majority of those in high society didn't mind staring openly as she passed. She'd felt their eyes on her the entire walk to the temple and even now as they settled in their usual seats. Not even the sacred space of the gods kept the others from gossiping.

Liana settled on the bench with her family, Hannah and Charlotte on either side of her.

"The temple at the castle was beautiful," Hannah commented. "Both are worthy of the gods, but I preferred the privacy of the temple at the castle. Did you get a chance to visit while we were there?"

Liana did not get the opportunity to visit the castle's temple during their stay after the attack by the lake. She was unconscious or too weak to attend worship during those days.

"I did not. However, I think I would agree on the privacy part," Liana stated. Everyone stared, not bothering to be discreet about it. She forced her chin high and shoulders back doing her best to ignore it all.

"Can you believe the king picked her over Mistress Yvonne?" a woman said loudly from somewhere behind them. Liana recognized the voice as Mrs. Notting, the mage baker's wife. The woman was as common as they came but was friends with everyone because of the bakery. That meant she had her fingers in everyone's business as well.

"I thought for sure he would pick her or the shifter. What was he thinking picking her? She is so peculiar and disliked. He needs a queen that the people will favor too." Liana knew that voice as well. Lady Sanderson, wife of Lord Sanderson, another mage on the council with her father.

Liana had not yet considered what it would mean for the people to not favor her as queen, to not have their support. If they did not, she couldn't fathom the repercussions although she knew it would make her life as queen far more difficult.

"It is still unseasonably hot for this time of year," Charlotte said loudly in an attempt to drown out the women. Liana paid her no mind, but Hannah played along.

"Quite so, sister," she agreed. "I wish I would have brought a fan with me."

Liana conjured their fans from home and absentmindedly handed them over. Stunned, her sisters said nothing as they took them and began to rapidly cool themselves.

"It's all very odd. I feel sorry for the chaps that bet on it too. No one picked the Monroe girl. There must be a lot of poor men," Mrs. Notting lamented.

All the calm Liana forced herself to feel in preparation for today fled in an instant. How was she supposed to ignore such blatant talk about her? The ladies weren't even trying to be quiet about it. All of it was expected - the stares, the gossiping. But the mention of a bet was too much. They had not even been at the temple for more than a few minutes and already she wanted to run home and hide behind her books. Wanted to hide in her room and never emerge.

People bet on her. Bet on her to lose.

It was one thing for people to fill their time with petty gossip. It was another thing altogether that they purposefully spent money counting on her failure.

Liana had not realized that magic sparked from her fingers until Charlotte placed her palm over Liana's clenched fists.

"Do not listen to them, Liana. They mean nothing. What they say means nothing."

"We both know that's not true. What they say means everything," she whispered. "They are right, no one will respect me as queen. They even bet against me, Charlotte." Liana could hardly stand the humiliation. If it weren't for her family surrounding her, she would have run home.

Damien must have thought of this though in all his scheming. Surely, he took into account that she was not well liked. Did that weigh into his decision to pick her, or did it not matter? Did his love outweigh his reason?

"You must make them respect you," Charlotte declared in a whisper.

Liana paused at her sister's vehemence. "How?"

"That is for you to discover. Although, if I were you, I'd be a queen they couldn't ignore. One that showed up time and again despite their belittlement to be what this kingdom needs... the queen it deserves."

Liana stared unblinkingly at her sister. Gone was the reserved high society girl. In her place sat an intelligent and cunning female. It was a side of Charlotte she'd rarely seen, her intelligence always hidden by an air of nonchalance and deference.

Liana took a deep breath, placing one hand over Charlotte's. "Thank you, sister. Your advice is very wise."

"I'm glad you have finally acknowledged my superior wisdom. Perhaps you will listen to me more often now."

Liana eyed her sister sidelong and found a playful smirk on her lips. "I have never listened to you before. I doubt that I will start now," she teased back.

Charlotte shook her head on a chuckle. "Hush now. The prayers are starting."

Forgetting all about the gossip being whispered around her, Liana smiled as she bowed her head in prayer.

***

After worship, the family took afternoon tea in their garden with Master Ranville, Ms. Jasmine, and Lord Dietrich. The older adults sat at the iron table while the Monroe children and Jasmine sat on a picnic blanket with pillows. Carlisle and William scarfed down their food before running off to play with Lord Dietrich's hound. They had another guest as well, the new mage student on scholarship by the name of Peter Smith.

He was a young man, probably about her age and, unfortunately, had not grown into his lanky height. Lord Monroe mentioned he came to the city for a wife, but he couldn't truly be looking for a wife so young. Most mage males waited well into their twenties or thirties, after they completed schooling. He was not an attractive male, but nor was he unattractive with sun-kissed cheeks and wheat blonde hair. He still had a ways to go to mature into his body which made it a lucky thing that he now focused on school rather than marriage.

"Congratulations on your scholarship, Peter," Lord Dietrich commented. "I remember my days at the school. Some of the fondest memories I have and some of the finest friendships I kept. Make the most of it," he advised.

"Thank you, Sir. It has been an honor to study at the mage school. I am among many talented mage."

"Right you are," he replied, raising his glass to toast.

"Did I hear correctly that you are also in need of congratulations, Lord Dietrich? An engagement to Ms. Hannah Monroe I believe."

Lord Dietrich smiled genuinely toward Hannah who blushed. "Correct again, Peter. The lovely Ms. Hannah will be my wife soon."

"When is the wedding? In fact, when are all the Monroe weddings?" Peter wondered.

Liana hid her eye roll under a long blink as she sipped from her glass of wine. There were plenty of other things to talk about, important things, yet they always spoke of the weddings or relationships.

"With three other Monroe's marrying this year, I decided to wait a few months."

Hannah gazed at him with stars in her eyes. "A winter wedding sounds magical."

Wesley slid his hand into Jasmine's with a smile. "We will marry after Liana and the king. Once their dust settles, we will have our moment in the spotlight."

Liana frowned at her eldest brother who just smirked back. She didn't want to outshine any of her siblings. She'd elope if Damien would agree.

"Master Ranville?" Peter prompted.

"I have not yet set a date for our wedding," he replied blandly. Liana looked to Charlotte who sat serenely beside her. Once they had a private moment alone,

Liana would ask about Charlotte's true feelings toward Ranville considering she always seemed so unaffected by anything he did or said.

"Ms. Liana, what of your wedding? You must be excited," Peter continued.

She gave him a polite smile. "Very excited."

"It is soon, is it not?"

"Yes, just three weeks."

"Fascinating," he replied. "I find it remarkable that you can marry a male of a different breed."

Liana sat a bit straighter at the accusation. "The King," she stressed his title in case he forgot who he spoke of, "is a vampire, but he is also a male just as you are. What is so remarkable about that?"

"Just that we are so different from them. I am surprised you would agree to marry someone that does not have the same values or beliefs."

Liana clenched her fists into her dress to hide any magic that might leak out with her anger. She took a steadying breath to keep a level head as Charlotte always did. If she were to be queen, she better start acting like one. "We worship the same gods. We breathe the same air. We value this kingdom's prosperity. We value each other. What else is there?"

"We do not worship the gods in the same way. Will you worship separately as a result? We have different beliefs on how domestic life should be led, how a home is to be run. Would you not be happier with a mage, a male you've been trained to care for?"

Liana gritted her teeth against the surge of anger coursing through her body. Magic screamed inside her to be let out, to pummel this pompous ass into the ground. Forcing herself to breathe, she glanced away from his irritating face to find Charlotte staring back at her. Her sister gave her a curt nod as if to say, let him have it.

"It is an honor that the king chose to marry our daughter," Lord Monroe interjected.

"How the King and I live our lives is none of your business, Peter. However, I must point out a fallacy in your beliefs. Female mage are not trained to care for male mage, that is not our divine purpose - to be servants to males. We are shackled and suppressed into believing the only thing we are good for is to be a wife and homemaker when in fact we are born with the exact same magic."

"That is the way of the mage, has been for thousands of years. Females are the homemakers. Aside from that though, he is a vampire. He will outlive you. And what of children? I know of no hybrid children. Which is probably for the best, they would not likely be accepted easily into society."

"Peter, you overstep with these questions," Lord Monroe scolded.

"I apologize, Lord Monroe, that was not my intention. I am simply curious. As I am sure most are since there are rarely any interbreed marriages, none that I've ever known."

There were so many things wrong with what he said. But her mind caught on one thing in particular. Her children wouldn't be accepted into society. They would end up just like her, the outcast, the ridiculed. They would suffer alone simply because they did not fit into the norm.

She couldn't help the magic that built inside her. It raged along with her bruised soul. She didn't notice her skin starting to glow.

"Liana," Charlotte said, kneeling in front of her and grabbing onto her hands. She tugged Liana until she stood which gave her enough time to take back control. "Let us go for a walk. The weather is pleasant, and I want to smell the flowers."

Liana glared down at Peter. "You best mind your words, Peter. You sound very close to following separatist ideals," Liana declared before pulling Charlotte with her toward the path. She erected a shield instantly, her guards falling into step behind them. "I'm going to murder that male," Liana growled.

"That would not be wise, sister. Even if you will be queen soon, murder is not an easy offense to acquit even if it is justified."

Caught off guard by her sister's wit, she snorted a laugh and some tension left her. "Justified, indeed."

"What unfortunate manners that boy has. Master Ranville said he could be the next Master based on his aptitude and skill."

"Aptitude for magic only, it appears. He could use more lessons on proper conversation and respect for others."

Charlotte sighed. "That is how a lot of mage men think, Liana"

"The fact that it is true does not mean it is right."

"You don't have to lecture me. I am a female mage too, in case you've forgotten. I understand the oppression just as well as you," she bit out angrily.

Liana sighed. "I am sorry, Charlotte. It makes me so angry that it has been this way for so long. The vampires and shifters do not treat their women this way and I only want that for us as well."

She nodded, her face somber. "Tell me about Master Ranville. Do you love him?" Liana asked. This was as good an opportunity as any to ask.

"Master Ranville is a successful man. He is just and fair."

Liana raised a questioning brow. "I have a privacy shield up, sister. You can tell me the truth. I already know he is successful and rich. Do you even like the man?" Charlotte glanced over their shoulders to where they sat then to her, uncertainty in her eyes. "Charlotte?" she questioned, concerned. "Are you having second thoughts? Do you need help breaking the engagement?"

Charlotte stopped short to face her. "There is nothing to tell, Liana. He is a wonderful man. I am lucky to be marrying him."

Her brows furrowed. "You don't have to be strong for me, sister. You can tell me anything." Gone was the ferocious woman advising her to be a queen, in her place stood a frightened female. "Has he harmed you? Threatened you?" Charlotte shook her head. "What worries you? Is he not to your liking? Perhaps Damien could find you a more suitable match."

Charlotte's lips pursed in anger. "Stop, Liana. Stop meddling. You get to live your fairytale ending but no one else gets that. I've accepted my life, now leave me be." As she turned to leave, Liana grabbed her arm.

"I only meant that vampires treat women better. Damien could help you find a better male. One that would appreciate your intelligence."

"I will not tell you again, Liana. Leave it be. I am marrying Master Ranville. Go back to your castle and stop meddling in my affairs."

Rooted to the spot, Liana could not believe her sister's words, her resentful tone far more concerning and hurtful. Just this morning she was supporting Liana, helping her with her upcoming role only to turn around and smite her for her, albeit unexpected, but nevertheless very good fortune. Liana had no part in making this happen. The king chose her because he loved her for some odd reason or another. Perhaps she was happy though, at least, as happy as she could be to marry despite rebelling against it her entire life.

Damien proved himself to be a ruthless leader but also a kind and gentle man when dealing with her. Charlotte must see that as her fairytale ending, which Liana had to admit, was quite true. But she only wanted that for her sister as well.

Mage males were the issue, so it seemed the most reasonable solution to find a husband that was not a mage. Charlotte clearly wanted nothing to do with that theory though. She couldn't understand why her sister would begrudge her happiness.

Not able to handle any more of this social hour she walked back to the house. No one stopped her. Neither did the guards when she took a dark cloak from the foyer closet and snuck out of the house.

Chapter Five

Liana needed to forget this afternoon and expend some magical energy in the process. It still roiled beneath her skin like a living thing bent on revenge. It wanted to pummel Peter for even suggesting that her children would be outcasts. Liana would never let that happen. If she were blessed with children that is. It was entirely possible that she and Damien could not conceive.

Children were not a dream of hers. She knew she would be expected to have them, but there was no burning desire for them. Until now. Until hypothetical children were no longer possible did she yearn for them. Yearn to protect them from all this terrible world offered. She could picture them. A boy with chestnut hair like her own and bright blue eyes like Damien's. A girl with her green eyes and Damien's black hair falling in ringlets down her back. They would be perfect. They would not be ridiculed or ostracized.

She found herself outside the building for the homeless. So enraptured by her own thoughts she hadn't realized this is where her feet led her. Glancing over her shoulder, she saw only two guards. One she recognized as the one from the night at Cassia's home.

"Stay quiet and stay by the door. They don't trust easily," she informed the vampires before opening the door. They took up positions along the wall, away from the door while she met with Grace.

"What are you doing here, Liana?" she whispered, pulling her into the corner which happened to be close to her guards. Grace looked them up and down sharply. "Who are these two?"

"As I'm sure you've heard, I'm engaged to the king. He insisted on guards."

Grace hummed. "We all heard the news. Congratulations, I suppose."

"Thank you. Now, I'm here to work. I apologize that I missed the last two weeks."

"Do not trouble yourself, girl. Your fiancé sent supplies in your stead."

Liana's jaw nearly dropped. "What do you mean?"

"He showed up with baskets full of food and supplies the night you were supposed to be here last week. We thought something happened to you since you've never missed coming here twice in a row. He said you had been ill and were recovering. You alright?"

"Fine," she answered quickly, still trying to understand what the woman told her. "What did he bring?"

"Everything. Food, clothes, blankets, bandages and salves."

"He did not tell me."

"Well, thank him when you see him next."

"What can I do?"

"Not much. I think there is one injury that could use mending."

"Fine. Take me to it."

"Hold on." Grace pulled Liana's hood further over her face to conceal her identity. Her power was a secret to the kingdom aside from a handful of people now and it needed to stay that way for now because although the list was ever growing, not everyone needed to know about her unusual power.

Liana healed two injuries, both inconsequential and would have healed easily on their own. With magic still coursing through her, she searched for anything she could do. Finally, she saw a pile of dirty, torn fabric heaped into a pile.

"What is all this?"

"Old clothes or blankets. We have the new items, and this stuff isn't worth saving," Grace explained.

Liana disagreed. She started picking carefully through, her magic cleaning each item as she went. Most pieces had multiple patch sites with new holes waiting to be fixed. She summoned the kit she normally brought with her and set to fixing it all. By the time she was done, they had plenty of clothes and blankets to go around.

"If you all don't want them, save them for the next person," Liana explained. Because unfortunately, there would be a next person.

"Thank you, child."

Liana nodded. "Life is not very predictable at the present time. I will try to be here weekly, otherwise, do you still have that parchment I gave you?"

"I do. I'll send word if we need anything."

"Good. I'll see you soon."

Liana left feeling no better than when she arrived. Her magic quieted but still wanted to be used. She was also not ready to go home yet. Which is why she found herself in a seedy pub in a not so gentle part of the city. Keeping the hood in place, she took a seat at a table in a dark corner.

"Sit down. You look suspicious," she demanded of her vampire guards. Reluctantly, they joined her. "A round of ale on the king if someone lends me some coins. I did not bring any money." The male to her right stood.

"I'll get us a round." He was the guard from the other night. Owen, if she recalled correctly. The burly man full of muscle stood taller than anyone else in the pub which made her feel safer because he was far too intimidating for anyone to try anything with them. His shaved head and the jagged scar along the left side of his neck didn't bode well for anyone either.

"What is your name, Sir?" she asked the guard on her left. He looked far more approachable with light blonde hair and calm blue eyes. His muscles were defined but not bulging. Much more reasonable looking.

"Asher, my lady."

"Just Liana, please." He nodded. "Are you typically on guard duty, or do you have a different role as a soldier?"

He leaned back in the chair, an easy air of nonchalance falling over him. "Owen and I are soldiers in the King's army, but we are also his cousin's. We have many roles that fall under our purview, the least of which is being a soldier."

"Cousins?" she exclaimed. They couldn't look farther from family if they tried. They all held the similar build of powerful vampire males yet where Damien was all dark, Asher was all light with a pale, yet tanned complexion, with golden hair and eyes.

"Yes, Owen and I are half brothers. Our mother is sister to High Lady Evangeline."

That was even more of a shock to hear Owen and Asher were brothers. He returned then with three mugs. She took the mug gratefully and sipped.

Nearly gagging, she hid her reaction beneath the hood. "What in the gods is that vile liquid?"

Asher chuckled. "It's pub ale. Nothing else quite like it but somehow the same in every kingdom... shitty."

Liana laughed at his description. "Shitty is correct."

"Yes, but it will get you sloshed faster than anything else." Liana gulped the vile liquid after that statement. "What's a young lady so eager to get drunk for?" Asher wondered and she sighed.

"So many reasons." Not that she wanted to get into any of them. For now, all she wanted to do was drink and forget this day with all its troubles, and that was precisely what she did.

Liana couldn't tell exactly how it happened but one moment she was nervously sitting with her two guards, the next she was shoving the patron on the piano away so she could play something more upbeat. Her fingers weren't as cooperative on the keys, but the song still came out mostly the same. A gentleman appeared beside her with a violin and began to match the tune. At the next song, an accordion joined the fun. Liana laughed and played, having the time of her life. When she looked back at the pub, nobody paid them any mind.

She shoved the piano stool away and set a spell on the piano to keep it going as she hopped up on the stool. "Come on you sad fools, get up and dance!" she yelled at the pub's patrons. Jumping onto the nearest table, the males pulled their drinks safely away from her before she started stomping the steps to the line dance.

To her ecstatic joy, Asher jumped on the table across the room and joined in.

"You heard the lady, dance!" he bellowed, and the music filled the pub, her magic amplifying it while the others slowly started to soften to the beat. A few stood, keeping their moves on the floor.

Liana jumped to the next table, her foot stomping and hands clapping. Someone else jumped onto a nearby table, their steps collectively gaining in strength and adding another instrument to the melody. She jumped to the floor to keep it going.

Liana laughed and yelled with joy as she spun and stepped around the room making sure everyone joined in. As she started the next song on the piano, the others followed accordingly, and they were back to it. At one point she danced along the bar, a few males helping her up then down when the barkeep shooed her off. She grabbed Asher and spun around the pub with him, her mind swirling and thoughts a blur. Song after song they danced, the pub alive with energy that it felt like magic pricking her skin.

"You're glowing!" Asher yelled in her ear over the music.

It took a moment for her to register what he said then struggled to pull her magic back from the surface. It wasn't the pub's energy tingling along her spine, it had been her own. Feeling dizzy after she stopped moving, Liana grabbed onto Asher.

"I need to sit." He led her back to their table where she lay her head down atop her arms. She groaned, the dizziness way worse while looking down. "You were not jesting about the ale," she complained. The chair beside her scraped against the floor far too loudly, making her wince. She expected to find Owen beside her since he disappeared a while ago. Her heart dropped into her stomach when she found glacial eyes glaring at her from beneath a dark hood.

He reclined in the chair although he was anything but relaxed. Shoulders tensed toward his ears, jaw clenched and set, while his fingers were laced together, his elbows resting on the armrests.

"Liana, what are you doing here?" he demanded on a growl. Her magic still kept the music going, everyone sloshed and dancing all over the pub. No one paid them any mind.

She opened her mouth, only nothing came out.

"You know the dangers we face, particularly now with the rebels. If you wanted to get drunk you do it in the safety of your home or the castle."

Disappointment and anger radiated off him in waves. The only reason she was here right now getting drunk was because she didn't want to go home. As she remembered all the reasons why, her lower lip started to wobble, her vision blurred by tears. Charlotte hated her and there was nothing Liana could do about it.

His scowl softened. "Liana?" he worried, which broke her finally. She did find her happy ending. She found Damien. Rather, he found her, but he was perfect. He truly cared for her and let her be the powerful female she yearned to be.

Sobbing into her hands, she barely noticed when he picked her up and walked out of the pub. Face buried in his neck, she clung to him. Clung to her love.

"What happened?" he growled.

Asher answered. "She was upset about something during their tea and left to go to some homeless shelter. Then we came here. That was all."

"What upset her at the tea?"

Asher blew out a heavy breath. "There was a lot to be offended by. I'm not sure which set her off. Maybe the fight with her sister."

The rocking of his fast walk did nothing for her dizziness and as much as she wanted to stay in his arms, she shoved away, nearly falling on her face before Damien righted her. She continued walking without knowing where they were. In a dark alley, she stumbled forward along the cobbled street.

"Liana, stop." She pulled out of Damien's grasp, her tears still falling. "Let me take you home."

"No," she sobbed. "Charlotte hates me. She hates me because of you," she slurred. "You are my fairytale ending and she is stuck with a mage that does not value a single part of her aside from our father's name." Damien righted her as she stumbled into the middle of the street then let go again. "Then you had the audacity to keep secrets from me."

"What secrets?" he demanded, his hand staying on her hips to keep her from falling face first into the street.

"About the homeless shelter. You brought them supplies."

"That was hardly a secret. I never found an appropriate moment to inform you. Nor do I need to inform you of every move I make to support my people and kingdom."

He had a point, but that's not what she focused on now. "There was plenty of time to tell me."

"Fine. I apologize for keeping such a heinous secret from you." She turned on him, falling right into his chest. He caught her easily.

"Do not patronize me, Damien." She shoved off him and righted her dress. To her, her movements seemed quick and caused her dizziness. She doubted they were quick at all though with how blurred her vision became with each movement. He slid his hands through his hair taking a deep breath.

"I apologize. Can we please go home now?"

"No." She started walking again. "The entire city gambled on my future, on your future. They gambled on who you would choose."

He sighed, sliding his hands into his pockets. "I am aware."

She gaped at him. "You knew?" she screeched. He simply shrugged.

"People gamble on everything."

Not able to handle much more right now, she walked away. "Liana, stop. Surely that is not what has you so upset."

She stopped. That was not what had her so upset, it was something else entirely. Something she didn't want to think about but couldn't forget. Damien stood before her now, his eyes probing.

"I wanted to kill him," she admitted through gritted teeth. Damien didn't flinch at the certainty in her tone.

"Who?"

"Peter." Just thinking of him, what he said, had her magic surging to the surface again. Her body glowed, lighting up the alley. Owen and Asher flinched while Damien stood steadily. "I wanted to kill him," she declared with a slash of her hand. A deafening crack filled the alley, the males flinched in unison. In the cobblestones beside them, her magic slashed a clean line.

Damien faced her wrath head on. "Why?"

"He said many things, but I will never forget what he said about our children," she growled.

He blinked slowly, the only sign he heard her. "We may not be able to have children, Liana," he said softly.

She ignored him. "He said they would be different. That they wouldn't be accepted." Her tears fell in earnest again. "No child of mine will suffer like I did, Damien. Do you understand me? Our children will be special, and they will be loved. They will never know what it is like to be different, to be tormented, or to be afraid of their own damned shadow. I'll kill anyone that hurts them," she declared, her fingers dripping with magic.

Damien stared into her glowing eyes. "Agreed, my queen."

Liana nodded and calmed her roiling magic. As soon as it left her, she stumbled. Damien caught her before she hit her knees, right before she vomited everything in her stomach.

Chapter Six

Confusion struck Liana when she woke in her bed. The pounding headache and awful taste in her mouth reminded her of what happened last night but she was uncertain of how she made it back to her house.

Groaning, she rolled over only to be stopped by a warm body. Squinting, the bright light of the day burned her eyes. Still, she could see the handsome vampire reclined beside her.

"How are you feeling, my little mage?" he taunted, knowing full well she did not feel well.

"Why are you here?" she croaked, her throat drier than dust.

"After your overindulgence last night, I stayed to make sure you did not choke on vomit in your sleep." She groaned again, embarrassment coloring her cheeks as she rolled away again.

"I am alive, thank you. You may go."

"Eager to be rid of me, my queen?" His arm slid over her waist, and he pulled her into his body, holding her. She did not comment on how good it felt to be held that way, or how content her magic was in his presence. Didn't want to hear his smug satisfaction either.

"I would rather wallow in my regrets alone."

He chuckled, the sound low and gravely in her ear. "Tell me you at least enjoyed yourself last night. In all my days I do not think I've seen a queen dance on pub tables and bars."

She was glad he could not see her face for how red it flushed. "How long were you there? How much did you see?"

"Oh, my little mage, I saw it all. I arrived just in time to watch you jump onto the first table."

She buried her face into her pillow. She couldn't believe she'd done all that. "How did you find me?" Grabbing the hand that lay over her, she threaded her fingers through his and held it against her chest like a pillow.

"Owen came to me. Said you drank him dry and needed more money to fund your bender."

"Oh gods. I do owe him for all the drinks. I'm not sure how many I had but it must have been a lot."

"I settled your debts, my queen. No need to worry."

She sighed, holding his arm tighter. "You truly are too good to me," she whispered, disbelieving that this vampire, this king cared so much for her that he fetched then tended to her when in need. Her views on men were everything that this man was not. He did not belittle her emotions. He did not silence her in any way. He did not ignore her. He held her tenderly every chance he could and made her feel cherished. Charlotte had been correct in that he was her fairytale ending.

All her life Liana resigned herself to a lackluster life where she had to hide her magic and practice in secret. A life where she catered to a husband and children while her own wants and desires were classified as odd and improper. With Damien though, he supported every odd thing she did.

The tears came quickly, and she could not stop them. His thumb breached her hold and brushed against her cheek.

"Why do you cry, my queen?" She rolled over and buried her face into his chest, clinging to him.

"I am so happy," she admitted.

"Happiness makes you cry?" he questioned. If she could have explained it to him, she would have. For now, she could only feel and perhaps one day she could explain it in words.

Her door swung open, making Damien freeze beneath her. "Rise and shine, Ms. Liana," Phillipa greeted, bursting into her room as she did each morning. She walked to the curtains and flung them wide, letting the light pour in. "You gave us all quite a fright last night. It was lucky that the king sent word that you were safe or else the entire house was going to go searching." She moved to the balcony doors and flung them open. "It smells like a pub in here. And vomit. You need a bath."

Liana sniffled as she sat up. Phillipa finally looked toward her and froze, her eyes going to the king beside her. "What do you think you are doing?" she scolded as she rushed to close and lock the bedroom door. "He should not be in your bed, child!"

Liana shushed her. "I know, Phillipa. I assure you nothing happened. He only ensured that I was well."

"That does not matter. You know you would be ruined if this got out, no matter if you're engaged or not."

Liana sighed. "I know, but I need him right now," she admitted. The maid inspected her red puffy eyes and tear-stained face. Coming around the side of the bed, she pulled the girl into a hug.

"You can talk to me as well, my sweet Liana."

"It is complicated."

"Doubtful," the maid snarked. "I raised you, child. I know everything there is to know about you, so you come to me the next time you think drowning yourself in ale is a good idea."

Liana chuckled then pulled back. "Agreed. I do not feel well."

Chuffing, she stood. "Serves you right. Now, I will prepare a bath. He better be gone by the time I get back. Your Majesty," she acknowledged with a quick curtsy before exiting the room. Damien pulled her back into his embrace.

"That went far better than I thought."

"Yes, luckily. Phillipa is a reasonable and tolerable woman though. She had to be with me as her charge." He combed his fingers through her hair.

"You make it sound as if you were a difficult child," he surmised, prompting for more details.

"Imagine me now but with little care to mince my words. I was a bit stubborn as a child."

Damien broke into laughter, shaking her entire bed. "You mean to say that you think you mince your words now and are not as stubborn as a brick wall?"

"Yes," she declared, affronted. Damien only laughed. Sitting up, she glared. "Were you supposed to be leaving?" He pulled her back into his embrace.

"Come here, my stubborn queen. I have a hangover cure for you."

"I do not want anything from you." The pointed look he gave her had her crossing her arms. "I am not stubborn," she mumbled.

"Whatever you say. Now, take a drink of my blood and feel better." That grabbed her attention. Once he mentioned that drinking his blood would keep her young for hundreds of years. She didn't know it would also cure hangovers.

His fangs appeared and he dragged his wrist across one. Careful not to spill, he held it to her lips. Closing her mouth around the wound, she licked the blood from his skin. It did not taste metallic as she expected but of sugary caramel poured over her favorite dessert. A moan escaped her at the flavor which in turn Damien growled. Her eyes snapped to his. Fully dilated she could hardly see any of the blue. She licked once more but the wound had sealed.

Her head still ached though. "I do not feel any better."

"You need more," he mumbled around his fangs. She grabbed his wrist before he could open his skin again and reached to touch one fang. Even though she was gentle, the sharp tooth pricked her skin. A droplet of blood welled, and Damien's lips closed around her finger, sucking it clean. Her breath came faster, eyes fixed on his mouth and the feeling of his tongue swirling over her skin.

"Show me how you bite," she demanded, holding her wrist up to his mouth. He shook his head fast and hard.

"No. I cannot endure that torture right now." At her furrowed brows, he explained, "If I bite you, I will not be able to hold back. It is a struggle already to not rip off this gown and sink myself into the welcoming heat of your body. If I bite you, the temptation will be undeniable."

She smirked deviously then shifted to sit on his lap. Hands gripped her waist, bruising the pale flesh. Beneath her she felt the hard length of him through his trousers and her thin nightgown.

"Why must you torture me?" he growled. She only chuckled. Grabbing his wrist again, she caressed the spot he bit into and sliced the skin open with magic. Blood welled quickly, her lips locking around his skin as she sucked his blood down. The flavor so intense she moaned again. She hadn't realized her hips moved until he growled, his other hand squeezing in a punishing grip. After a few more swallows of that delicious blood, she licked the wound closed, sealing it with magic.

"Did you just make magic come out of your tongue?" His chest heaved for breath. Licking her lips, she nodded, feeling the blood diffuse her body with power and energy. He groaned, his eyes rolling back as she ground down against him again.

"By the gods, I feel amazing," she exclaimed. Damien rolled them. As she landed on her back, he leaped out of the bed his entire body taught and ready to launch back at her.

"I must leave, temptress. Come to the castle this afternoon. You start your training with Master Kinley," he declared before rushing out the balcony doors.

Liana licked her lips again. It would be no trouble at all to drink that sweet nectar for the next few hundred years. No trouble at all.

***

After a bath and some food, Liana felt back to normal, even better than normal actually. Vampire blood did wonders to make her feel well, possibly stronger than before. Phillipa accompanied her in the carriage on the way to the castle, her four guards followed as well.

They were led through the castle to a courtyard she had not seen before. On the backside of the castle, it stuck to the structure as if someone thought to add it on after it had already been built. Three sides were exposed to the mountains beyond, the grand arches giving a breathtaking view. A stone balustrade and matching arches opposite the perimeter of the courtyard delineated the walkway from the grass-covered lawn which then led upward to a vaulted ceiling. That is where she found Damien and a host of onlookers as he sparred with four other vampires. Each held a sword as they battled. Although they moved faster than the average male, she could see that the four males attacked Damien.

Unsurprisingly, he held them off with the rumored skill of his brutality as a warrior. She hadn't seen much of this side of him and thanked the gods she saw him now because, although his skills were impressive, it was his shirtless torso that caught her eyes. Clad in only trousers and boots, she watched as his muscles rippled and stretched with every movement, sweat glistening over all that dark skin.

Damien felled two opponents in quick succession which brought on a round of applause from the gaggle of courtiers watching. To her disappointment, most of them were women. She'd met most of them before while attending her father's endless business and political dinners. Some of the ladies were fine, the shifters and vampires much kinder than the mage females, but at that moment, she hated them all.

While she stayed here previously, she did not have much chance to encounter many of the courtiers. Whether that was by Damien's design or the gods, she was thankful for it. She couldn't stand the lot of them.

The epitome of high society folks, all they did was flit about this castle and their grand homes with nothing better to do than gossip and fawn over the king. She would not tolerate that when she was queen though.

The females eyed her fiancé and giggled amongst themselves. There were mage, shifters, and vampires alike in the group, all of them not taking their eyes off the King. Liana recalled that much gossip about the King, aside from his ruthlessness, came from his lack of female bed companions. At least, companions that he kept a secret.

The male was one hundred years old, she knew he was not celibate, definitely not after he played her body like an expert. To see these women here, all eager and willing to take him to bed, likely already had taken him to bed, set her teeth to grinding. It made her wonder if he planned to take other lovers after they were married. Many males did, although they kept quiet about it. Kings especially had harems of women at their beck and call. That she would not stand for either. Perhaps if she had married Keeper Olivier or some other mage she would not have cared. But Damien... he was different. He was only hers.

"Liana," Phillipa whispered, her delicate hand gripping her forearm. "Your magic," she warned as she was so used to doing. Phillipa had been the only one to see her uncontrollable magic. It was her that taught her some semblance of control as a child so it would stop leaking out.

Liana took deep breaths, reigning in her temper and magic. Act like a queen, she repeated Charlotte's words in her mind. Act like a queen. No longer could she let her temper get the best of her. Just like with Damien's courtship, being queen was all about playing the game. You had to be smarter than your opponent, and if you weren't, still act as though you were.

She strode onto the grass with her head held high. The ladies' whispers intensified as they caught sight of her. Damien still focused on his two remaining opponents. Stopped a few feet behind him, hands planted on her hips, she waited for their fight to end. Closer now, it made it more difficult to ignore the wide expanse of flesh that made up his shoulders and then tapered down to a narrow waist, the curve of his muscular ass peeking out as his pants rode low on his hips.

Damien finally ended the duel, his opponents flat on their backs. Cheers followed to which he bowed.

"A pity they inflate your ego when I worked so hard to deflate it," she snarked. He turned slowly to face her, a cocky smirk lifting his lips. Gods, she wanted to kiss that mouth and launch a spell at it all at the same time.

"Lovely to see you again, Lady Liana."

She erected a privacy shield. "Why did you bring me here?"

His brows furrowed at her tone. "What upset you in the hours since I left? I thought I put you in a rather pliable mood."

She glared. "You overestimate your ability to impact my mood, Your Highness," she lied. He was the most influential person on her mood unfortunately. "You summoned. I am here."

His smirk faltered. "Truly, tell me what bothers you, Liana." She failed miserably at playing queen. This was not how a queen would act. This was a petulant child throwing a tantrum. She took a deep breath and unclenched her hands.

"Nothing, I am not bothered. You mentioned training," she prompted.

Damien nodded to his soldiers as they bid him farewell, their sparring session over. "Master Kinley will begin your training. I do not think it wise to hold off any longer given the incident by the lake and the mercenary the other night." She nodded in agreement. "Are you going to be okay with this considering your past?" he questioned in a whisper.

Liana had yet to ask Phillipa about that, still too terrified of whatever happened. "I'll be fine, thank you for your concern."

He gave her hand a light squeeze in reassurance then led her over to the walkway where the simpering ladies and a few gentlemen waited. Thankfully, he pulled his shirt back on.

"That is all for today, everyone," he said in dismissal. The ladies eyed her with jealousy as they scampered off. Only Master Kinley remained and a few guards, two of them she recognized as Owen and Asher. Phillipa joined them as well.

Damien hopped onto the balustrade, feet dangling down and leaned back on his hands. "Master Kinley, if you would be so kind, Ms. Liana is ready for her first lesson."

The mage walked onto the grass leading her into the center. "I saw what you did by the lake. I would like to start by testing your power to see how strong you truly are."

This is what she was afraid of, that they would start poking and prodding at her to determine her strength. To see why she was so different.

Glancing to Phillipa, she found her maid sitting beside Damien, her brows furrowed in concern. Liana's hands broke out into a sweat. Fear gripped her at the thought of someone testing her magic. Uncertain as to where this fear came from, she gulped, pushing it away and knowing that it had something to do with her mysterious past. "What kind of tests?"

"A few simple spells to get a better sense of your power." He took a step closer, one hand reached toward her. She took a step back and glanced at Phillipa again.

"I... that's unnecessary. I am strong. Let us move on," she declared. She sought out Damien. He was her comfort now, her safe haven, and each second that passed made her more desperate for that safety.

He raised a single brow as if to ask if she were alright. Completely the opposite in fact. She felt ready to run again. Concern marred his face as he slid off the balustrade.

"It is a simple test done on all young mages. It will not harm you," Master Kinley implored.

Damien stood ready to intervene, the unspoken question asking if she needed help lingering between them. Staring into those eyes, the ones full of concern but also support she found her courage once more. Act like a queen, she told herself again. A queen was fearless.

"You mean, it is a test performed on all male children," she corrected, then brushed off her skirts to steady her hands.

Master Kinley frowned. "Yes, only male children."

She took a deep breath. "You may perform the spell." Fisting her hands at her side, she locked her knees as he approached. He lifted his palm up to her, waiting. She wiped her sweaty palm along her wool dress before clasping his.

Master Kinley whispered the spell quickly. She braced herself knowing that what came next would not be pleasant. But that thought gave her pause. How could she have known? She'd never been tested before.

His magic slithered into her veins, her magic retreating from the foreign presence. Receding into the very core of itself, her magic writhed angrily, coiling like a snake ready to strike. Liana locked her muscles, eyes clenched shut as she begged her magic to behave. They couldn't react like last time. They had to stay calm.

Kinley's magic poked at her magic, and it lashed out in warning, readying for a death blow. He jerked in her hold.

"Calm, Liana. I will not hurt you." She gritted her teeth, control over her magic tenuous. She felt threatened and so did it, the magic doing everything in its power to protect them both. As Kinley's magic slowly approached her own, she felt it, felt the need to kill, to protect. With a yell, she yanked as hard as she could on her magic just as it lunged for him.

Her body hit the ground with a thud, her eyes staring up at the sky unseeing. Phillipa's face appeared above her, shaking her.

"Liana! Can you hear me? Liana!"

Liana couldn't hear her as her vision went black.

Chapter Seven

Blackness was the first thing she registered. Then she felt her magic, an angry and livid thing beneath her skin before a rush of images surged through her mind.

Memories. They were her memories from so long ago. But this was the first time she ever remembered them.

And they explained everything. She finally remembered the event that made her so terrified of discovery.

It happened when she was only a child of six years old. She'd been wandering around the city by herself performing little spells here and there, her magic as powerful as any boy she knew and always eager to be used. Phillipa left Liana with her sisters hours ago while she tended to Liana's laundry. The moment the woman had gone, Liana snuck out of the house. She was known for wandering off unattended, but usually returned before it got dark. Most often they'd find the young girl hidden away in the garden somewhere. Sometimes she escaped into the city to spread her magic to the world.

Naïve and ignorant, Liana loved using her magic and boasting about it. Phillipa and her mother warned her to not use it. Lady Monroe had punished her more times than she could count so eventually, Liana did hide her magic from her mother. Phillipa never harmed her though and even helped Liana learn to control it.

On a lovely spring day, the young girl skipped through the city, not paying any mind to where she was going while she used her magic, reviving dying plants and flowers to make them vibrant again.

A rough hand grabbed her small arm just after she brought an entire window box of herbs back to life. Such magic should have been impossible for a child, let alone a female child. Liana almost screamed until she caught sight of who it was that had hold of her.

It was Master Ranville, father to the Master Ranville she was familiar with in present day.

He grabbed her off the street and tugged her into a secluded alleyway.

"You're Monroe's daughter, aren't you?" he questioned. Liana didn't fight his hold, not recognizing the threat yet. "How were you performing that magic?" She didn't answer knowing that she would likely be punished if he told her mother. He grabbed her hand and said a spell, the same spell Master Kinley just tried to use on her adult self in the castle. His magic barreled into her own feeling as if she were trampled by a horse. Going limp in his hold, she whimpered.

"How can this be?" he whispered reverently, his eyes shining with glee. "A female with so much power. More power than anyone I've ever tested."

She didn't even sense the knockout spell before it struck her unconscious.

Everything that followed after, flashed through her mind in pieces; locked in a cell, questions and beatings. Nothing seemed too vivid aside from the remembered pain before her vision went black again and her surroundings trickled into her senses. Flat on the grass, she lay in shock at the revealed memory.

"Liana!" Phillipa shouted again then slapped her cheek. She rolled away from the woman and sat up, scared to look at the damage she caused. Out of the corner of her eye she found the guards surrounding Master Kinley. One of them held him up as he drank from Damien's wrist. Pale as a ghost, he did not look like he would make it despite the vampire blood he drank.

Closing the distance, she crawled to him and grabbed his ankle blasting her magic into him. She'd nearly killed him. If Damien hadn't fed his blood to the man, he probably would be. Her magic revived him completely, his face filling with color and he let go of Damien's wrist.

"By the gods child, are you even human?" Kinley exclaimed breathlessly.

Someone else's voice echoed in her ears, a haunting voice that had her magic pulsing in response. "You have the power of a god," Master Ranville's voice whispered in her mind and she flinched in remembered pain.

Liana stood on wobbly legs, Phillipa steadying her. "You shut your mouth," the woman snapped. "Liana is perfectly normal," she insisted, rubbing a hand up and down her back forcefully.

Kinley got to his feet, the vampires helping him. "She is anything but normal. I've never felt power like hers. It doesn't feel right."

Liana stared at the ground, flinching again as *his* phantom voice yelled in her head, "Where did your power come from? Who blessed you with it? Did the gods finally send our savior?"

Phillipa held her tighter. "This was a mistake. I never should have let this happen." She tried to lead Liana away, but she couldn't move. His voice still haunted her, his fists pounding against her flesh and his magic forcing its way in as he tried to coerce her magic out.

"What is it, Liana? What is wrong?" Damien questioned, as he let go of Kinley and moved toward her. His hands held onto her arms while she stared at his chest, nothing around her registering, her mind still lost in the past of her memories.

When she finally broke out of the dungeon Ranville kept her in, Phillipa was the first person to find her. She told her maid everything then Phillipa made her forget. Made her forget what she did and what had been done to her. It was not enough though. Her magic remembered and left her with a life-long fear of discovery. It was the reason why she'd always had this innate fear of discovery... because she'd been discovered before.

Liana gasped, her body finally catching up to her memories. Tears poured from her eyes as she shoved away from Damien and her maid, betrayal hitting her hard. "What did you do?" she accused the woman. Phillipa's eyes widened at her anger. "You made me forget!"

Realization dawned, tears filling Phillipa's eyes. "I protected you."

"No! You stole my memories."

"I protected you. You were only six years old!"

Damien stepped between the pair and interjected, "May I suggest we move this somewhere more private." He tried to settle a comforting arm around Liana's back, but she flinched under his touch and her magic's volatile reaction to it. Right now, it was riled and on guard for anything. Although there was no threat here, it seethed beneath her skin like a living thing, the memory of her torture too fresh.

Damien didn't attempt to touch her again. "Kinley, privacy please." Master Kinley stepped into their circle and erected a privacy shield. "You need to remove the memories of everyone outside this circle."

Master Kinley nodded, not questioning his king or the illegal magic. He began whispering the spell which appeared as a sphere of glowing white between his hands. Once the spell was complete, he turned and launched a piece of it at everyone still in the courtyard.

"That is all for the day," he dismissed everyone. "Liana, Phillipa, Kinley, follow me."

As he strode out of the courtyard, Liana looked to her tearful maid. Brows furrowed in concern, Phillipa pleaded with glossy eyes. Liana knew this was coming, suspected that Phillipa had knowledge of her past and perhaps took her memories. It was another thing altogether to know that it was true.

Liana followed Damien, not sparing her maid another glance. It seemed as though she would be getting her answers today whether she wanted to or not.

They settled in a sitting room down the hall from the training courtyard. Liana would have admired the touch of dark wood throughout the room in such contrast to the gray stone of the castle. Would have admired the intricate detail carved into the bookcases or even the armchairs. Would have traced the perfect stitching along the edges of the green velvet chair she sat upon if she had not been so upset.

Phillipa sat in the matching chair opposite Liana, an oval wooden table between them with a vase of fresh jasmine in the middle of it gently perfuming the air. Damien sat upon the edge of the sofa, elbows on his knees and looking as if he were prepared to jump into battle. Master Kinley stood stiffly near the door, his presence not entirely comfortable for Liana.

"Liana, would you care to begin? What happened in the training yard?" Damien began, dictating himself as the mediator of whatever was about to be revealed.

She looked away from them both, memories pummeling her once more. Every second of every day she spent in that dungeon became fresh in her mind as she remembered the lost events.

"I remember everything," she whispered, her voice small and weak just as she'd been as a child in that cell.

Phillipa's breath stuttered as she breathed in. "I am so sorry, Liana."

"Do you want to tell us what happened?" Damien asked, his tone cautious.

Wrapping her arms around her middle, she curled in on herself. The only thing she wanted to do was curl up in her bed and hide beneath the covers. Now it all made sense. Now she understood why her magic reacted so dramatically when someone discovered her power. It was because of him.

"My sweet girl, you don't have to bear this alone. I am here for you. We are here for you now," Phillipa implored.

Liana hugged herself tighter, unable to look at the woman that was like a mother to her. "You should have let me keep my memories," she accused.

"I tried to. I didn't even think of hiding them in the beginning. But you suffered so greatly, even months after it happened. When you came back, you were suddenly withdrawn, and your magic spiked out of control too often. I had to do something."

Liana swiped angrily at her own tears as they began to fall again. "You could have helped me another way."

"You were drawing attention to yourself, and there was still an investigation into his death. I didn't have time to do anything else."

"Then you should have told me when I was older!" she yelled at the woman, her anger fueling her magic which sparked from her fingertips.

Phillipa let her head fall. "I didn't have a chance. My magic is not strong, and you broke through my spell without even realizing what you'd done and remembered all on your own when you were eleven. I let you keep them. You did not handle it well, so I took them away again." Liana didn't remember that much. "And again, two years ago, you broke through my spell. I thought you were handling it better because you were older. Then, one of the servants startled you and you nearly killed them with your magic."

Liana shook her head vehemently. "I would never."

Phillipa cried, "But you did, and I took your memories away again."

"What are you talking about? What caused her this trauma?" Damien demanded. Liana couldn't look at him either. She couldn't tell him what she'd done. That she was a murderer. Twice now she'd killed someone, the first one she only just remembered, and add on to that, she nearly killed an innocent servant. It did not sit well with her that she had, or that she did not remember it.

She glanced at her maid. "I don't recall any of that. I don't recall any of the times I've remembered previously."

Phillipa pulled a handkerchief from her bodice and wiped at her nose. "After you came back, you told me what happened. You told me about the dungeon and the beatings. You were covered in bruises and broken bones."

Damien growled, then he shifted closer but didn't reach for her.

Liana looked to her fiancé finding his eyes nearly all black and his fangs descended. He was at the edge of his control, his vampiric side at the forefront simply from listening to her story. Knowing that they could both use some comfort, she moved to sit beside him on the sofa and threaded her fingers through his.

"I healed you as best I could before presenting you to your family," Phillipa continued. "I lied to them. Told them you got lost in the forest for four days so they wouldn't suspect you. Your disappearance and his death were too coincidental, and I feared what they might do to you."

"Tell me," Damien growled. "Please."

Liana leaned into his side, resting her head on his tensed shoulder. She didn't want to speak these words, didn't want to relive any of this, but he needed to know. He needed to protect himself from whatever would happen if someone discovered what she'd done.

"When I was six years old, the former Master Ranville saw me performing magic on the street. I'd revived an old herb garden. He tested my power as Master Kinley just did which revealed how powerful I am. He took me to his home where there is a dungeon with two cells, and locked me in one for four days so he could beat and starve me into telling him who I was."

Damien vibrated with anger beneath her touch but said nothing.

"He kept calling me a child of the gods. He said I was their savior, a divine gift to the mage. I had no idea what he meant and still don't but that didn't stop him from threatening me and my family while torturing me. The cells blocked magic which is why I couldn't escape. On the fourth day though, when he came in to beat me once more, I stabbed my fork through his eye and stole the keys. As soon as I was out of the cell, my magic lashed out of my control and..." She gulped, looking to Phillipa for reassurance, forgetting for a moment that the woman had betrayed her. Her tortured eyes overflowed with tears.

"And killed him. I killed Master Ranville then ran home as fast as I could despite all my broken bones and bruises."

"I had to hide the truth from everyone," Phillipa defended once Liana finished. "If people came looking at you for his death, they would have discovered your magic too and I couldn't let that happen."

"How did you learn to hide her memories?" Damien demanded to know.

"Liana became so withdrawn and flinched at every sound that her family started to worry. So, I snuck into Lord Monroe's study one night to find the spell that would hide her memories of the events. I did it that night, and the next morning she was back to herself, although she would still panic if someone caught her unaware while doing magic. She kept breaking through my spells though, and I had to keep doing them over."

Liana understood the reasoning behind Phillipa's betrayal. She would have preferred to know, however, given the history of her reactions to the knowledge in the past, perhaps it was best she hadn't known until now.

A steady growl rose from Damien. "I'll kill him."

"I appreciate your loyalty, but the man is already dead," Liana pointed out.

"I meant the current Master Ranville."

Liana sat up to look at him. "He never hurt me."

"Perhaps not, but he must have known something. He must still know something."

Liana looked at Phillipa with worry. "Although he is not my favorite person, the current Master Ranville has never been unkind toward me, nor has he said an ill word about me."

"Frederick would have already been sixteen years old when you were taken, and plenty old enough to have known what his father was doing. At the very least, he would know of his father's beliefs in the foolish savior fantasy."

The women exchanged confused looks. "You seem to have heard of this "savior" before," Liana noted. "What does it mean? Where does it come from?"

Damien tensed beneath her hold on his arm. "It is just an old wives' tale, a bedtime story told to children in the old days when Triaedian was first created."

Phillipa shook her head when Liana looked to her for answers. "Tell me the story," she insisted from Damien.

"It's nonsense. Just a fairytale about a child of the gods that was gifted to the people to spread power and prosperity among us. I did not think there was anyone left that still told their children such foolishness."

Liana did not quite believe that was the end of the explanation. "You are saying that a man kidnapped me out of some misguided belief in a children's tale?"

Damien shook his head and stood, slipping out of her grasp. He planted one hand at his hip, the other smoothing over his sweat-soaked hair. "I cannot say for certain, however, if he did, he was obviously mad. It is more likely that he took you for your power alone. The mage males, especially one in such a position of power would have been eager to use you."

Liana's magic pulsed within her, a feeling of unease creeping into her mind. "What use would he have for a child?"

"You were powerful then and would have only grown more so. He probably sought to keep you locked in that cell forever and mold you into a weapon," Damien explained.

"A weapon for what?" Phillipa exclaimed while Liana gulped at the reminder of her wretched cell.

"A weapon for power. If the mage controlled you, controlled all that power, they could have taken the crown from the Ashwood line for good. The mage would rule Triaedian and we would all suffer for it. We'd become another segregated kingdom just like all the others."

Her eyes snapped to him. He stared at the floor, his mind clearly whirling with possibilities. How quickly he turned from concerned about her, to concern about his throne. She didn't let her mind turn to such thoughts though, didn't let herself come to false conclusions about the direction of his thoughts. All she wanted was for him to hold her and make her forget any of this happened in the first place.

"Liana is not a weapon. She is just a girl," Phillipa defended. "And not all mage prefer segregation."

Damien paused in his pacing. "I am well aware of what Liana is and is not. And, although not all mage prefer segregation, the ones that are powerful enough to seek my crown, do which I will not allow."

Liana's magic coiled around her like a protective cocoon, like a snake readying to launch at any threat. Damien made it sound as if this was a present problem when in fact, it happened thirteen years ago.

"She may still become a threat if someone were to capture her or control her mind," Master Kinley added.

"I will never let that happen," Damien growled.

Liana took a steadying breath, her thoughts getting wildly out of control, just as their conversation. Her magic was not so easily calmed with all this talk either. It would never let anyone capture her again nor would it allow anyone to use magic to control her mind.

"Regardless of what happened in the past, no one controls me now and no one will ever capture me again."

Liana walked toward the window, the view of the mountain side so close to the castle. Lush green filled the glass from the grass and full trees still soaking up the summer sun. She wished she could be out there instead of inside with this stifling conversation. Out there where she could process her newly revealed memories and torture.

Strong hands settled gently upon her shoulders. "Liana?" Damien questioned, his breath hitting the back of her neck making her shiver. She dropped her arm, threading her hands together. "What do you need?" he asked, uncertainty clouding his tone.

She shook her head as the tears began to form again. A sniffle and an angry swipe at her face had his arms encircling her, his solid body pressing into her back. "I do not know," she admitted. "I do not know what I need other than this to never have happened at all."

His lips brushed against her neck before he hugged her, settling his chin upon her shoulder. "You are strong, my love. You will face this with courage, and I will help however I can."

"Oh, not so worried about your crown anymore?" she chided.

A heavy sigh hit her cheek. "You are the most important thing to me now. I am still king though, and I must consider all avenues."

She sighed and leaned back into his embrace. He was right. Of course, he was. He had an annoying habit of being right often.

Her voice was quiet and vulnerable when she asked, "What am I to do now?"

"Now, you learn to deal with what happened so that you become stronger from it and keep living." He stressed the last word, giving her a gentle squeeze as well. "Learn to live without the fear of your magic being discovered."

That sounded impossible. Never did she envision a life where she didn't have to fear the oddity of her magic.

"That sounds so peaceful," she hummed.

"And we will work through this together." She closed her eyes against the tears that welled at his words and nodded. Together.

Even after the truth was revealed, that she had killed her kidnapper without even trying at six years old, that she nearly took the life of a servant by accident, he still wanted her. Even after he discovered just how truly broken by her past she was, he wanted her.

He lifted his head and kissed her temple, still holding his arms in a tight embrace. "How about a tour of your new home to distract you for a moment?"

A smile split her lips. "This is not my home yet," she pointed out.

"In three short weeks, this will all be your home."

A daunting thought she realized as she still gazed out at the side of the mountain beyond the window. This would be her home soon because she would be married and become queen. A different kind of fear threatened to overwhelm her which she shoved down as best she could. "A bit large for my tastes," she jested.

Damien chuckled. "Ah yes, I believe if you had your way, you'd live in a tiny, secluded cottage in the woods where you could smite men in private for the rest of your life."

Grinning over her shoulder, she let him see her amusement. "You know me so well, my king." His hand cupped her cheek, his thumb brushing over her bottom lip.

"I do know you, my love." His words were serious once more despite his previous teasing, and when he bent to kiss her lips, she gladly met him halfway.

A throat cleared loudly before she could deepen their kiss.

"I do not need to remind you both how inappropriate you are being," Phillipa interrupted.

Master Kinley provided a grunt in agreement.

Damien blew out a heavy breath. "Did I say three *short* weeks?" he asked. "I meant, an eternity until we are married."

Despite her red, puffy eyes, despite her freshly revealed memories of torture, Liana found herself laughing.

Damien was everything she wanted and never knew she needed. With his help, she would keep her memories this time.

This time, she wouldn't break.

Chapter Eight

Liana found herself riding in the family's carriage toward the castle again on this overcast day. Rain drenched the ground last night leaving them with a slow ride and a bit of a chill to the air which was such a relief after all the blazing temperatures. Summer should almost be over, thankfully, with fall just around the corner. Liana loved fall. Loved the cooler temperatures and the changing of the leaves, which were still at least a month or two from changing. Mostly, she loved how cozy and cheerful the city became. And not too much longer, they'd begin to prepare for the Fall Festival with all the lovely decorations lining the streets.

"Liana?" Phillipa questioned, trying to get her attention once more. Right, she'd asked a question. One that Liana did not want to answer.

She had not decided yet on how to handle Phillipa's deceit and illegal magic usage which meant she avoided the maid all of yesterday once they'd returned from the castle. The older woman made it difficult though because she hovered all night to ensure Liana coped well with her memories.

Liana wanted to be upset with the woman, thought she should be upset, but she felt nothing. All she knew was that she now had to deal with memories of a torture that felt fresh in her mind once more. If she never forgot about her kidnapping, Liana didn't know how she would have grown up. Would she have lived in worse fear every day, or would she have eventually coped and been fine? She'd never know and didn't feel like dwelling on that considering she felt content with where she was at in her life.

"I am not sure what will happen with Master Kinley today," she answered the woman finally. "I am willing to train with my magic though. I feel fine."

"If you want to stop at any point, you just tell them so."

Liana nodded, not quite sure if she'd have the courage to go through with today. Damien told her she did not have to train if she did not want to. This was important to her though. She wanted to learn more defensive magic. She wanted to be able to defend not only herself but Damien and the kingdom as well. There was all this magic inside her and she did not want to fail anyone again simply because she didn't know how even though she was plenty capable.

Once they stopped outside the castle, a servant helped Liana step out of the carriage and directly into Damien's outstretched hand as he ran down the stairs with vampiric speed. It still amazed her how quickly he could move.

"My queen," he said with a smirk as he took her hand and kissed the back of it. Her magic immediately calmed, her shoulders relaxing for the first time since she left him yesterday.

She raised a brow, eyes roving over his disheveled state of dress. The white tunic he wore stuck to his sweaty skin while his boots and trousers were covered in dirt. His dark hair sweat-soaked and also caked in dirt.

"Once again, I am not yet queen. And if I were, is this any way to greet your queen?"

He stepped closer, a grin and a glint of wickedness in his icy eyes as he whispered, "You will always be my queen." She shivered at the promise in his words, a brief yet consuming image of him on his knees as he worshiped his queen properly. "And as for my state of dress," he continued, taking a step back and breaking the spell of desire that took no effort for him to spin around her, "You caught me in the middle of training. I would have changed if I had the time."

Liana raised her chin then made to walk past him. She paused, their arms brushing and looked up at him from under her lashes. "I could aid you now to take these dirty clothes off." She smirked when she noticed the clenching of his jaw then flitted passed. She did love teasing him.

Steps crunched on the stone as he trailed her. "And what of the clean clothes? Will you help me into those?" he said only for her ears as they walked up the stairs.

"Maybe. Once I've had my fill of you."

He chuckled low and gravelly. "I've been in your presence for not even a minute, and you've already turned me into a drooling mess. Why must you always make things so sensual?"

She scoffed. "Me? You started it. I am merely playing along."

"Temptress," he whispered, his tone promising without any hint of malice.

He led her through the castle toward the training courtyard. They passed many guards and a few courtiers that stopped to bow as the king walked by.

"How are you feeling after yesterday?" he asked, his steps measured for her sake.

"I am well, considering."

His eyes lingered on her despite the assurances. "You look tired, my love. Are you sure you are well?"

The dark circles beneath her eyes from the lack of sleep she endured last night were impossible to conceal. She fell asleep without trouble last night, but it was the nightmares that kept her awake.

"In truth, I did not sleep very well. Nightmares," she explained.

"I will get you a sleeping tincture," he declared. "You do not have to train today, Liana. You may rest."

She shook her head. "I want to train. I need to." He stopped to face her. Eyes examining her tired countenance and tense shoulders, she hoped he saw how much she needed this. How much she needed to do something productive, to forget about her past for a moment, to finally take control of her magic.

He slipped his hand into hers and squeezed before releasing once more. "I'll be off to the side." He didn't need to say, in case you need me, because his presence alone was support enough. "There is something else I must tell you."

His hesitant tone didn't bode well.

"My grandfather arrived last night. We didn't expect him, but he will be staying until the wedding."

"Why do you make it sound like such a dreadful thing? Do you not enjoy his presence?"

"I love the man, but Grandfather is a bit cynical, and he can be a bit tough on those that are marrying into the family."

"Tough? How so?"

"He likes to test you all, to make sure you're fit for the royal line or some other asinine reason."

"Well now I have no wish to meet him," she snarked.

He turned her down the hall that led to the training area. "It will be fine. Just be yourself and do not let him intimidate you."

That was easy for him to say considering he wouldn't be on the receiving end.

"And which grandfather is this? Vampires call all their great grandfathers the same, correct?" She'd spoken about it once with Felix when he asked her to send magical messages to his own father and grandfather regarding Cassia's pregnancy.

"Grandfather Luciano. He is my great, great, great grandfather."

Liana stopped walking and stared at him in open disbelief. "You're telling me, I am about to meet the fifth king of Triaedian? I am not prepared for this!"

He chuckled at her dramatics.

"I am serious, Damien. I cannot meet him right now. I am not at my best after a restless night and everything that was revealed yesterday."

His brow softened and he pulled her into his arms. "I understand. However, I do eagerly want to introduce you. He was an integral part of my upbringing and transition into a vampire. I love him like a father and wish for him to meet the woman I am madly in love with."

She frowned at him. "Don't try to sweet talk me, Your Majesty."

"Please, Liana. I will protect you from his inquisition today but I want to introduce you."

She sighed, rubbing her fingers into her temples. "Fine. But if he hates me, I'm not going to do much to change his mind. I don't have much energy to care right now." If the ancient vampire hated her, found her lacking for any reason, she was beyond caring at the moment. She had too many emotions and memories to deal with after she finally remembered her past.

"No one could ever hate you." She knew Damien declared that with all honesty but she was not so disillusioned. Many people hated her for no reason other than being different.

"Let's go then."

Walking with their hands linked, he led her into the courtyard, Phillipa trailing behind. There were far fewer people in attendance today, none of the courtiers lingered, only a handful of soldiers scattered along the balustrade watching the fierce battle unfold between Asher, Owen and who she assumed to be High Lord Luciano Ashwood.

Liana greeted Master Kinley with a polite half-curtsy before watching the battle.

Asher and Owen were fierce fighters but the older vampire had far more experience and held them off easily. Their movements were so fast that she could hardly see until she whispered a spell that allowed her to perceive as quickly as a vampire did. She didn't understand fighting or swordsmanship, nor did she have to. Luciano clearly bested them with little effort.

After watching Damien yesterday, she doubted he would be able to beat Luciano either.

Their match quickly came to an end, the soldiers having gotten rowdier with every clang of swords. They cheered at the defeat of Owen and Asher, both vampires laid out on the grass.

Luciano sheathed his sword into the belt around his trim waist then helped the soldiers to their feet. The pair may have been Damien's cousins on his mother's side with no blood relation to Luciano directly, but she could see the camaraderie in their jesting as they walked toward her and Damien.

Asher took a few jogging steps and gathered her in an unexpected hug. "Lady Liana, such a pleasure to see you again," he said with an easy smile and mocking bow. "Come to dance for us once more?"

Liana chuckled even as her cheeks reddened and her eyes dashed toward the imposing figure beyond him. "Asher, be a gentleman and forget that night at the pub, will you?"

He grinned. "Never. I will always remember the night my queen danced atop pub tables and got kicked off the bar."

Liana groaned. "I am not queen yet, even still, you should not tease a lady so."

Damien crossed his arms, leaning against a pillar with one of those damned brows raised. "Aren't you always telling me you're no proper lady."

Eyes narrowed, she sent him a glare that only set him to laughing.

"Come on children, play nicely," Master Kinley interjected as if he were their father.

Damien shoved off the pillar and placed a hand on Liana's back. "Grandfather, allow me to introduce my fiancé, Lady Liana Monroe."

He stood in equal height to Damien, not appearing anywhere near his seven hundred and something-year old self. The man looked closer in age to her own father with the only gray in his black hair peppering his temples and thick beard. Those eyes though, an earthy brown closer to Ramone's coloring, they held a different story. Hard and guarded from his long years, Liana found only sorrow in them.

Liana gave him a full curtsy. "A pleasure to meet you, High Lord."

He grunted. "You are younger than I imagined." Liana did her best to keep her face blank. He made an obvious sniff toward her being and scrunched his nose. "You look and smell like a frightened animal. If I scare you so easily, perhaps you should rethink this engagement considering I'm not nearly the scariest thing you will face as queen."

Liana barely refrained from letting her jaw drop. No one had ever spoken to her so bluntly. Damien had come close but never so rudely. Fury boiling, she let her magic rise to the surface.

"Grandfather," Damien chided. "Can you please tone down the intimidation. She does not need to be tested like…"

"Do not tell me what to do, boy," Luciano interrupted. "I will protect this family and Triaedian as I see fit."

"Yes, but, Liana has been through enough…"

"No, Damien." Now Liana was the one to interject. Lifting her chin, she let her magic bolster her with anger and power. "You do not need to defend me against this male. If you want to test me, Sir, be my guest." She turned to Master Kinley who looked nearly as pale as he did yesterday when she nearly killed him. "Let's train before I decide to test my power on the pompous males of this kingdom that continue to think me weak and belittle me any chance they get." Her eyes fell on Luciano as she said this. He merely stared back.

Walking onto the grass, she took slow, even breaths to calm down a bit. Anger still fueled her and that was never a good result when her magic was involved. Master Kinley stood opposite her while she kept her back to the ancient vampire, not wanting to see or acknowledge his presence. So much for good first impressions. Shaking her head, she breathed again then shoved him out of her mind on the exhale.

"Let us begin with basic combat spells," Master Kinley started. "I am told you know some basics so mimic me as I go. If I say one you are unfamiliar with, stop me." She nodded her understanding, and they began. Engrossed in the work, she finally forgot who inhabited her audience.

The first twenty or so were familiar, then they weren't, and they had to slow down. He would say the spell, hands following the appropriate motions then letting it go. She mimicked him, reciting the spell over and over until she had it memorized then actually performed it. It was odd how the spells would hit a shield before it reached the walkways and be absorbed. She'd felt the power the moment she stepped into the courtyard but couldn't place it. Finally, she asked as they walked toward their audience.

"It is a self-sustaining shield that keeps all magic inside this courtyard, so any onlookers remain unharmed. Any magic that hits the shield is absorbed to keep the shield powered," Kinley explained. "The shield can easily be altered to keep people and weapons in or out during a duel as well." Liana nodded. It would be a valuable tool especially in a duel to keep any outside interference from entering.

"Are there many real duels? As in fights to the death?" she wondered.

"Not as many as I'd like," Damien declared with a cocky grin as he stepped down from his perch on the balustrade.

Asher snorted. "You banned fights to the death, you boring, old bastard."

"Who are you calling old?" he growled lightly at his cousin. Asher merely laughed.

"Lady Liana, perhaps you could take him in a few rounds. See if you can best our king."

Not one to sit out on the fun, Liana jested with the males ignoring Luciano who lurked nearby. "That would be an unfair fight," she pointed out with a grin directed at Damien.

"He'd take it easy on you."

"I meant for him. I'd crush him under a spell in a heartbeat."

Asher howled with laughter. Even Owen cracked a grin.

"Perhaps we should teach you some defensive maneuvers," Damien said, his smile faltering. "In the impossible event someone ever dares to touch you and somehow prevents you from using magic, I'd like you to know basic combat skills."

Flashes of that cell bombarded Liana's mind. Clearing her throat, she nodded. "That would be agreeable. Let us begin now."

Damien took a few steps into the courtyard and gestured for her to follow. "First and foremost, you need to know how to escape a hold. Asher, come demonstrate."

The soldier sauntered toward Damien and at the last second, moved too quickly for Liana to see, grabbing Damien in a chokehold. She gasped, her magic flaring to protect Damien out of instinct, but reeled back as Damien twisted and kicked at the back of Asher's legs to pin him to the ground.

"You'll never best me, cousin," Damien taunted to which Asher just chuckled.

"One day," Asher promised. Damien let him go then turned to Liana.

"Let us begin with teaching you how to get out of a hold." Damien gestured her forward. She took a step toward him, and he circled to her back where he wrapped his arms around her, his hand slowly encircling her neck so as not to terrify her.

"If someone grabs you like this, there is a simple way of getting free." He dropped his arms then demonstrated the moves on Asher so she could see. He did it again much slower then walked her through it, step by step.

He came up behind her once more and resumed the position. "Go slowly and show me how you'd get out of this hold."

Feeling him behind her, feeling his fingers upon her throat and his lips so close to her neck was doing things to her that were certainly not appropriate for the moment. She couldn't help but tease him though. "I rather like where I'm at actually," she quipped, and leaned back into his solid body.

A huff of a laugh brushed her neck while his fingers gripped ever so slightly tighter around her neck. "Temptress," he warned and said in whispered words, "I'll remember this when we're finally married."

Nibbling on her bottom lip, she grinned. "Promise?"

He groaned behind her. Taking advantage of his torment, she executed the moves, not bothering to go slowly as he suggested. She stomped on the inset of his foot while grabbing the thumb of the hand that latched her throat and yanked downward. Twisting in the direction of the arm she pulled, she spun out of his hold and dropped his hand.

Hands planted on her hips, she gave him a triumphant smirk and mocked his signature brow raise with one of her own.

Asher chuckled beside them. "Who knew it would only take a few teasing words to fell our king!"

Damien spared him a glare before setting his sights on Liana. "You think you're clever?"

"Usually," she quipped, still smiling.

"That won't work twice," he challenged.

With a shrug, she pretended to pick at her nails. "I'm sure I would come up with something equally as distracting next time."

"Give it your best try." Before she could blink, he moved with vampiric speed and trapped her in the same hold.

She zapped him with a jolt of magic which only had his arms tightening around her. "No magic," he growled. With a roll of her eyes, she executed the moves once more. It wasn't as forceful this time since he wasn't distracted but she still performed them correctly and got out of the hold.

"Now, if this truly were the case and a vampire caught you like this, you'd need a weapon. Our strength is too much for you and this move would not work. Owen, show her how to get out of this with a weapon." Damien played the captor while Owen taught her how to sneak a weapon out then disable Damien.

"Does this mean I must be armed at all times as well?" she asked. Owen handed her the dagger which was smaller than the length of her forearm but still deadly if used properly.

"It would be for the best," Damien agreed. "I will get you some weapons."

"And where would I keep them so that they would be in easy reach for such an attack?" Owen kept his blade in a sheath buckled around his waist, a longer sword on the other side. "Perhaps I could set a new fashion trend with a decorative holster around my waist," she jested.

Damien set his jaw. "I'll think of something. For now, show me you know what you're doing." His arms came around her and she smirked again. Asher's eyes narrowed on her.

"She's got this devious look in her eyes, cousin," Asher warned.

She erected a silencing shield around just the two of them. "I could always get a holster to strap around my thigh." Her hand slid against his muscular thigh, rising higher. "Just here, I think. But it would be difficult to reach beneath all these heavy skirts."

Damien growled but kept his attention on her. "You fight dirty, my queen."

Not waiting another moment, she attacked. At the last second, she withheld the injuring blow of the blade but still nicked his skin to prove she'd be capable of doing it.

"Excellent," Damien declared, his wound already healed. His arm snaked around her waist and pulled her tightly against his front. "And I will be remembering each and every time you have teased me. Expect retribution."

She showed her teeth in a grin as she lifted the dagger's tip to his neck and pressed hard enough to get one drop of blood. "I expect a lot, my king." She brought the dagger to her mouth and licked the drop of blood off. He tasted just as sweet as she remembered. The blue of his eyes disappeared, consumed by black as he focused solely on her lips.

His mother's voice stopped him as he moved to kiss her. "Liana, if you are done torturing your betrothed, I need you for a dress fitting." Liana glanced over to the High Lady standing at the edge of the courtyard with her lady's maid and Phillipa. The latter looked decidedly upset, her ire directed at Liana, but she was used to that. Luciano still lurked in the shadows, his eyes focused solely on her.

Liana pulled out of Damien's arms and handed the dagger back to Owen. The vampire kept his hands behind his back.

"My lady, I believe the dagger is yours now," Owen said.

Asher chuckled. "Yeah, not after that show." Her cheeks reddened realizing how bold and inappropriate she'd been.

Damien stepped up behind her and reached for the dagger. "I shall keep it safe for you."

She escaped his reach and stepped away from the three vampires. "This is mine now. I shall keep it with me."

He crossed his arms over his wide chest. "You cannot walk around holding a dagger. It will appear as a threat."

"Then I will keep it safe for now, where I can easily access it." Without a thought, she placed the dagger against her right forearm and whispered a spell. The dagger sunk into her skin, morphing into black ink before disappearing completely. The males stared down at her empty hand speechless.

"Where did it go?" Asher questioned.

She crossed her arms defiantly. "Into my body, where I can keep it safely hidden for now."

"How?" Master Kinley asked, his voice full of disbelief. "That is no spell I've ever known. Where did you learn it?" he asked, accusingly.

It took her a moment to realize that they all seemed uncertain of her. All except Damien. She looked to him for guidance because she couldn't think past the worry that yet again, she was caught, that she did something wrong. Panic surged within her, her magic at the ready within a beat of her racing heart. Her eyes focused on movement to the side. Luciano emerged from his dark corner to stare at her arm, his brows furrowed in either anger or concern.

Looking for the quickest escape, she readied to sprint out of there, her magic already prepared with a shield.

"Quite clever, Liana," Damien said as he took her by the shoulder gently and turned her toward the castle. "Now, go. My mother is impatient and you don't want to be on the other end of her wrath."

He kept his arm tightly around her shoulder as he walked with her. He must have heard her heart pounding, smelled her instant fear.

"You speak lies, Son," High Lady Evangeline said, her voice raised for Liana to hear, the vampires could hear just fine. Damien led her over to his mother and Phillipa.

"I'll see you tomorrow." He gave her a kiss on the forehead before giving his mother a polite kiss on the cheek as well. "Mother," he said reverently but with a smile. "Please do not torture my bride too long," he teased and left with a wink directed at Liana.

"Ugh, he is so dramatic," High Lady Evangeline complained before looping her arm through Liana's. "Now, let us try on your gown and finalize details for the wedding. Not much time yet left to go."

Slowly, her magic calmed by the lack of response from everyone else and Damien's quick diffusion of the situation.

"Quite right, High Lady," she addressed politely despite the new nerves that seized her. It wasn't fear over Damien, but the actual wedding and having so many look upon her. She dreamed of a small wedding with only family in attendance. That would never be reality though considering she was marrying the king and it was meant to be the grandest event in all of Triaedian's history.

She sighed, resigned to her fate as a public figure for the rest of her life wherein she would always be the center of attention, or at least gossip.

Whatever the High Lady planned for the rest of the afternoon, at least it would distract her from thinking of yet another faux paus she committed in front of the others. Her fingers brushed absently over the place where the dagger disappeared. Just like with her spells, it was hidden from view, and only she could call upon it to be revealed. It was not natural the things she did. They came far too easily and she could deny her oddity no longer. She perhaps was the strongest mage to ever been born yet the least prepared for dealing with that responsibility. For now, she'd take it one day at a time. She'd learn her magic. She'd learn to control it, to push it to its limits and become a formidable opponent to any that threatened her happiness or her kingdom.

Chapter Nine

Terror seized her body as she heard the opening click of the lock in the dungeon door a few paces away. Everything ached and stung already, her breaths shallow to lessen the pain of her expanding chest. Master Ranville strode up to her cell after locking the door behind him. He hung the torch in its place on the wall to light the bleak area then shrugged out of his dress coat and hung it on a rung of her iron barred cell. When he began rolling his sleeves up, her body began to shake with fear.

"Have you decided to give me answers today, Savior?"

Tears poured down her face, the cut on her lip stinging from the salty liquid. "I don't know what you're talking about," she responded, her young voice broken and small.

"You do. You know exactly who and what you are. I need to know which god sent you. Which god's powers do you possess?" He unlocked her cell then stepped through, the spell to prevent magic shimmering slightly as he stepped through it before going invisible once more.

A wince set her bones to aching as the iron door clanked closed. She'd been here for days. Endless days of solitude locked in darkness without any inkling of the sun's presence. She only assumed it was night because Master Ranville was here, and he worked with her father during the day.

Her father. What must he think of all this? Did he know she was missing yet? Did her family search for her? Surely they would be, or at least Phillipa would be. Liana knew she had a knack for sneaking away from her guards, but it had never been this long.

"Tell me girl, which god is your father?" he asked, his frame towering over her like an omen of death.

"My father is Lord Monroe," she answered as she had countless times before. This man was crazy, she realized that. There was nothing she could do though. He blocked her magic somehow and there was no way out.

Pain lanced up her spine and into her skull where it felt like knives were stabbing from the inside out. Her scream echoed off the stone walls until Ranville released the spell. She slumped to the ground, her childish body just a lump of fabric on the floor.

"Which god is the father of your power? It was not the man that gave you life. His power is nothing like yours. No, your power is nothing like other mage. Your power is divine. Which god blessed you with it? And why a female? It would have been better served by a male."

Liana simply cried. She tried answering his questions before. He never believed her. She had no idea what he spoke of. His boot came at her and it was all she could do to curl up into a ball. The blow landed to her shins, nearly cracking from the force. A sob broke from her.

A bell tinkled through the cramped dungeon, the sound mockingly bright and cheerful. "Well, it appears I am being summoned for supper. I'll be back to finish this." He stepped out of the cell and locked her inside before donning his coat once more. "If you answer my questions, perhaps I will bring you something delicious to eat."

Her stomach growled at the taunt. He'd barely fed her at all in the days she'd been here. Measly bread and water when he remembered to bring it.

"Even if you don't want to answer me, I'll keep you in this cell until you're old enough to control. Old enough for me to train your magic to become what the Savior was meant to be. Perhaps I'll even find a way to rip that magic from your useless body to use it myself. That sounds like a wonderful idea, don't you think?"

Once again, she didn't answer him and he stalked out of the dungeon, extinguishing the torch to leave her in utter darkness.

Liana gasped as she woke. Sweat drenched everything, her hair and gown sticking to her unpleasantly. Tumbling out of bed, she gasped for air as the nightmare lingered in her mind. It was less of a nightmare and more of a memory. She hadn't remembered everything so vividly before, but that dream was more real than she thought possible. Even the pain lingered deep in her bones. Needing air, she flung open her patio doors.

Cool night air swept in, her sweat-slicked skin chilled instantly. It tortured her once more to recall what had been done. It made her angry more than anything though. Angry that he had been able to just take her like that. Angry that he thought he had the right to and more than angry at whatever ludicrous ideas he believed in that made him think it was okay to torture her like that. No beliefs ever justified such treatment.

Liana stayed on the patio the rest of the night, needing the cool air to soothe her raging soul and keep her awake. She feared falling asleep again. Feared reliving that torture again.

***

Yawning, Liana rested her head against the carriage as they ambled toward the castle again. She didn't attend training yesterday because it had been worship day which she spent with her family. Last night, she woke from another nightmare, more of the same as the previous and kept herself awake by making potions and salves for her secret customers. It left her feeling awful though with the lack of sleep, and the memories were making her so jumpy.

At breakfast this morning, she nearly hit Henry with a spell when he suddenly announced the post had arrived. She hadn't been paying much attention to anyone, so his abrupt announcement had her on edge. Luckily, she reeled back her magic, and everyone was safe.

She did not look forward to training today despite wanting to learn. All she wanted was peaceful, dreamless sleep.

"You look tired," Phillipa pointed out unhelpfully. "Are you sure you feel well?"

Her maid worried over her more so now that Liana knew the truth. She knew the woman worried that Liana might not deal with the knowledge of her kidnapping well again. There was no reassuring the woman that she would be fine in time despite Liana's many attempts.

"I am well, Phillipa." She offered the maid a smile.

Phillipa wrung her hands together in her lap. "You seemed a bit quiet at breakfast this morning. And supper last night. You are withdrawn even now."

"Phillipa, I am well. I simply did not sleep enough. Please, stop worrying over me."

By the time they arrived at the castle, Liana was surprised Phillipa had any skin left on her fingers with how hard she wrung them. The woman clearly didn't listen to her charge.

Damien didn't greet her this time which is why a guard led the way to the training courtyard. Courtiers lined the balustrade once again, watching the males fight, more like drooling over them. Liana rolled her eyes at the pathetic waste of time. There were far more in attendance though today and High Lady Evangeline was among them, her group of admirers close by. Liana made sure to stay on the outskirts of it all and behind everyone, so she was not noticed.

She realized why the audience had grown when she spotted two males fighting in the center of the courtyard. Nearly identical specimens wearing only their black trousers to reveal darkly tanned skin and torsos corded with muscle, Damien and his father fought one another with swords. Liana didn't think of Ramone as being overly fit beneath all his courtly fashion, but this male proved her so very wrong. Damien stood barely taller than his father, but each looked as if they were sculpted from stone.

Father and son sparred jovially, their smiles and laughter at such odds with the parrying of their swords. Their taunting words were not quite humorous though and even had Liana blushing at the vulgarity.

Each managed to get a few nicks on the other, neither landing a killing blow. Liana watched raptly despite her judgment of the other courtiers. She couldn't look away from her fiancé, the tantalizing body that would be hers soon.

When they finally called their match to an end, a thunderous applause came from the soldiers standing around the courtyard and their courtier audience. They took mocking bows and when Damien stood, his eyes found hers as if he already knew she was there.

"The show is over for today, exit the courtyard," he instructed everyone before walking over to retrieve his shirt. Ramone skipped his shirt and smothered his wife in a hug. Evangeline protested even as her arms wrapped around his neck, and he peppered her with kisses. Her courtiers excused themselves quietly and left with the rest of the soldiers.

So enraptured by the love between the former queen and king, Liana hadn't noticed Damien walking toward her. When he snaked an arm around her waist, she jolted away, her magic lashing out as well. It gave him a sting of pain on the arm before she could pull it back.

"Oh, Damien. I apologize. I didn't realize it was you."

He stared down at her beneath that heavy brow. "I apologize, my love. I did not mean to startle you." His hand cupped her cheek, his thumb brushing over her cheek. "Are you well? You look pale."

Glaring up at him, she declared, "You must never tell me such things. I am a lady, and I am always pretty."

She expected a smile, but he still stared back, features tight with concern. "You are always pretty to me, but I can see the fatigue in your eyes."

She sighed. "I did not sleep well, that is all," she reassured then glanced back at his parents who were still in an embrace, Ramone sans shirt. "Your parents seem deeply in love."

"They are. Which is partly why I waited so long to find a wife. I wanted what they have, true love."

Liana did not need this right now. She could not handle his tender words on top of her own frazzled emotions. "And how is that search? Did you find your true love yet?" she teased to keep from crying.

"So cheeky," he said, his thumb brushing over her bottom lip.

"Perhaps you should not have put your shirt on. Now I am only distracted by your father." She glanced in his direction, the sweaty male's torso still on full display. "I see you inherited more from him than your title." She bit her bottom lip for effect.

He growled, pulling her chin to look only at him. "You tease me to the point of pain, little mage."

Those words were like a bucket of water thrown over her. Tease to the point of pain. Torture to the point of pain and far beyond it. Bones breaking... her mind flayed open. Endless moments in which she pleaded for it all to end.

Flinching, she pulled out of his grip. "I apologize."

Brows furrowed, he reached for her once more. Body taut, she let him get close while she tried to calm her racing heart and twisted mind.

"Truly, Liana, you worry me. What is wrong?"

She could lie to him, tell him everything was alright. But he knew the truth, knew she was struggling with something.

"I've had terrible nightmares for the past few nights. I believe I am just tired and skittish."

As Damien began to respond, someone interrupted. "Good morning, Your Majesty, Lady Liana."

Liana stiffened when she beheld who stood beside them. She never thought much about Master Ranville but with recent memories resurfaced, the likeness between him and his father were undeniable. They were so similar that Liana couldn't find the difference in her haze of terror. She squeezed Damien's arm too tightly, her breath coming faster. Magic surged beneath her skin preparing to defend her.

Damien shifted, blocking most of her from Frederick's view. "Master Ranville," he said with a polite nod of his head. "We shall speak later, for now, we have business to attend to. I'll have my cousin, Owen, escort you out."

She couldn't see Ranville's face anymore, but she knew the proud man would not have appreciated the dismissal.

Their steps faded then Damien wrapped his arms around her.

"They look so similar," she explained in a whisper of her voice, clinging onto his sweaty shirt. His hand smoothed over her back, up and down rhythmically to comfort her.

"Shall I get rid of him? Truly, I've never much liked him anyway."

She balked, gaping up at him. "You can't just kill people like that."

He raised that infernal, haughty brow. "And why not? I am king and he has offended my queen by his presence alone. Justified by my standards."

She scoffed but fell back into his embrace. "Your standards are extremely concerning."

"I believe it is you that is concerning because I simply meant I could send him away, perhaps to Sapphire Cove or to the south, to the desert perhaps. You are the one that assumed I would kill him."

"Well, if the reputation fits," she remarked, her heart already calming.

"There is some truth to that," he admitted. "I would be far more satisfied watching the life drain out of his eyes."

Footsteps approached their quiet moment. "Should we be concerned about you two quietly plotting murder over here?" Ramone questioned.

Damien's reply was quick. "Only if you plan on trying to stop us."

Ramone laughed then clapped a hand on his son's shoulder. "Come, we are eager to see what our new queen is capable of with that magic."

Liana glanced at Damien, panic flaring in her eyes. "They are going to watch?"

His hand continued along her back, never faltering. "I will make them leave if you do not want them here."

After a few deep breaths, her hands stopped shaking. "No. No, it's fine. I just... I hate being the center of attention."

"You are always the center of my attention, and you do not hate that," he retorted with a smirk. Rolling her eyes, she shoved him away.

"Insufferable king." He merely laughed and followed her into the courtyard.

Master Kinley followed, ready for their lesson of the day. Liana noted with relief that High Lord Luciano was nowhere to be found today.

They began with more defensive spells, this time, testing how far her shields could expand. They all knew her explosive magic from that day on the lake managed to reach for at least a mile, it would be another task completely to be able to expand a controlled shield to her greatest potential.

Ignoring her audience, Damien's parents and Asher, Liana created a shield around herself which was as easy as breathing. For so long she'd been able to create shields, of all manner as well. Sound shields. Protective shields. Shields to hide her from view. Perhaps her fascination with them stemmed from her past, her need to feel protected. She suspected a lot she did stemmed from that repressed fear.

For now, this one would strictly be a protective shield, one that would keep anything or anyone from penetrating. If in battle, no one would be able to pass through from the outside nor would any weapons like arrows, spells, and spears.

A glowing orb of gold appeared around her which she quickly expanded to encompass Damien and Master Kinley. It kept going, no sign of faltering as it bypassed the walkway. When it passed through the walls, they looked up to watch it expand into the sky.

Liana felt a twinge of pain in her chest, in the place where her magic felt coiled within herself at all times. It was a warning. A warning that she was reaching her limit. She slowed, keeping her magic open and feeding the shield until the tug was too much.

Master Kinley gaped up at the sky, his head leaned all the way back. Damien's eyes fell to her own, a smug smirk filling his face.

The pride in that one look filled her chest with so much that she missed out on from so many others. Every time she looked to her mother with a new potion or showed her father a difficult spell and was met with only scolding instead of the praise she deserved.

Liana extinguished the spell and gave a slight shrug of her shoulder when Master Kinley just looked at her. "What next?" she questioned.

And so they went for the rest of the morning and into the afternoon. Master Kinley presented her with a task, and she would respond easily. Even if it were a new spell, he would merely have to explain it once before she was able to perform it with ease. They worked through the midafternoon.

"Should I have food brought to us or are you two finished showing off your magic?" Damien called out from the walkway.

"I am ravenous," Liana admitted. All that magic worked up an appetite, even a bit of a sweat as well.

The High Lord and Lady, as well as Asher and Owen opted to join their meal which was served in a private garden on a higher-level patio. Phillipa sat on her own by the entrance while they sat beneath a canvas to block the sun in the center of the garden. Servants just finished setting the food out and pouring wine when their group arrived.

Before she could even sit, High Lord Luciano strolled onto the patio and silently claimed a seat opposite her. It put him in direct eyeline of Liana and any semblance of ease she felt disappeared. His dark eyes haunted her every move. Despite his presence, Liana dug into her meal, her stomach gurgling loudly enough for all to hear.

"Liana, you might consider moving to the castle early," Evangeline suggested.

She paused mid chew, her gaze darting to Damien who appeared the picture of nonchalance. "Why do you say that, High Lady?"

"Please, Eva will do just fine while we are alone like this. And I would think living in the castle would be far easier for everyone considering we still have things to discuss about the wedding, your magic training, and we need to begin your regency lessons."

"Regency lessons?" Liana asked, gulping.

"Do you know anything about being a queen?" she retorted.

Liana's cheeks flushed as she shook her head.

"Do you know anything of what it takes to rule a kingdom, let alone one that is home to a variety of people and beliefs that you have to hold together?"

Again, she shook her head.

"There is a matter of safety to consider as well. Although the rebels have been silenced once more, there will always be some threat and with you traveling so far each day, and predictably so, begs for trouble."

"Right you are, dear," Ramone interjected.

"Then it is settled. You will move into the castle within the next two days," Eva said with finality. Liana couldn't argue, didn't know if she should or if she even wanted to. Being closer would be beneficial on all accounts. She would not have to waste the time it took each day to travel to the castle. She would be moving in two weeks either way. There was no point in delaying.

She glanced at Damien to see if he had any thoughts on the matter. She did not want to become a nuisance to him. The grin on his lips didn't bode well for her though. She braced herself for whatever was about to exit his mouth.

"It shall be a pleasure to have you so close."

Asher snorted a laugh to her right.

Eva tutted. "None of that, Son. Liana will stay in the room beside your father and I. We will keep a close eye on her while she is here."

"You ruin all my fun, Mother," he teased while Liana's cheeks flared with embarrassment. As much as she would have loved to be closer to Damien, it was probably for the best that they'd have his parents as buffers between them because with each passing day, it became that much more difficult to resist the temptation they both toyed at.

Eva did not rise to her son's teasing, instead, bit into a crunchy piece of apple.

"Thank you for the suggestion, Eva," Liana said, her tongue halting over the informal use of the high lady's name. It would be something she'd have to get used to, just like a great many number of things it would seem. She'd have to get used to living in this castle. To the luxury of being queen that went far beyond even her wealthy upbringing. To the heavy weight of responsibilities she'd yet to comprehend. To be a wife.

There was much still to do, and Liana wasn't quite prepared for any of it.

"I suppose there will be no more pub visits once you are queen then," Asher commented to which Liana smacked his arm out of habit. She was used to doing that with Carlisle all the time. Asher merely laughed at her actions.

"I told you to forget about that," she mumbled through gritted teeth.

"No one will ever forget that," Owen interjected. Her jaw dropped. He was supposed to be the serious one, the one who took his duties so seriously above all else yet here he was teasing her with his brother.

"Forget what?" Ramone questioned.

Liana was quick to respond. "Nothing."

"She got pissed at a pub and started dancing on the bar and tables," Asher revealed to which Damien and Ramone chuckled. Liana's face flamed.

"It was not my finest hour." She avoided looking in Luciano's direction, avoided his undoubtedly disappointed look.

Damien took her hand in his beneath the table. "It was all in good fun."

"It sounds reckless," Luciano interjected.

"The three of us were there to protect her, Grandfather."

"How would a group of vampires have protected the people from her mage power though? She is obviously more powerful than any mage in Triaedian. What would happen if she lost control while drunk?"

Thoroughly reprimanded, Liana let go of Damien's hand to pick at her nails. She had been a bit uncontrolled. Her magic gouged a crevice in the road without her bidding.

"Liana is not a fledgling, Grandfather. She is plenty controlled." She appreciated Damien defending her even if they both knew he lied. She was anything but controlled.

"And you are a fool blinded by love. She is a fledgling in mage terms. Only nineteen years old with the power of a Master, and of course, in mage tradition, completely untrained because she is female."

Her breath stuttered out of her. Magic simmered beneath her skin, rising to defend without her permission as always. She'd only encountered the ancient vampire for a few hours the other day and already he understood her. Understood what the others ignored or were in denial about.

"She has trained herself," Damien defended. "You were not there when we were attacked by the rebels. Liana saved everyone and defeated their entire battalion with little aid from my army."

"From what I hear, she exploded with uncontrolled power that knocked out their army and ours."

Damien growled beside her.

"Still wrestling with your vampire, boy," Luciano taunted, and Liana was getting quite tired of the cantankerous, old bastard.

"First of all, it is my army, Grandfather, you are no longer the King, and I will not allow you to antagonize Liana." Damien fisted his hands but not before she saw his fingers morph into taloned claws.

"You cannot live in denial about the danger she poses to us all. Vampires are the least sensitive to sensing magic and even I can feel her vibrating with it the more upset she becomes."

Damien leaped to his feet, his chair tumbling backward. Ramone rose with him, a hand to his son's chest that rose and fell too quickly. Luciano merely sat back. Knowing he was right, Liana breathed deeply, shoving her magic down as far as it would go.

"And you have gone lax with your own training, boy. Your vampire is ruling you again. If you both don't get control, you're doomed and you'll bring us all down with you."

Liana slid her hand into Damien's after forcing it open. "Damien," she called lightly. His head snapped toward her, his eyes nearly all black, fangs filling his slightly parted lips. "Calm, Damien," she said, her fingers stroking along his forearm. His eyes fell closed, his chest rising and falling slower.

Eyes narrowed on Luciano, she took a moment to consider her next move. This ancient vampire clearly had far more experience than both of them, and he only spoke truth. His truths cut deeper than either of them wanted to acknowledge though.

"If you truly care about Damien and Triaedian, then I suggest the next time you speak to me you choose to use your words for guidance instead of instigation. I am young. I am untried by your standards, but I am not a lost cause. Nor do I appreciate your insults."

Luciano didn't seem to hear her, his eyes focused on their joined hands and Damien's face. Her fiancé calmed the moment she touched him, his fangs retracted slowly afterward and his eyes following until his vampiric side was held at bay once more.

Sensing she wouldn't receive a reply from the former king, she nodded her head towards Damien's parents. "I shall take my leave. Thank you for your hospitality. I shall ask my parents their thoughts on the move and get back to you." Pulling Damien with her, she strode away from the table. Phillipa trailed them as soon as they passed her.

No one spoke until they reached the main staircase, and that was when Damien pulled her back and held her against the stone wall, away from prying eyes. Phillipa gasped but stayed quiet.

Damien leaned in close, his nose brushing against her neck as he inhaled. "Grandfather has always been my biggest hero, but you just pulled his throne right out from under him. I'm amazed by you, Liana." His lips claimed hers in a fierce possession. Liana accepted him eagerly, wanting so much more but he pulled back just as abruptly. "Go now while I can still control myself. Pack your things, and I shall send a cart and servants to transport it all here."

Biting her lip, she attempted to recenter herself. "Um, yes, okay. I will see you tomorrow."

Smirking, he gave her a wink before running off with vampiric speed.

Phillipa quickly linked her arm through Liana's and tugged her toward the stairs. "Hopeless fools in love," she tutted.

Liana chuckled then sighed. She certainly couldn't argue with her maid.

Chapter Ten

Liana prepared an entire speech to give to her parents the next morning. All night she tossed and turned as she crafted the perfect string of words to convince them to let her move to the castle early. She doubted her mother would care, in fact, the woman would probably help pack her bags if it meant throwing her at the King for whatever he pleased. Her father would take convincing because as most male mages, he stuck strictly to the belief that all females remain chaste until their wedding. Moving into Damien's home, even if it is a massive castle, would appear uncouth. Still, she spun a very eloquent argument on why she would benefit from moving into the castle early.

While they all sat in the drawing room on this dry morning waiting for breakfast, all the windows open to let in the fresh air, Liana rehearsed her speech. Her father sat at his desk reading through and answering letters with Wesley aiding him. Carlisle and William played a game of blocks while Charlotte played a piece on the piano. Hannah sat beside Liana with a book and Lady Monroe busied herself with needlework on the sofa opposite Liana.

Liana's hands twisted in her lap as she gulped, preparing herself.

"Father, Mother, I must speak with you," she began. Her father turned from his writing desk while her mother just gave a hum of acknowledgement, her focus still on the needlework in her hands. Her siblings tuned in as well.

"As you know, I've been training at the castle each day. The High Lady would also like to start lessons with me and thought it best if I move into the castle to save time. There is also a concern of safety with everything that has been happening. It is a great risk traveling back and forth each day."

Henry entered to deliver the mail, looking as pristine as ever in his butler's uniform, and gave her a brief moment to breathe as he handed the letters to her father.

"Breakfast is ready, my Lord," Henry informed before leaving.

Distracted, Lord Monroe sifted through it all, handing a letter to Wesley then to Liana. She took it absently, noting only the swooping lines of her name on the front.

"What are you asking, dear?" Lady Monroe questioned.

"May I move into the castle prior to the wedding? The High Lady invited me personally, and I would have my own chambers, of course. There is so much to learn though and the commute is too far and dangerous."

"She has a point, Mary. It would be safer," Lord Monroe commented while already reading through his mail. Liana stared at her father, surprised he capitulated so easily.

"You want to leave us so soon?" she complained.

"No, Mother. It only makes sense to go. It is only two weeks early, anyway."

She shook her head. "Give me a moment to think. We can discuss this over breakfast." She stood, addressing the others. "Come now."

Liana sighed. That was as best as she would get for now. Flipping the letter over, she broke the plain wax seal and slid out the small piece of parchment. As she read the few words written there, her heart skipped a beat then dropped out of her chest.

Do not marry the king, or you shall suffer a fate worse than death.

There was no signature, no indication who sent it. Only a few words that managed to freeze her entire body with fear. Magic roiled beneath her skin, sensing the threat Liana so clearly felt.

Hannah gasped from beside Liana. "Papa!" she cried, grabbing onto Liana's arm. Lord Monroe snatched the letter from her hands, taking only seconds to read the threat.

"Guard!" he screamed, one of the vampires arriving instantly. "Secure the house, Liana has been threatened. I will send word to the King." As he scribbled something on a blank parchment on his desk, he ordered, "Mary, take everyone down to the kitchen. Have the servants secure the area."

Lady Monroe gathered her children, shoving them toward the door. She pulled Liana off the sofa, dragging her along as Lord Monroe sent the message via magic. They were ushered through the kitchen and down into the cellar with the servants.

As soon as Lady Monroe gave the order, the servants locked the iron door they just entered and ensured the door to the outside was locked as well. There were no windows and no other points of entry. In a matter of a minute, the entire staff and her family were locked inside all while her frantic magic battered against her control to be let out, to protect her.

Liana clamped down on her magic, begging it to calm down. Lamps were lit by magic and the family settled at a small table and chairs while the servants huddled in groups, either standing or sitting on stools and cushions.

A servant set a cup of tea before her, the calming scent of it doing little to ease her nerves. Lady Monroe held William in her lap while rubbing a hand over Liana's back. "It will be okay, sweetie. Your father will protect us," she promised.

He should not have to protect them. This should not be happening. She should be out there helping. But she found that she could not move. What good were her lessons if she always froze in the face of danger?

Footsteps pounded down the stairs followed by a specific patterned knock. A servant opened the door to Wesley. Damien rushed in after him, and to her surprise, Luciano. She stood, meeting him. His hands framed her face as he looked her over, eyes dilated and frenzied.

"Are you hurt?" he asked in a growl, his fangs out. She shook her head, holding on to his arms. He pressed his forehead to hers, taking a steadying breath. "Stay here until we figure this out. Grandfather will stay here to protect you. I will retrieve you later." He stepped back, his eyes back to normal, his fangs gone.

He disappeared up the stairs again with Wesley, the servant securing the iron door while Liana sank into her chair, ignoring the ancient vampire that settled into a corner away from everyone else. If anyone realized who he was, they made no mention of it, ignoring him just as he did of them.

From Liana's perspective, it was as though the gods were against her from the moment she'd been born. They cursed her with this power and left her to live a life in seclusion and fear. Then, when she finally had a chance at happiness, her entire relationship with Damien had been rocky from the start, one thing after another interfering. This was just the latest in a string of challenges. Although they would get through it, she wished they would stop. She was tired of being scared.

Hours passed before anyone returned for them. The servants lounged at the table with them, the others on the floor. Food was served at one point although Liana couldn't eat much with her stomach in knots. At some point, Liana was so bored that she started summoning objects requested by others. She summoned knitting supplies, books and parchment, even a chess board for Carlisle and Chef to play. Liana studied the spellbook Master Kinley gave her when they heard steps on the stairs again.

The knock was different this time, but the servant still opened the door. Her father appeared this time with Damien.

"It is safe," Lord Monroe declared. "You may exit and take what remains of the day to rest," he told the servants.

"Liana, come," Damien ordered, holding his hand out to her. Ready to leave, she didn't balk at the order. Grabbing her book, she slid her hand into his. "We are going to the castle. I'll send for your things when they are packed."

"What about my family? Are they safe here?"

"We believe the threat is only to you. If you leave, they will be safe. I will leave guards to be sure."

Liana looked back at her family. "I will see you all soon. I love you all," she said in farewell before following Damien up the stairs. Luciano followed on her heels. When they reached the front door, Damien picked her up and ran all the way to the castle, his grandfather following. It was no wonder he showed up everywhere so quickly as they arrived within seconds. He set her down just over the threshold of the entrance while Luciano continued on, not stopping with them.

"Welcome home, my love." Despite the turmoil of the day, she smiled up at him.

"You are my home, Damien." He raised that damned brow.

"Feeling overly sentimental?" he teased. She laughed at herself, spinning on her heel with a shrug.

"I thought I would try it out. I don't think it suits me." He snuck up behind her, pulling her into his body to whisper in her ear.

"It soothes my aching heart to hear such words, but I also enjoy the attitude."

She spun in his arms. "I am pleased to hear it. You, on the other hand, could improve on both fronts." She patted his chest then strutted away, his laughter following her.

"Build me up, huh?" he called out.

"Then knock you back down," she finished, her hips swaying with each step up the stairs. He appeared beside her, caging her against the wall.

"What am I going to do with you, temptress?" he taunted, his hand resting at her throat, thumb brushing over her pounding pulse.

A familiar throat cleared followed by, "Stay far away," Eva declared.

"Mother, honestly, you have the worst timing."

"I am the only thing keeping that girl from ruin in the eyes of the mage community. No one else cares if you bed the girl or not. You'll be thanking me soon."

Damien took his mother's hands and placed a kiss on her cheek. "Thank you, Mother. And as you've so directly pointed out, I cannot be trusted. Will you please show Liana to her temporary chambers?"

"Excellent idea, my boy. I'll put her right next to your father and me. Come along, dear."

"Why does it feel like I'm being punished for your wandering hands?" she whispered to him.

"This is entirely your doing. If you were not so tempting..." he whispered back only to be interrupted by his mother.

"Do you not have somewhere to be, Damien?" she called over her shoulder, still walking down the hall. Chuckling, he gave Liana a quick kiss to her cheek.

She couldn't keep the trembling out of her voice as she called to him, "Damien." She tugged him back into her arms as he made to move away. "Who sent that letter? Was it the rebels?"

A heavy sigh escaped him before he wrapped his arms around her completely. "It could have been anyone. We were unable to track it to whomever wrote it."

"Who else aside from the rebels would want us apart though?" she pressed, her magic still uneasy beneath her skin.

Damien smoothed out the lines of worry crinkling at the corners of his eyes and gave her a gentle smile. "Do not trouble yourself with this, Liana. I will protect you from any and all threats."

Liana frowned at him. "If you knew me at all, Damien, you would know that I dislike when males try to placate me." She shoved him off and walked up the few remaining stairs to follow his mother down the hall. She stood patiently at the far end of the hallway, pretending not to listen, although with those vampiric ears, she heard it all.

"Liana." Damien grabbed her hand, pulling her back around. Pulling out of his grip, she crossed her arms over her chest. "My love, I know I cannot placate you, but it is not in my nature to let my wife worry over my responsibilities."

"Your responsibilities? I would think that my safety would be my responsibility, and I'm not your wife yet," she declared, her magic fueling her sudden anger.

"Semantics," he retorted. "And your safety is my responsibility. It is my top concern." He seemed to grow before her eyes, his chest broadening, his height looming over her. Even his eyes grew dark with shadows of the creature that lurked inside him. "Keeping you out of harm's way is all that matters to me." That last word ended in a growl as he stalked her toward the wall.

Liana gulped, her steps faltering as she backpedaled. She'd only seen Damien like this one other time. After she'd run into the forest and that mercenary caught her. He'd looked the same then as well. Eyes wild with rage, features sharpened into a creature of death with fangs made for the ultimate predator.

Arms caged her against the wall once more, except she shook with fear instead of need this time. His nose dipped to her throat, dragging along the tender skin.

"When are you going to realize, Liana, that you have become the most important thing in my life? When are you going to realize that I will protect you at any cost? That I will kill first and ask questions later of anyone that dares utter a word against you."

Despite her fear, despite the cold nervousness that had her magic twitching and ready to protect her, Liana loosened her tight shoulders and breathed deeply.

"There is that overbearing, ruthless king the rumors speak about," she said, her heart pounding out of her chest. "I was beginning to think it was all truly just gossip. There was no way my tender-hearted fiancé was this menacing monarch the kingdom spoke of."

He growled, pressing his body into hers. Liana kept her eyes on his, the blue she loved just a sliver around the black. "Tender-hearted?" His hand drifted over her shoulder to encircle her throat. With the slightest bit of pressure, her magic reached out of its own volition and latched onto his wrist. He spared the flare of gold magic a glance, not threatened in the slightest. His thumb nudged at her chin, her head lightly hitting the wall as she was forced to look up at him.

"Do I feel tender now?" he growled, his hard body flush against every inch of her own.

Never one to back down from his challenges, Liana urged her magic forward, urged it to slide up his arm, over the collar of his shirt. Her magic still sought to protect her but let Liana alter its feel, let Damien feel desire as it slipped beneath his collar and caressed down his chest, down the ridges of his abdomen.

He shivered beneath her touch which had her smirking. "So tender, my king."

"Temptress," he growled before his mouth was on her. He captured the surprised cry that escaped her, swallowing it down as he slanted his lips over hers.

Liana couldn't think, could only feel as he consumed her, consumed every thought and feeling. Falling into his embrace, she lost control of her magic, wrapping her arms around his waist to desperately hold onto his dizzying yet grounding presence.

Before she could lose herself completely, he broke away. Panting, they stared at each other, eyes wide.

"Liana," he groaned, bending over as if hurt. "Your magic," he managed to say.

Surprised, Liana focused on her magic, finding it slithering all over him, exploring and lighting up beneath his clothes. Liana latched onto it, taking back control and pulled it off him. Instead of roiling with the need to protect, for once, her magic purred happily, content like she'd never felt before.

Damien leaned over with his hands on his knees still breathing heavily.

"Are you hurt?" she worried, although her magic didn't feel as though it hurt him.

He groaned and slammed her into the wall once more. His mouth ravenous upon her own, she closed her eyes to follow his lead as he nipped at her lip and soothed it with a kiss.

"You are going to undo me," he breathed, resting his forehead against hers.

"I didn't mean to... my magic... I lost control," she tried to explain, her thoughts still frazzled.

"You may lose control whenever you wish, temptress." He gave her a gentle kiss before putting a bit of space between them. He was back to himself, those glacial blue eyes bright and teasing once more.

Liana struggled to gather her thoughts, finally recalling what started this to begin with. She brushed down her skirts and cleared her throat in an attempt to calm her racing heart.

"Yes, well, if you had not lost control, nor would I. And before you go vampire on me once more, let me reiterate that my safety is my concern. You do not withhold information about my safety."

"There is nothing we know for certain about the letter, Liana," he said, running his hands through his hair and taking a moment to compose himself. "I did not mean to make you feel managed. All I wanted is for you to not feel scared because I will keep you safe, my love. I will protect you from all threats."

"That is a touching sentiment, however, you cannot make such a promise. You are the King of Triaedian. There will always be a threat and you cannot promise that you will catch each one unless you lock me up in one of these towers. You must keep me informed so I can also stay alert and on guard."

That damn brow rose, accompanied by a smirk. "Locked in a tower? That sounds promising." He leaned forward as if to trap her once more. Liana shoved him away and took a step toward the hall his mother disappeared to.

"That is not amusing in the slightest, Damien," she warned. She'd never let herself be locked up anywhere ever again. "Now, I will take my leave, Your Majesty," she said formally just to rile him some more. Turning, she didn't curtsy. She rarely had during their courtship and now that she would be his queen soon, she wouldn't start. She saw them as equals and would not be bowing to him, especially not when she currently needed to emphasize her point. He supported her independence from the beginning, she wouldn't let him stop now.

Although she still worried about her ability to perform when she truly faced danger, that would just have to be something else she had to work on. Instead of cowering in fear, she'd have to learn to react with action, to defend herself and others unlike today when she merely froze. Straightening her shoulders as she walked, well aware of Damien's eyes on her, she added that to the ever-growing list of things to do.

When she turned the corner, Liana was not surprised to find Eva waiting at the end of another long hallway. Arms crossed and leaning against a wooden door at the very end of the hall, she had that same imperious brow raised just like her son.

Prepared for whatever scolding the woman wished to dole out, Liana strode toward her. Standing before Eva, she planted her hands on her hips. "Well, what tongue-lashing have you prepared?" she asked boldly when the older vampire simply stared at her.

Eva smiled, cold-cunning shining in her eyes. "You did well for one so young and naïve."

Liana opened her mouth to argue about her naivety, but Eva held up a hand to stop her. "What you have yet to understand about vampires, Liana, is that we are more alike with shifters than with mage. Inside us lurks a creature, a predator ready to pounce. Because that is what we truly are at the basest level of ourselves, predators. We were created to be the perfect hunters and in turn, the fiercest protectors." She pushed off the door and circled Liana with unearthly grace. "When something we love is threatened, our creature side takes over. It takes control of whatever humanity we have and turns it to ash so that we can protect with lethal accuracy."

Liana shivered thinking back to when Damien ripped that mercenary's head from his shoulders. There had been none of the man she knew in that vampire's face, only a ruthless, killing calm.

"My son is no exception although he has sought to control his baser instincts with an iron fist. With you, his control slips so easily. It worries him. Worried because his creature is especially cruel and merciless."

Liana had no idea. He hadn't talked to her about any of this.

Eva continued, uncaring of Liana's turmoil. "He has waited so long to find a wife and much to our surprise, he chose you, a mage. The most vulnerable of all the species, with the shortest lifespan. Even the shifters live at least two-hundred years. You are so much more breakable than a vampire wife would be."

Liana once thought Eva to be kind, or at least thought the woman liked her. She was not so sure anymore. Fisting her hands at her sides, she stood there as Eva circled her once more. "My magic is powerful. I can protect myself," she declared.

"Of that I have no doubt," Eva purred. "Which is one of the reasons my son chose you, the strongest mage to have ever been born."

Her words struck a nerve as she recalled similar ones from so long ago. Words shouted at her in the darkness of a cell with pain wracking every breath.

"He loves me," Liana said through gritted teeth. She wouldn't let this woman manipulate her. Damien loved her, he didn't care about her magic.

"Of course he does, dear. But that does not negate the fact that he also covets your power." Eva stood before Liana now, her face blank without a hint of malice despite her words.

"Why are you telling me this? What game do you play?" Liana questioned, unable to figure this woman out.

Eva's eyes narrowed. "Are you strong enough to stand by his side? Are you strong enough to become the Queen of Triaedian and face the trials that come with the title?" She paused, letting her words sink in before she finished with, "Are you strong enough to not run from his vampire when he inevitably, fully loses control?"

Anger surged through Liana's veins. Not anger directed at Eva though. Anger because the woman was correct in questioning her. Was Liana ready for all of this? Was she strong enough to survive it all and not drag Damien down with her?

There was one thing she was certain of, and that was her love for Damien. That man supported her from the very beginning. With just one look, he devoted himself to her, to caring for all her broken pieces. He gave her what she needed when she had no idea what that was. He continued to challenge her to become better, face her fears instead of hiding from them. He taught her to open her mind beyond the misguided beliefs she held so steadfastly to about men and their society. He made it so easy to fall in love with a decent man.

And just now, she had been scared when he lost a bit of control, when his vampiric side took hold. But she didn't run. She met him face to face. She challenged him just as he always did for her. She loved him, every part of him, and that would never change, even if she didn't fully understand everything just yet. He did the same for her as he stood beside her, guiding her through the turmoil of remembering her childhood trauma. Even before that, when she exploded with magic by the lake, he did not call her a freak, did not ogle her like some prized possession. He only showed her kindness and understanding.

Liana stepped up to the High Lady. Nose to nose, Liana stared into eyes that were just a shade darker than Damien's. "I may not know how to play all your courtly games but I do know that, no matter the circumstances, I will never run from him. I will stand by his side to face whatever challenges come our way. And if he should ever lose control of his vampiric side, I will be there to bring him back."

"Your attempts at teasing or seduction will not always be enough," Eva countered, which had Liana's cheeks heating with embarrassment. Of course she heard them just down the hall.

"It may not, but I know Damien, and he would never hurt me."

"He wouldn't mean to. His vampire only wants to protect you, but sometimes that means doing things you may not like. He was not kidding when he said he'd lock you in a tower."

Liana's palm twitched as she desperately told herself not to slap the woman. Eva didn't know of her past, didn't know how much that one comment stung, but it didn't lessen the blow or her need for retaliation. But that was exactly what Eva aimed to do, wasn't it? She wanted Liana to lose control, wanted to push her and test her.

Taking a step back, Liana took a deep breath and raised her chin defiantly. "Damien understands me, and I understand him. We know what our limits are and how to act with one another. He may be your son, but he will be my husband and you will not try to come between us or turn me away from him like you are now. I know what I am getting myself into, you don't need to remind me." Eva raised that damn brow again. "If that is all, shall we start my regency lessons or shall we wait for another time?"

Eva's smirk turned sinister. "Oh, my dear, we have already begun." She turned and waved for Liana to follow as she walked through the wooden door she leaned against before.

Liana squared her shoulders and followed the conniving woman. It seemed as though her lessons would never end.

Chapter Eleven

The servants worked quickly to move her belongings into the castle. As promised, her quarters were beside Damien's parents, not that she minded much. She quite enjoyed waking in the castle and having breakfast with Damien and his family. Sometimes Asher and Owen would join, or they'd be out on duty somewhere. Unfortunately, Luciano was always present as well. The only benefit was that he barely spoke and he'd stopped insulting her. He also disappeared after breakfast, not to be seen until supper every evening.

Liana found it far more convenient to not have to travel so far each day, and it allowed her to study and practice far longer. Today though, she made it a point to ask for an escort into the city to run a few errands. Damien protested at first, stating that the servants would get whatever she needed, but Liana insisted on going herself. She wanted to chat with a few friends and such.

Damien countered that he thought she didn't have any friends, which he was not entirely joking about. Eventually she convinced him to let her go as long as she took Sasha and Owen as guards.

So, the four of them, including Phillipa, sat in the carriage, ambling toward the city in the early morning. Phillipa carried three satchels full of potions and trinkets, all the latest orders from her secret business.

"It is a pleasure to see you again, Sasha. May I ask where you have been? I haven't seen you around the castle," Liana questioned.

"I was visiting a friend in the north, my Lady."

"Oh, how nice. I've never been anywhere aside from Sancta Valles and Sapphire Cove. I hear the north is just as beautiful if not a bit more barren."

"To the far northeast, the forests lead way into rocky and grassy landscapes upon the mountains. The northwest is mountainous but far more lush and the coast is far steeper with the entire border being cliffs."

"Fascinating. One day I shall travel there to see it for myself. You'd come too, Phillipa."

"I'm not much for traveling, Lady Liana."

"Yes, well, I suppose Damien will be fine enough company then." Phillipa snorted a laugh, pulling one from Owen as well.

"I doubt you'd be able to leave him behind," Owen commented.

Smiling, she looked at Sasha. "Where do you suggest we visit first then?"

"Port Salvus would be my first destination."

Liana recognized the name. It was the first landing site of the original founders of Triaedian. They sailed from distant kingdoms in search of a new land where they could create their own kingdom of unity. Damien's ancestors were on that ship, the first vampires to set foot on this land they claimed as Triaedian.

"I would love to visit." She'd always wanted to go but her parents weren't much for traveling either. They'd never let her go alone either. It wasn't exactly safe to travel as a single female anyway.

"It is a far journey," Owen warned.

Liana shrugged. "It would be worth it." And it would. Her magic hummed in agreement, feeling a draw toward this place that was the first village that started it all.

When they arrived on the outskirts of the city, they stopped at the homeless house where she kept her face concealed and only allowed Sasha in because she appeared less threatening. There was not much for her to do but she did leave behind a few games for the children to entertain themselves with. She even relinquished one of her old dolls to a little girl.

Next, they rode into the city's wealthier districts to stop at Bacchus and Helen's bakery. Owen led the way, Sasha following closely.

"How did I know this is where we were headed next?" Sasha commented as they entered through the front door.

Liana didn't respond to the question and met Helen with a hug.

"My dear, you have been missed," Helen greeted. "Congratulations though, future Queen." She teased with a curtsy.

"Please, Helen, I cannot deal with curtsies just yet."

Laughing, she slung an arm over her shoulder and led her toward the back. Bacchus dropped the dough he was kneading and swallowed her in a hug.

"So good to see you, darling girl."

Cheeks flushed and a smile filling her face, Liana felt herself calm. This was normal to her. This was routine and comfortable. Something she sorely missed in the past few weeks.

"A pleasure to see you both."

"Here, sit. Everyone, please," Helen gestured, already pulling up additional stools around the tiny table in the back of the warm kitchen. "I've got croissants for everyone."

"No, Helen, please. I didn't mean to interrupt."

"Nonsense. We have loads to fill you in on," she gushed, stacking a plate full of the delicious pastry. After setting it down, she kept working beside her mate as they filled her in on all the latest shifter gossip.

Liana laughed at most of it. Some was good news, some awful. But she saved the worst for last. "Which brings me to the unrest among the community."

Owen and Sasha didn't move a muscle but Liana sensed their entire attention shifted toward Helen now.

"Ever since word got out about the attack on you and the king by the lake, people have been more suspicious. It seems talk of breeds and segregation is all that anyone cares about now. I know of a few customers that no longer come here because you and the King frequent us."

Liana frowned. "I'm terribly sorry to have caused problems."

"Don't you worry about it for a second, sweetheart. You've brought us more business than any of those fools that left. Besides, I don't want to serve any rebels anyway."

"You know the butcher across the lane and two doors down, my great uncle?" Bacchus questioned then kept going. "He said the same thing. He's lost a few customers because he supports you and the King."

Liana shrank into her seat. She had no idea her marriage would be so problematic. "I never intended for our marriage to cause such a divide. If anything, I thought it might inspire change, perhaps even more acceptance."

Helen clucked her tongue. "It's no fault of yours, Liana. People are who they are and nothing you do or don't do is going to change them."

"Maybe, but it sounds like our engagement has already caused a divide among the people. What will our marriage, and perhaps even children do? What will become of Triaedian if a half-mage, half-vampire sits on the throne?"

Magic curled in her palms sparking everyone's attention while her worry rose.

"I suppose your child would face much adversity but they would be more powerful, would they not?" Bacchus pointed out.

Liana looked to Owen. He was there the night she lost control over the thought of her imaginary children suffering as she did. Now she remembered why she'd been so tortured and distraught through the years, but still, they would be born different from everyone else, not just powerful like her.

He saw the panic in her eyes and laid a hand on her forearm. "Do not think about it, Liana. You know your child would be loved and protected by all of us."

Liana swallowed thickly. There was no guarantee they could even conceive, a child was hypothetical. The threat upon her marriage was not.

"What are we to do if our marriage is already creating a rift among the breeds?"

No one had an answer.

"We did not mean to upset you," Helen said. "You marry that vampire and forget everyone else. Your relationship will inspire others to do the same."

Liana agreed, yet couldn't ignore that it would also enrage others as well. She stood, taking one satchel from Phillipa. Placing it on the counter, she gave Helen a hug.

"Please deliver these last few orders and let everyone know that I won't be able to continue this."

"Of course, sweetheart. You keep your chin up and forget those rebels. You and the King are stronger than them."

With a reluctant smile, she nodded and left with her entourage in tow.

They silently walked down a few blocks toward Claudius's fabric shop. Her guards were focused on their surroundings while Liana's mind reeled. She had no intention for her marriage to cause such strife. More than ever she wished to just run away and disappear with Damien, far away from court and politics.

Moving on to their next location, Claudius was busy with customers when she entered, all of them taking too long to look and comment about her. She left him a note and the satchel before leaving once more. When they made it to the back entrance of Felix's blood bar, Owen finally stopped.

"You are not going in there, Lady Liana," he declared.

Sasha walked past him. "It's fine." She knew her way up the stairs and found Felix on the third floor with Cassia and her children. A few homeless vampires occupied the second floor.

Cassia ran to her immediately and hugged the air out of her chest. "You amazing female. There is not enough thanks in the world to bestow upon you."

She patted the woman's back gently if not a bit awkwardly. "You are welcome, Cassia. How is the little babe?" She led her to where Felix sat with the baby girl.

"Good morning, Liana," Felix greeted with a smile.

She smiled back at the blind vampire and rested a hand on his shoulder. "Good morning, Felix. How is your granddaughter?"

"Perfect, of course. Would you like to hold her?" He lifted the babe and Liana scooped her into the crook of her arm. She was only weeks old and still adorable.

"Perfect, just as you said."

He smiled proudly. She summoned cushions for everyone and sat on the floor.

"I heard exciting news, Liana. Is it true you are going to marry the King?" Liana nodded at Cassia's enthusiasm, not feeling as happy about it right now.

"I am. That is not something we need to discuss though. What about you? How are you feeling?"

"I'm wonderful, thanks to you."

Liana merely hummed in response as she gazed down at the precious baby in her arms. To think that she was born into a world where people would hate her based on who she chose to love was unthinkable. Liana hated this world. Even in a land that prized diversification, they were still separated.

Felix must have sensed her melancholy and he reached for his cello. "A lesson, Liana?"

Liana handed the baby to Phillipa and grabbed the other cello before sitting on the stool. She followed his lead, playing a cheerful tune that didn't hit quite right within her. She played for the others, still stuck in her own mind.

When Felix abruptly stopped the song, Liana did as well, curious.

"Someone new is coming," he warned, getting to his feet and grabbing the dagger at his waist. Liana erected a shield around everyone staring at the stairs with bated breath. When Luciano appeared on the stairs, her shoulders dropped but her shield did not.

Felix dropped to one knee. Owen and Sasha gave polite bows of their heads.

"As you were," he declared, stepping into Felix's home without permission.

Felix stood. "High Lord Luciano, it is an honor to be in your presence again."

"You as well, Felix. I'm pleased to know you are doing well and that my grandson took care of you after your injury."

Felix bowed his head but Liana scoffed.

Earthy brown eyes latched onto hers. "Something to add, mage?" He didn't respect her enough to call her by name.

With a saccharine smile she shook her head. "Oh, nothing at all." Only that it was she who pulled Felix from the depths of his melancholy, not Damien. "Did you follow me?"

"I did," he responded without shame. "I've been following you since I first arrived. I'll admit, this is the first time someone has surprised me in quite a long time, the last time being when Damien transitioned, although I should have seen that coming considering what he is."

Her brows furrowed. "What he is?" she repeated for clarification. He didn't offer any.

"It struck me as odd that a mage seemed so close to those shifters at the bakery, then your delivery to the fabric dealer. Now, here, at an old Royal Commander's home. If I didn't know you were a naive little girl, I would suspect you were up to something."

Cassia and Phillipa gasped at the insult.

Felix took a step in front of her. "High Lord, I beg your pardon, but Liana is the kindest and most loyal person I've ever met. She saved my life and just weeks ago, she saved my daughter and granddaughter. You don't get to speak to her like that in my home."

Liana appreciated his support, not that it would do much good.

"Is there a reason you came to insult me yet again? If you'll get all of it out now so we could all move on with our days, that would be swell. Although, I'd just as soon swallow poison than indulge you further, but you are Damien's grandfather after all."

The ancient vampire actually smirked at her in response. "No more insults, Mage. I am simply curious about you. You are the first puzzle I haven't immediately cracked in too long. You've got me intrigued."

"Let me relieve you of that intrigue then because I am a simple mage female that just wants to live her life in peace."

His brows lifted. "Then why did you agree to marry the one person that could never grant you that?"

He had a point. She'd said so herself many times. With a sigh, she sat back down on the stool then dropped her shield. "Cut it with the insults, old man, or we're going to have problems. Felix, another song." Ignoring the ancient vampire, she chose a classic song full of passion. It was up to the listener to determine what kind of passion that was, for now, Liana felt it through anger.

Luciano leaned against the wall near a window, occasionally looking out. He watched her mostly, his eyes always slightly squinted in her direction. Used to being watched and scrutinized, Liana ignored him. After one more song, Liana decided to get back to the castle. It neared midday which left plenty of time to practice her magic.

"Felix, Cassia, I've brought the rest of those orders with a list. I included a pile of other sun protecting charms, rings, bracelets, and the like for any that may need them in the future." Phillipa handed the last satchel over. "I left a few vials of blood filler as well because I will not be able to keep doing this. With everything changing, I doubt I could keep up with it, nor would it look good if news got out that the Queen was giving out free services."

Felix hugged her. "We understand, Liana. You've done more than enough already. The cello will be here waiting whenever you'd like to visit. Now, why don't you go relax for a while with that fiancé of yours."

She huffed a laugh. "Unlikely. Thank you all the same."

Cassia hugged her goodbye before they all filed down the back stairs. When they got to the carriage, Luciano made Owen ride outside with the driver.

"If you are going to stare at me the entire ride, I will put up a shield you cannot see through," she snapped at the former king, her nerves already frayed.

"How long have you been providing free services to all of Sancta Valles and the homeless?"

She shrugged. "It wasn't all of Sancta Valles, just the inner city. I've never traveled to the outer villages." He dropped his chin, his stare expectant. Leaning to look out the window, she watched the forest go by as they left the city and started up the long path to the castle. "Since I was a child."

"How did you first start?"

If the suspicious vampire needed honesty in order to accept her, she'd give them to him. It didn't make any difference to her.

"I roamed the city alone too much as a child. I first stumbled upon the homeless during those times. I was always dirty and my clothes torn from playing outside, much to Phillipa's disdain, so they didn't see me as too out of place, and when I performed magic for them without a price, they never questioned me. It wasn't until I met Helen that it became an organized thing."

Liana remembered that moment fondly. She'd snuck away from Phillipa yet again and ran right to the bakery with the coin she'd pilfered from Wesley's allowance. Helen eyed her skeptically when the girl arrived alone and a mess as usual. While waiting in line, she discreetly repaired many of the rickety tables and chairs around her, even the displays when she got close enough. She went back every day that week to buy a different pastry and while she sat there, her magic begged to be used and she spruced up whatever she could.

"Bacchus was in the back when we all heard a clatter and scream. After Helen rushed back there, I heard her scream and ran to help. Bacchus tripped as he was refilling the wood for the oven and went face first into the fire. I healed him quickly and the rest followed."

He seemed to wait for more. "What did you gain from it?"

She flung her hands up in defeat. "Why does there always have to be something gained or some ulterior motive? I was a bored child with too much magic."

"And too little caution," Phillipa interjected, earning a glare from Liana.

"She is right. You were lucky you were not snatched off the streets and used for your power."

Flashes of her memories pummeled her. Of Ranville throwing her haphazardly into that cell. Of pain and fear consuming her.

Magic rushed into her hands, sparks dripping from her fingers as she tried to breathe through her panic. Darkness clouded the edges of her vision. Distantly, she heard Phillipa's voice trying to talk her down. The memories were too loud though. His voice overpowered all others. The memories shoved reality aside, forcing her to relive the torture she endured after being snatched off the streets. She lost the battle to stay present, to force the memories aside and fell into her own mind.

Darkness consumed her, the stench of damp earth didn't bother her too much anymore considering she couldn't breathe through it anymore, so swollen as it was and clogged by tears and blood. Her breath hiccuped in and out in a jarring rhythm to all her injuries. Curled on the floor, her small body hurt so much.

"Liana!" Someone screamed at her and she flinched. If only she had her magic to protect her but these bars prevented her from using it. That left her feeling far more empty and despondent than being in the cell, the absence of her magic. It had always been a comforting blanket around her soul for as long as she could remember, now that it was gone, she felt it so keenly.

"Liana!" Someone shook her shoulders and she blinked. Vision blurred, she blinked again. Light pierced her eyes and she flinched away. Her body responded and instead of pain, she felt only soft grass. Grass. That wasn't right. Grasping onto it with all she had, dirt sank beneath her nails and she opened her eyes.

She wasn't in that cell. She wasn't a child anymore.

"Liana?" his voice penetrated the fog, sounding uncertain.

Her magic reacted to him first, calming enough for her to gain her bearings. Kneeling in the grass, she found him beside her, the carriage behind him and the others hiding behind it except for Luciano who openly stared.

"Damien?"

He pulled her into an embrace. "I've got you, love."

Closing her eyes, she wrapped her arms around him. She knew exactly what happened, and shame consumed her with the realization of her panic. "Did I hurt anyone?"

"No."

A relieved breath escaped her. "Your grandfather is really going to hate me now."

"Yes, well, I'm not particularly fond of him right now either."

"He didn't know. Nor is it his fault that I'm unstable."

He hugged her tighter. "You're not unstable. You've only remembered this trauma for a week. That isn't nearly enough time for anyone to recover from something like that. You need time."

Pulling away, she stood to address the others. "Right, so, any chance you all will forget that happened?"

Luciano widened his stance and crossed his arms.

"Thought not," she grumbled. "Well, I do not want to explain it. If you have questions, ask Damien. As for me, I'm going to find Master Kinley for training." She climbed into the carriage, her hands and nails caked with dirt. A quick spell had them clean once more.

Phillipa climbed in and Liana urged the horses forward with more magic, not bothering to wait for anyone. The driver startled from what she could hear but didn't stop.

Chapter Twelve

Two weeks passed quickly in the castle, which was Evangeline's intent as she kept Liana busy at all hours of the day. When she was not at magic practice, she either studied magic or sat for queenly lessons with Eva. Lessons included everything from table etiquette to memorizing all the top families in the kingdom to the art of subterfuge which took up a surprising amount of time. It was those lessons in particular that made Liana feel out of her depth with Damien. She thought she'd been playing the game of seduction so well, but there was so much yet that she needed to learn if she were to stand at Damien's side as an asset rather than a liability.

Being queen came with so much responsibility and risk that she'd only guessed at before. The true scope of what she must be, especially in times such as these when there was so much unrest among the people, threatened to overwhelm her. She had no choice other than to endure it and prepare to the best of her ability.

Each day left Liana exhausted with no time to sneak off and visit Damien. She had not seen him much since moving to the castle, either by design or circumstance. Likely by Evangeline's design.

The daunting lessons were manageable though, especially with Phillipa's presence. Phillipa brought all her things from home and now lived with her in the castle as well. Liana considered herself blessed to have the woman with her because she cared for Liana better than the girl could for herself. She kept Liana fed and looking presentable when the young woman couldn't be bothered to care, not when she was so busy. Phillipa helped her study with every free moment. When she combed Liana's hair or dressed her, the woman would test her knowledge or act as a sounding board when Liana needed to talk something out from her books.

Liana was especially grateful for the woman's presence on the nights that she woke from nightmares. Phillipa would be there to comfort her and rock her back to sleep as she'd done so many times in the past when Liana was just a young girl. She did not have nightmares each night, but they were regular enough that she needed help with them. As much as she felt she'd moved on from her kidnapping, the fear and pain from the experience lingered.

Other nights she dreamed of her fiancé. Those were the moments that she was glad he was not near, and the former king and queen slept nearby or else she'd be tempted to pull him into her bed once more to see what else he could do to make her feel as if her soul might explode from her body. Luckily for them both however, there was never a moment where they were left alone.

The only other constant in her life these days, much to her dismay, was Luciano. He lurked around every corner if he didn't outright follow her. He made his presence known mostly during her magic practice. She knew he tried to intimidate her, but she became a master at ignoring people throughout her years of being a pariah in the mage community. It was no different to ignore the former king and her fiancé's grandfather, at least that's what she told herself.

Two weeks were gone though and in two days it would be her wedding day. Today, they were tasked with greeting the rest of the Ashwood line that traveled to get to Sancta Valles. They'd also be rehearsing the procession and ceremony in detail tomorrow to ensure everything went smoothly on the wedding day.

Phillipa helped her into a lovely pale blue gown and pinned half her chestnut curls back. When she exited her room, Sasha waited outside the door.

The soldier bowed. "I am to escort you to the King's dining hall, my Lady."

Liana hadn't been sure where to meet with everyone and was thankful for the soldier. "Oh, very well then." As the guard walked, she and Phillipa followed. Glancing around, she couldn't see any sign of Luciano, not that she trusted her senses when it came to that vampire. He likely hid somewhere close by, always watching.

"Have you seen High Lord Luciano today, Sasha?"

"I have not, my Lady."

Lowering her voice, she also erected a privacy shield. "You do not sense him nearby, do you?" The guard shook her head. "Good, because I've had enough of him."

Sasha smiled, not bothering to hide it. "I've heard that before, my Lady. You should know that he is a tired, cynical old man that wants to die. He doesn't care much for social standards or niceties anymore."

Liana's steps faltered at her blunt observation. "Oh?" was all she could muster.

The guard smirked. "My great uncle has lived a long life. His mate and daughter were killed centuries ago which left him with no desire to stay in this life, and he prays everyday that the gods reunite him with his love. Until that happens, he has vowed to keep the rest of his family safe, including from themselves and their choice in spouse."

"That is terribly depressing," Liana commented. "Are you related to Damien as well then, if High Lord Luciano is your great uncle?"

"Not by blood. My great, great grandmother was the sister of Luciano's mate."

Her head spun at the thought of the royal line's family tree and just nodded for simplicity's sake. "Yes, well, your great uncle is a huge thorn in my side."

Phillipa snorted a laugh, even Sasha broke a grin before smothering it.

When they turned another corner, Damien walked toward them. Her eyes caught his immediately, a smile blooming on her face to match his. Dressed in his formal jacket and trousers, he wore his crown and his hair down as was expected. Her heart skipped a beat whenever she saw that handsome face.

He stopped in front of her and offered his hand. Liana placed her right hand in his which he brought to his lips with a slight bow.

"My beautiful bride, I came to escort you the rest of the way."

"Wonderful, then you can prepare me for the family drama we are about to enter into."

He placed her hand in the crook of his arm and led her onward, Phillipa and Sasha falling a few steps behind. "We are not a family prone to drama," he said with a straight face.

"The royal family of Triaedian is not prone to drama? I've told you never to lie to me, future husband."

Damien laughed. "Alright, I may have fibbed a bit. We do tend to keep out of the gossip as much as possible though."

"Yes, well, what am I walking into? Any major issues I should avoid?"

"Do not ever mention swimming to Grandmother Marina, she abhors it. Otherwise, just be ready for lively debate."

She groaned, too nervous about impressing a room full of Triaedian's previous monarchs and her groom's family. "We could run away right now and elope on distant shores where we will never have to worry about the crown or rebels, or me impressing your family."

Damien tugged her to a stop, his brows furrowed. "Do you truly not want to deal with all of this?"

"Not entirely, but I'll be fine," she rushed to reassure him. "My nerves are speaking for me, and that was supposed to make you laugh, not worry."

His hand cupped her face, thumb brushing along her cheek. "I do not laugh when my bride is so upset."

"Stop being such a gentleman. Tease me back, make me laugh."

"I am not a court jester, you cannot command me to entertain," he teased as requested.

She leaned into him. "Then I command you to kiss me."

Fingers gripped her chin lightly and tilted her head back. "Anytime, temptress." It was a brief kiss before he pulled away. "Now, stop fretting and let things play out as they will. You'll be fantastic, my love."

Sighing, she resigned herself to this breakfast.

As they approached the King's formal dining hall, which they used only once before, Liana heard the voices of new guests. Keeping her shoulders back, she pasted a pleasant smile upon her lips. When they stood in the doorway, arm in arm, the chatter ceased and at least thirty vampires turned toward them.

Liana had not expected near this many people for a meeting of his family, then again, with the long lives of vampires, she was surprised there weren't more.

"Good morning to you all," Damien began while Liana kept a death grip on his arm. His hand patted over hers to hide her white knuckles. "It is a pleasure to welcome you all back into Sancta Valles Castle, and even more of an honor to introduce to you my bride, Lady Liana Monroe."

Liana gave a small curtsy as Eva instructed her to do so. Licking her dry lips, she kept her smile in place. "Thank you all for traveling so far to help us celebrate our marriage." Surprised that she actually made it through that without stuttering, Liana took a deep breath, forcing the air into her tight chest.

A handsome man so similar to Damien but moreso to Ramone approached, a warm smile

on his broad face. He was much darker than them, appearing as if he spent the entire summer on the coast. Liana recognized him from one of the many portraits of him around the castle. In fact, all of the family present she had seen at least once, if not a hundred times depicted in one painting or another.

"My boy!" he greeted before pulling Damien into a fierce hug. He slapped his grandson on the back in a manly gesture then gripped his shoulders while his wife appeared beside him. "I'm surprised you finally convinced a girl to tolerate you, son. We nearly lost hope."

Liana couldn't help the real smile that replaced her fake one at his grandfather's teasing. Damien took it in stride though.

"Don't celebrate yet, we still have to get through the wedding in two days so don't screw it up for me, Grandfather."

The former queen elbowed her husband out of the way. "Oh sweetheart, we've missed you so much," she gushed and smothered Damien in a hug. "How have you been? Are you drinking enough?"

Liana was so enraptured by the obvious love between them that she didn't see High Lord

Armand until he'd already wrapped his arms around her. In a slight moment of panic, her magic surged to protect her.

"Welcome to the family, Liana," he squeezed her once more before letting her go all while she forced her magic to calm down. She could only nod at the burly man before High Lady Marina also gathered her into a more delicate embrace.

"Welcome, Liana," she greeted, giving her a gentle smile from behind sea blue eyes and waves of golden hair, so unlike her husband.

Eva's parents greeted them next. They each gave Damien a hug, deciding to only nod towards Liana. Eva said they would do that though. They were reserved people with newcomers and it would take them longer to accept her.

Eva's sister and husband followed with a polite bow and curtsy.

"Happy to see you again, Auntie, Uncle," Damien greeted with a nod.

Ophelia leaned in to give her nephew a double-cheek kiss. "It's always nice to visit, especially since my boys decide they are too important now to visit their mother. Where are they anyway? Did they know I arrived last night? They didn't even come say hello."

"I'll be sure to send them to the south more often so they'll have an excuse to visit," Damien supplied gracefully, avoiding the fact that Owen and Asher were absolutely avoiding this breakfast.

"You're such a doll. I'd always hoped you'd rub off on my boys." Her husband gently guided her away with a grateful nod.

Next came his paternal great grandparents with hugs for him and polite nods to her.

There were so many of his family considering vampires could usually only conceive one or two children if they were lucky. But they all showed for this momentous event. Great aunts and uncles, cousins and spouses with their children. Liana counted forty-six in total.

High Lord Luciano stepped up last although they were well acquainted and reunited. He held his right arm out and Damien clasped his forearm in a warrior's greeting. "Grandfather," Damien greeted, his voice low and reverent in a way she'd never heard him use before. Damien mentioned that Luciano played an integral part in his upbringing, not that she'd had time to ask him about it further.

"Morning," he greeted.

"How has your morning been?"

"Terrible. The gods continue to curse me with life." Liana didn't react to his blunt words, having already heard them from Sasha. At least the soldier had been honest and not spouting lies.

"Perhaps we can unburden you from your curse for a few days with our celebration of marriage. I thought for sure you and Liana were getting along so well."

Liana glared at Damien for his joking while Luciano actually cracked a smile.

"She has been an unexpected source of intrigue I must admit. You as well, boy. I never thought anyone would be brave enough to bring a different breed into the Ashwood line," he stated outright.

Liana kept her face blank, her magic starting to writhe beneath the surface of her weak control. Now would not be the time for her magic to react without her permission. After all the torment he put her through since his arrival, his words were not welcomed. Especially not in front of his entire family.

"About time it happened," he grumbled before downing his drink. He strode off without another word, leaving Liana confused and shocked. The vampire didn't hide his dislike for her yet there he stood, giving the closest thing to approval as they'd likely get. It didn't make any sense.

Liana glanced at Damien but he just watched his ancient grandfather walk away with a pensive look. A quick shield hid her words. "Dare I ask what that was about right now or shall we table that discussion?"

"Table it," he murmured, then she dropped the shield.

The large group took their seats among the two long tables. Damien sat at the head of one, Luciano sitting opposite him, while Liana sat to his right. Eva thankfully sat beside her with Armand and Marina on the opposite side of the table. Most of the former monarchs sat at their table as well, with the rest of the extended family at the other table.

Liana began to relax after the food was served mostly due to the fact that Damien's grandfather, Armand, was a master storyteller. He regaled them with tales of his retirement all along the coastal cities and villages of Triaedian. Liana ignored the light chatter of others, opting to fall completely into the stories of international trade and adventures.

Too soon though they all exited the dining hall and ventured toward the lake for an afternoon of fun. She tried to not recall the last time they spent an afternoon at the lake, the day they were attacked and Charlotte almost died, the day she revealed just how powerful she was to everyone.

Damien helped her into a boat and offered, "I assure you there are far more guards out here than before. We are safe."

They were about to push off when Luciano stopped them. Damien moved to sit beside her while Luciano took his seat and offered to row.

"How did you meet?" he asked simply, the question completely random. He'd already had almost two weeks to interrogate them, yet now he had more questions.

"At the opening ball of the courting season," Damien replied.

They drifted into the middle of the lake, everyone else rowing steadily along in different directions.

"You haven't known each other for long."

Liana couldn't help the scrunching of her brows. Did he think they should have waited for marriage? What did it matter how long they'd known each other anyway? Liana knew plenty of couples that didn't meet until their wedding day.

"Plenty of time to get to know one another, Grandfather."

"I wonder if you've told each other everything though. In a union such as yours, where most are uncomfortable with the thought of interbreeding, you have to be an unbreakable unit. No secrets, no lies."

Liana felt the shift in the conversation and erected a silencing shield. Luciano nodded at her. "You can speak plainly with us, Luciano. I have no secrets from Damien, nor do I have any ulterior motives in marrying him. Ask what you want to know of me and let's be done with it."

It wasn't exactly the decorum Eva taught her, but it was a strategic move on her part.

A ghost of a smile tilted Luciano's lips. "Alright, has he told you about his vampire?"

Her bravado faded quickly as she looked to Damien. Jaw clenched, he glared at his relative.

"I do not think we need to get into the gritty details, Grandfather. She knows enough."

"If she does not know everything, then she does not know enough. The greatest danger to you both will always be lack of knowledge because you are each powerful beings in your own right... together you'd be unstoppable. It is the knowledge that will be your downfall."

She took Damien's hand in her own. "I will know everything in time, and none of it will change my mind about him."

"Touching." Luciano's tone left much to be desired as he stowed the oars and let them float. "That sentiment will get you killed though. You fight for as much knowledge as you can get and as quickly as you can. Your husband will be your first source. Tell her of your youth."

"Now is not the time," Damien denied.

"There will never be a right time. Just as there will never be a moment you can waste. You tell everything to each other now, before it is too late."

Liana couldn't help but think of his late wife and perhaps that was why he was adamant about not wasting time.

"While you may have a point, we can handle this on our own. You do not need to be present," Liana countered.

Luciano gave a quick jerk of his head. "No, this is too important. Damien, tell her."

Damien looked anywhere but at them, and after a heavy sigh, he started. "When I grew into a man, my vampire side became more aggressive, more dominant. I had the temper of a child with a hairpin trigger and the strength of a full-blooded vampire in the throes of rage. My parents and grandparents did everything they could to help me tame the creature inside of me, then they called in Master Kinley's father to see if there was any magic that could help. It did for a while, before I grew immune to it."

He sighed, scrubbing a hand through his hair. "Then they contacted Grandfather Luciano, the oldest, meanest, and most ruthless vampire alive. I was terrified but my vampire took it as a challenge."

They both laughed at that.

She tugged on his arm. "What happened?"

"My vampire took one look into his eyes and calmed down."

She glanced at the infuriating vampire. "You are intimidating, but why would that calm

him down?"

"Because his creature recognized that it was no longer the most powerful in the room. He recognized that I'd be the only one strong enough or have enough courage to kill him if he ever lost total control. After that, Damien was able to fight for more control over himself."

Liana gasped. "Kill you? Why would they kill you? Can you not just knock him out or something?"

"At a certain point, a feral vampire doesn't return. It's the same with the shifters. If they can't shift back, they have to be put down in order to save everyone else. I'm sure they do the same to mage who can't control their power or have lost their minds."

When Eva spoke of Damien's creature as if he would undoubtedly lose control at some point, Liana never guessed at something like this.

"Well, it is a good thing he has me now because I will not let that happen."

The ancient vampire leaned back, his hands gripping the side of the boat. "You may think that, but even if you are the love of his life, you won't be able to stop a feral vampire. You wouldn't have been able to even if you were a vampire."

Liana's magic surged to defend her in spite of her attempt at control. It filled her veins in a flash, a faint glow emanating from her skin. Luciano's eyes narrowed, roving over her arms.

"You know nothing of the power I hold. You know nothing of us, and I won't let anything happen to Damien, including your threats of murder by your own hand."

"He didn't mean it like that," Damien interjected but Luciano merely smirked.

"Perhaps there is one other that might be able to kill you, grandson." He saw her in a new light, mischief entering his eyes. "I've been watching you during your practice. You are the most powerful mage I've encountered and even now, sitting this close... I couldn't fathom that it was this much. I can actually taste it on my tongue, feel it in the air." He ran his hands over nothing but air. "In all my years, I've never felt magic like this before."

Liana shoved her magic as far down as it would go. Feeling like a fool, she folded her arms. "You goaded me."

"Ah, but I did," he admitted. "And you responded perfectly. You did also need to know about his vampire. That could have been a worse situation if it happened and you did not know."

Glaring, she tried so hard to stay calm, to keep her composure. "I'd love to show you more of what I can do. Perhaps you'd like to take a dip in the lake." She raised her hand toward him, his body lifting off the seat until Damien shoved her hand back down.

"Alright, my little mage, that is enough demonstration for the day. No one is dressed appropriately for a swim anyway."

Luciano laughed. "Do it, mage. Show your husband who has the power."

With a tight smile, Liana guided the boat back to the dock with a gust of magic.

His brows rose. "No spells or incantations?"

Ignoring that question even though it caused a spike of old panic, Liana stood and created invisible stairs of air to get her gracefully off that wretched boat. "Should you feel the need to test me again, Luciano, do not." She strode off the dock keeping her chin held high. A tent had been set up by the servants, blankets and pillows placed carefully about with trays of sliced fruit, meats, and cheeses. High Lady Gabriella and High Lord Quentin were the only ones sitting beneath the tent, the others out in the boats. She sat near them out of politeness.

Liana downed a glass of wine not bothering with the snacks.

"What did Grandfather do to put that sour look on your face?" Gabriella asked ruefully.

"Insinuated that we were going to fail and that I wasn't good enough for Damien."

Quentin refilled her wine glass. "He does it to us all. He nearly took my head off during a duel to test if I could protect his granddaughter. Told me I failed and that if I wanted to marry Gabriella that I'd have to train until I bested him."

"How long did that take?"

"One torturous year." He let out a relieved laugh. "But it was worth every minute of torture." He stared lovingly at his eternal bride which hid Liana's flinch at the mention of torture.

With her high-strung emotions it seemed as though her own memories were closer to the surface, her nerves on edge. She shoved those thoughts away. They were in the past.

"I'm lucky I only have to endure a few weeks in his presence."

Gabriella held her husband's hand, her own countenance shifting into sadness. "He means well but he has been through too much to be anything but the hard man you see. Grandfather is the most caring man I've ever met. He raised me after my parents were killed. He has just been through too much and doesn't want any of us to endure the same so he pushes us to be better."

Liana had been through her own trials, not that they compared to losing a wife and daughter. The cell flashed before her eyes, darkness consuming her vision just as Damien sat beside her. She jolted, spilling her wine. A simple wave of her hand had the stain disappearing.

"That is wonderful magic," Gabriella commented. "I wish I had it when Armand was a child. He spilled everything."

"Our son did have a knack for getting into sticky situations," Quentin added, which had Luciano huffing in annoyance.

"He was almost harder to break than Damien. His creature was not fierce enough, always playing tricks. I nearly kicked his ass into another continent before he understood the brutality of this world."

"Or you simply created another brute out of a once kind soul," Liana snapped, her magic surging to the surface once more. The soft glow of her skin caught all eyes. Damien grabbed her arm which she yanked out of on instinct.

Breathing heavily, she forced her vision to focus on the tray of food in front of her and not the beatings she endured as a child.

"Liana, what is wrong?"

Shoving to her feet, she stumbled out of the tent toward the castle. Damien caught up to her and she let him support her while attempting to breathe.

"What is it?" he asked again.

She shook her head, gulping down the bile that tried to rise. "I don't know. I cannot stop thinking about that cell, those fists upon my flesh." She collapsed to her knees, Damien following. On instinct, she erected a privacy shield around them and wrapped her arms over his shoulders. He held her easily. "I feel like every word today triggers my memories. I cannot stop them."

"I've got you, Liana. You're safe in my arms right now. Those memories are the past."

Her body trembled in his hold, her magic surging, ready to protect.

"I need you to slow your breathing down. Try to match it with mine. Ready, big breath in," he inhaled slowly. "And blow it out." He did this a few more times with little help before changing tactics. "In just another day you will be my wife. I will truly get to call you all mine and finally worship this body as I've been planning for months. First, I'm going to kiss you senseless until we've both had our fill then I'm going to take my time peeling you out of your wedding gown. After I slide the fabric off your body, I'm going to lay you down and trace every part of your body with my lips. I'm going to kiss away any memory of anyone else's hands on you aside from my own."

Her breath hitched, her body finally calming.

"There's my little mage," he cooed. "First, I will mark the spot where I'm going to bite my claiming mark into your neck." His lips pressed gently beneath her ear. "Then I'll trail them to the other side." Nibbled gently with his teeth which had her shivering. "Before I find my way to..." He pressed a kiss to the swell of her breast.

She pulled away, her mind completely focused on him now instead of the memories.

"Thank you." She let out a heavy breath. "I felt as if I were drowning for a moment."

"We don't have to talk about this right now, however, I think it is important that we address this sooner rather than later. Flashbacks are one thing but you were consumed by panic."

Pressing her nose into the crook of his neck, she just breathed him in. "I know. I'm not sure what happened. I kept hearing words or things that reminded me of it all then this happened. It doesn't help that I keep having nightmares as well."

"It can be difficult to deal with trauma, especially after it was hidden from you for so long." Rubbing his hand up and down her back, he soothed her further.

"Thank you for calming me. I can only imagine what your grandfather will have to say about this. I can already hear him now…"

Damien pressed a finger to her lips. "He does not matter in this moment. Only you, and you are not quite calm if your teasing is any indication."

She frowned at the man that knew her far too well. "What do you expect of me, Damien? I'm doing my best and that vampire antagonizes me at every chance."

His hand slid up to her neck, his fingers sliding beneath her hair while his thumb brushed against her jaw. "I expect nothing. I only want you to feel safe and comfortable. I'd like for you to rejoin my family when you are able because, despite what you think of my grandfather, I value his opinion and I'd like for the two of you to get along. I want all of my family to enjoy your company just as I do."

"Yes, well, you enjoy my company for very inappropriate reasons and if they all lust after me as you do, we might have a problem."

Chuckling, he took a step back to entwine their fingers. "There's my little mage. Now, come, I believe my father promised to best his father in a fencing duel and we do not want to miss that."

Liana scrunched her nose. "I hate fencing."

He smiled back, secrets in his eyes. "You'll like this kind of fencing."

Dropping her shields, she let him drag her back to the tent, not certain she believed him.

Chapter Thirteen

The fencing match proved to be entertaining and nothing like she was used to. Instead of rigid rules, the vampires sparred without the usual uniform, preferring just their trousers and shirts, and didn't follow any guidelines. At least, none that she could tell. They simply went at it, darting all over the place and grunting or yelling at each other. Some of the foul things that left their mouths had her laughing even as she blushed.

Damien laughed right along with everyone else as well, his mood more light and carefree than she'd ever witnessed before. When they were alone, he let his kingly mask fall, but now, with his family all around, it added another level of safety to the air that left her king relaxed.

Liana loved seeing him this way. She loved that he looked so at ease. This is how she always wanted him. Never did she want him stressed by his responsibilities or weighed down by his crown. That was inevitable though, all she could do was try to relieve him of some of that stress. Sliding her hand into his, she rested them in her lap, her magic floating with happiness beneath her skin.

Damien took his eyes off the fight. "What is that look for?" he questioned, his body leaning into hers.

With a smile she shook her head. "Nothing, my king." There was far more that she wanted to explain. With the many prying ears around them though, she'd hold her thoughts for a private moment.

Sliding his free hand to her neck, his thumb brushed her jaw before pulling her into a kiss. His lips were gentle on hers, just a brief caress, yet so full of love. She rested her head on his shoulder as they turned back to the fencing match, where Armand chased Ramone back down to the lake. Ramone led him around the entire lake before returning to the tent with vampiric speed.

"Still faster than you, old man," Ramone teased his father before replacing his foil in the stand it came from. Armand did the same before launching at Ramone.

He tackled his son to the ground and held him a constricting hold. "But not stronger," he boasted. Ramone struggled a bit before Armand relinquished his hold.

"Yeah, yeah. We all have our strengths and weaknesses," Ramone said to justify his loss.

Damien barked a laugh which had her sitting up. "I'm stronger and faster than you both," he goaded.

Father and son glanced at him then at each other, some private conversation passing between them before they launched at Damien. He tensed behind her but she held him still and erected a shield around herself and Damien, the former kings hitting it painfully. Armand fell backward while Ramone crumpled to his knees holding his broken nose.

Liana leaned back into Damien, letting him support her as she forced a serene expression on her face. "And it appears that I am faster and stronger than all three of you."

Everyone laughed except for the pair still collecting themselves.

"How wonderful it is to have a mage in the family," Gabriella exclaimed, still laughing.

"Mother," Armand complained. "A bit of support would be appreciated."

The former queen waved him off. "If you want to play like children, I am certainly not going to intervene on your behalf."

Armand grinned as he turned his attention to his wife, pinning her within his stare.

"Don't even think about it," Marina declared, sipping her wine. The vampire creeped up to her while she set her glass down then pounced, laying her back on the cushions she sat upon before kissing her. The rather indecent display had Liana turning away.

"Getting onto better topics of conversation," Damien started then asked his great grandmother, "How are the vineyards in the south, Grandmother?"

Liana knew Damien held vineyards to the north, it was no surprise that his family owned more.

"Quite well. I heard yours suffered some damage this past season. Is it true?"

"Yes. A bit of a fire. I suspect it was intentional although no one has been apprehended. Luckily, my foreman caught it before too much was ruined. We won't suffer much loss."

"What of the situation with the rebels? We've all heard the tale of the great vanquisher, Lady Liana," Quentin asked with a teasing tone at the end.

"I've been wondering how you all heard. We kept it pretty quiet from the rest of Sancta Valles so who told you all?"

Gabriella snorted a laugh. "Ramone told Armand…" Damien groaned at the news which had Quentin laughing. "And Armand told everyone else in the family."

Liana huffed. "And here I thought that I liked your grandfather's elaborate tales."

"Our son does love to regale everyone with a good story, and yours was quite impressive, Liana," Quentin said seriously.

"Of course I told them!" Armand defended. "My new granddaughter is a gods-damned force to be reckoned with."

Liana's blush was less about the attention and more about the endearment that she was already a part of the family, that Armand considered her a granddaughter. Their family was far different than she imagined in the very best of ways. They were so open and warm with one another. It was a family she'd love to be a part of.

Liana smoothed her skirts down. "Yes, well, I am just happy that everyone is alive and well after all that." Damien took her hand in his again, giving it a reassuring squeeze which had her magic relaxing as well.

"As for the rebels," Damien began, answering their question. "They have been nullified for now. As always though, we keep an ear to the ground for any news."

Liana couldn't help thinking about the threatening note she received just weeks ago. The rebels were diminished, not nullified. They would regroup and they'd deal with them again.

Quentin refilled his wife's wine glass then his own. "For Triaedian's sake, I sincerely hope your marriage will steer us toward the end of separatist ideals."

"It will take generations," Luciano added on. "It will take generations of mixed marriages and children of those unions for any lasting change to happen."

Liana frowned at the pessimist. She did not want to think of how many more centuries it would take for Triaedian to actually become the united kingdom it was always meant to be.

"So you think children will be possible for us?" Damien asked his grandfather.

"You know the prophecy as well as I, you know it is inevitable." Luciano gulped back his wine then refilled it before plopping a piece of thinly sliced meat into his mouth as if what he just said was not completely mind-altering.

Damien tensed beside her.

"What prophecy?" she asked.

Luciano halted mid chew, his eyes darting incredulously to his grandson. "You are not serious, Damien, are you? You did not tell her?"

"It's just an old-wives' tale, there is nothing to tell."

Luciano glared. "Do not test me, boy. That prophecy is the first thing written in the Book of Kings. It was written by the original founders of Triaedian, spoken to them from the gods themselves. Do not belittle it so disrespectfully."

Damien clenched his jaw, looking anywhere but at Liana.

"What does it say?" she demanded, looking at Luciano.

The vampire did not hesitate to answer. "The tenth vampire king will usher in a new era of diversity for Triaedian. He will become the strongest Ashwood in history in order to unite the kingdom with the aid of the promised savior as his wife. Their children will be the start of a new generation. A generation of peace."

Liana stopped breathing.

It wasn't the part about children that had her anger surging. Promised savior. That's what Ranville called her in that wretched cell. That's what he screamed at her as his fists beat into her flesh and when his boot landed in her gut.

She turned to Damien, betrayal curdling in her gut. "How could you not tell me? You told me it was a children's tale," she accused.

He shook his head, "It's all just a fairytale, Liana. It's not..."

She cut him off sharply. "Is that why you picked me? Is that why put on that farce of a courtship with the other two even though you chose me from the start? You knew all along what I would be to you. That I would make you the strongest Ashwood king in history."

Tears bit at the back of her eyes, her throat clogging as the full force of Damien's deception hit her.

He grabbed her by the shoulders, kneeling in front of her. "Don't go down that path, Liana. That is not what happened. I've never believed in that ridiculous prophecy. It doesn't explain who the savior is, and it's all just hopeful ramblings from ambitious pilgrims."

She shoved off his hands. "But you are the tenth king and Ranville called me the promised savior. How much more specific could it get?" she spat at him. Climbing to her feet, she stalked out of the tent toward the castle.

How quickly everything could change. Within minutes her peaceful joy was shattered by a single lie. It was everything she feared from the beginning, being used as a pawn for males in power, and this was the worst thing she could imagine, being a pawn for the king.

She would pack her bags, grab Phillipa and run as far away as possible from all of this.

Damien sped in front of her, her steps faltering.

"I knew this was all too good to be true," she seethed, stepping around him. "You've been manipulating me this entire time."

He growled, grabbing her arm. "Don't you dare accuse me of such things." The seriousness of his words had her pausing. "Everything I have done, everything I have said has been to convince you that we belong together. I love you, Liana. And not because of some gods-damned prophecy."

"Why did you not tell me then?" she nearly screamed at him.

"Because I knew you would react this way. I knew you would doubt me."

"Now you're a prophet as well? How rich." She seethed, her magic boiling beneath her skin which now glowed with a faint golden hue onto Damien's olive complexion.

He growled again, his eyes flashing with anger. "You were the most distrustful person I'd ever met, Liana. I had to hide my true feelings toward you because you didn't believe that I could love you without some ulterior motive."

"Yes, you've already said as much. You pretended to use me because that's what I expected of you." He explained this already the night he rescued her in the woods from that mercenary. "But you knew all along who you were meant to become in that prophecy and I fell right into your schemes."

"Gods, Liana, please, just listen to me. I never believed in any of that. It doesn't even explain who the promised one is. No one has ever known. When I met you, the prophecy was the last thing on my mind. I only thought of it again when you remembered what Ranville did, when he called you the savior. And after all that was revealed to you, the last thing I wanted to do was tell you about some ridiculous dream someone had of a future they wanted to come true. I knew you would take it to heart, that you would question my intentions."

"Congratulations on being correct, Damien, because I am questioning everything between us," she declared, magic dripped from her balled fists and scattered across the grass harmlessly.

His eyes narrowed on hers as he stepped closer. She held her ground, not giving an inch at his intimidation tactics. "I don't know how I can convince you that the prophecy means nothing to me. The only thing I ever cared about was being a good king until you came along. The moment I saw you in that ballroom I knew we had a connection. When we spoke in that alcove, I knew I would love you for the rest of my life. There was never a thought in my mind about using you for power. I didn't even realize the extent of your power until that day by the lake, and by then, I was already hopelessly in love with you."

A tear spilled over her lashes. She wanted to believe him. Wanted to pretend this afternoon never happened. But he had kept this from her on purpose. Even lied to her that the savior bit was just some old wives' tale. That was something she could not forget.

Shaking her head, she swiped the tear away. "I don't know what to believe."

"Believe that I love you, Liana," he declared, trying to wrap her in his arms. She stepped away and erected a shield around herself. Damien's jaw clamped shut, his teeth grinding as he looked away. When he stepped into her space once more, their noses practically touching, she stared into pained eyes. "If I did not love you I would not be so open. You would not have felt my arms around you so often or my lips upon your flesh. If I did not love you, if this was for your power alone, you would only know the King of Triaedian, you would not know me, Damien."

She knew of what he spoke. She saw how he acted as king, so rigid and blank. Her Damien was warm and pliable. Always ready with a grin and teasing remark. Yet she couldn't quite accept that he kept this from her. What if his change in attitude was choreographed? What if it was a tactic to lure her in?

"I cannot do this." She turned to stride away.

He grabbed her arm once more. She didn't turn back. "Liana, please. I will do anything to convince you of how much I love you. I only kept that prophecy from you because I knew it would cause you pain."

Tears fell faster now. "I just need some time, Damien." Pulling out of his hold, he let her go. She went straight to her room where Phillipa waited, reading a book.

"What happened?" she asked, tossing the book aside as she hurried to meet Liana's tear-stained face. She wrapped Liana in her arms and let her cry. Eventually, she guided her to the sofa to sit and had tea delivered.

"Phillipa, what do I do?" Liana asked after relaying the knowledge of the prophecy and Damien's deceit.

The maid sipped her tea calmly before setting it down. "What is there to do?"

Liana blinked. "Do I still marry the King?"

Phillipa frowned. "I think it would cause great pain if you were to call off the wedding."

Her eyes widened. "You don't think Damien would hurt me, do you? Could he force me to marry him?"

Her maid sighed, lips pursed as she stared at her young charge. "I meant it would break both your hearts. Liana, I know you have grown up being distrustful. I know you have not truly felt love from those that should give it freely and with abundance. But you are not a child anymore. You need to accept your past, learn from it, and grow." She reached over to cup her cheek in a tender gesture before returning to her lap. "I know the King loves you. There is nothing I am more certain of in this world than that. I will not disagree with what he did either because I have done the same. We withheld information to protect you. That may not have been the right thing, but I do not think it makes us villains either."

Phillipa took Liana's hands into her own lovingly. "You have a tendency to lean toward extremes, my dear girl. If someone is good, they are not infallible. And if they are bad, they are still capable of kindness and love. Please just remember that. Damien is a man hopelessly in love with you, and he is the King of Triaedian, yet he will still make mistakes. That is no reason to question his motives."

She strode toward the door, leaving Liana to her own thoughts.

*****

Damien found her later that day still secluded in her bedroom. He knocked before entering and found her sitting on a stool in front of the fire, practicing magic. She was only mindlessly playing with the fire while her mind tormented itself, going back and forth about Damien and his deceit.

The object of her ire sat behind her. "I am truly sorry, Liana. You must know that I only ever want you happy and protected. It was never my intention to make you feel deceived."

She couldn't look at him. Wouldn't look at him because she knew one look into those loving eyes would wilt her resolve.

"The intention doesn't cover up the fact that you purposefully lied to me though." She blew out a breath then turned to face him. Sitting on the edge of the sofa, he leaned forward to rest his elbows on his knees, his hands clasped tightly. "I believe that you love me. I believe that what we have is real. I believe you are not just using me for power. What I cannot wrap my head around, is the fact that you kept something so important from me."

"Keeping this from you has been one of the most difficult decisions of my life," he professed. "I knew that if you ever found out, it would hurt you. But telling you about it would have hurt you more. I didn't want you to know that someone kidnapped and tortured you as a child over some ridiculous words some ancestor of mine wrote in the hopes of a better future."

She stood with her anger rising swiftly once more. It had truly never left but waned in the previous hours. "Perhaps you think that knowing would have hurt worse, but at least I would have you and Phillipa to lean on. Now, you are the one that hurt me and I don't want your comfort, that is hurting me more than anything else."

That was a lie though too.

All she wanted these days was Damien's loving arms wrapped around her. She wanted to feel his warmth soaking into her skin and drown herself in his scent day and night. Even now she wanted to drop into his lap and never face the world again despite feeling irked by him.

"There did not seem to be a good option so I chose the one I felt was the lesser of two evils."

"You chose incorrectly."

He stared at her for long moments, his icy blue eyes contemplating. "You may think so. That is not how I see it."

At a loss for words, she could only stare back. They'd had plenty of serious discussions in the past few months, none of which ended in this frustrating stalemate. Usually one of them would end it with a witty remark or innuendo. There would be nothing of the sort to end this one.

"What are we supposed to do now?" she asked, uncertainty clouding her thoughts.

His brows furrowed before he stood to meet her. His hands reached out to take hers but stopped halfway before dropping away. "What do you mean?"

"How do we move past this if we don't agree?"

"We are allowed to disagree on things, Liana. Unless this is something you cannot move past. In that case, I'd say you should leave me, but I doubt I'd be able to let you go."

She shook her head and reached out to take his hands. "Even if I should leave you, I don't have the strength to do it." And that was the bold truth. For all her posturing of independence, of not needing any man to live a happy life, she managed to fall in love with the only man that could put all those thoughts to shame.

"Can you please promise to tell me things in the future though, no matter how hurtful you might think them?."

His hands squeezed hers. "That will go against my very nature to do so, but for you, Liana, I will try."

Chapter Fourteen

The next evening, after a very long day with Damien's family and her own for the rehearsals at the temple, Liana was beyond ready for bed. They spent the early evening practicing their vows for the wedding ceremony as well as her vows for her coronation which would be held right after the wedding.

A feast had been prepared for them after everything, and while watching her family and Damien's interact offered quite the entertainment, the only thing she longed for now was peace and quiet.

Damien and Liana walked arm in arm toward her room, Damien carrying her slippers considering she kicked them off at the base of the stairs before traversing. He had merely chuckled and picked them up instead of leaving them for a servant. He walked her into her bedroom, leaving the door open. Setting her shoes down, he pulled her into a hug.

"Tomorrow you will become my wife. Finally."

Smiling, she rested her head on his chest, her arms around his waist. "I cannot wait for it to be over."

"Do try to sound like you want this, or at least pretend."

Chuckling, she looked up at him. "Of course I do. I just do not want to wait any longer was all I meant."

"You and me both, temptress," he said, his voice low. He kissed her, slow and sweet, and full of promises for what was to come. Too soon though he stepped back. "I've got something for you." He pulled a long velvet box from his coat and held it open to her.

Inside the box lay a stunning necklace of gold upon navy velvet. The linked bands of gold were about as wide as two fingers and etched with a simple design of short dashes along the top and bottom rim. Each piece curved gently so that it would lay flat around her neck. Beneath each slat of gold draped a thin braided chain, a small diamond at the center of each chain.

"It is gorgeous."

"In vampire tradition, the female will wear a decorative band of fabric around her neck to symbolize that she is taken, essentially, that no one else can bite her neck, which is a sacred place to bite for mates. I thought this necklace would be a pleasant compromise."

She nodded, pulling him in for a kiss. Little did he know what she had planned for her wedding attire tomorrow. "Here," she said, summoning his gift. Her box was simple in comparison, made of thin wood with no engravings. "I suggest you open this tonight, and most certainly in private." He peaked beneath the lid, his brows furrowing. "Read the note," she said with a wink.

"Color me intrigued. I must leave you now, my stunning bride, before I devour you."

"Enjoy your gift," she called out to him with a devious smirk as he walked out. Damien wouldn't know what hit him until it was over. She had not known what to get the vampire. He was a king and already had whatever he desired. She did not want to buy him anything, partly because it would be bought with his money, but also because nothing seemed worthy of him. Nor did he cherish material things. He never bothered with flashy clothing unless the event required it. He did not flaunt his wealth like the other royals, nor did he speak of money like the others. So, she gave him the one thing he could not have. Well, the one thing he could not have *yet*. That would all change after the ceremony tomorrow.

She bottled a memory of her own. One that took incredible courage for her to give up let alone perform.

Last night, after Phillipa left for the evening, Liana plucked up the courage to do this for Damien. She stood before the floor length mirror in her bedroom in only a thin sleeping gown. A candle flickered on the table beside her while she stared at herself in the mirror. She'd been sure to secure herself with a privacy shield that blocked not only sound but scent, ever aware of Damien's parents nearby. A locking spell on her door also kept her secured or else she might not have garnered the courage to do this.

Even now, standing there and ready to create this memory for him, she had to remind herself that this would drive him wild. So, she put her nerves out of her mind and thought only of Damien. Thought of all their stolen, heated moments and snappy innuendos. Thought of the intense need they'd both been holding at bay.

Keeping all that at the forefront of her mind, she slowly dragged her right hand along the length of her left arm toward her chest, her eyes tracking each slow inch in the mirror. Fingers drifted across her chest, briefly caressing her neck and collarbones before sliding over her breasts with just a teasing caress. As she did so, she imagined it was his hands on her; she wanted him to imagine the same when he watched her memory.

She didn't linger long before reaching to undo the braid she always slept in. The soft waves hung heavily over one shoulder, her fingers combing through them briefly before reaching for the ties of the sleeping gown.

One slow pull of the strings undid the tie, the sleeves falling off her shoulders. She turned away from the mirror knowing this would drive Damien crazy. He wouldn't be able to see her anymore in her memory which would be through her eyes only.

She let the fabric fall to her waist and looked back over her shoulder. In the mirror, the candlelight flickered around her silhouette while casting the softest glow along the expanse of skin on her back. Slowly, she let the fabric slip down as she watched, pretending it was Damien's eyes tracking each movement.

Inch by inch, her backside came into view. When it reached the tops of her thighs, she paused before letting the fabric fall completely. She kicked the fabric aside and took a steadying breath before turning around. First, she turned to the side, keeping herself concealed with her arms, looking at herself for a few seconds before brushing the mass of hair to her back. The candle rested on a table behind her, which only allowed the dark silhouette of her front to be revealed in the mirror.

No male had ever seen her body before and her heart pounded in her chest as she felt nervous about revealing it to Damien. The fact that she was alone emboldened her to do this, and the knowledge that it would drive Damien wild had her continuing. She lifted her hands into her hair, ruffling the waves while arching her back, putting her entire profile on view for him. The curves of her body were enticing even to her as she looked her fill, letting him look too.

Finally, she turned to the front, dropping her arms to her sides. Her eyes traced down her body as if they were Damien's, as if he were the one standing before her seeing her naked body for the first time. The low light left her pale skin looking dark, the details of her body hidden.

She started with her neck, arching to the side as she ran delicate fingers over the sensitive skin, imagining it were Damien's lips there. She snapped her eyes open, not realizing they'd fallen closed. She gave him a sly grin in the mirror before those fingers dipped down to the center of her chest, her focus fastened on the movement. Both hands lifted to cup her breasts, feeling the sudden heaviness in them as her breath sped up. She brushed her thumbs over peaked nipples as he had done to her before then let her hands drift down her abdomen, eyes lingering on her breasts for another moment.

Hands slid down her belly then apart before fingers traced the dips along her sides that gave her a womanly figure. She let them trace down again, falling to the tops of her thighs then sliding upward and inward, caressing the soft thatch of hair protecting the rest of her from view.

Done with her teasing, Liana summoned a chair behind her and sat on the edge at a slight angle so that she was not fully facing herself. There was still something she wanted to keep a secret from him, even if she was fully naked already and he had touched her there once before. She hesitated with doubt for a brief moment before leaning back. All it took to encourage her was to remember the burning hunger in his eyes when he'd made love to her with his fingers. This was for him, she'd told herself. This was all for him... and a little bit for her.

She cupped her breasts again, toying with them as he had. The angle of her position cast most of her body in shadows which she quite enjoyed. It made her feel less exposed even though she bared nearly everything to him. She kept one hand on her breast as the other slid down her abdomen and between her thighs. Struggling to keep her eyes open at the first caress of her fingers, her eyelids dropped low, only slits allowing her to see what she was doing to herself. Color rose on her cheeks at how scandalous all this was, but she couldn't stop. The idea of Damien seeing this urged her on.

Legs parted slightly and back arched, she mimicked everything he had done to her. She let her head drop, hair tickling her back as she circled the overly sensitive part of herself that he paid particular attention to. Panting, she forced her eyes open again, being sure to look at herself fully.

Confidence surged in her veins. She had to admit that she looked like the temptress Damien always claimed her to be, just enough on display to entice while the rest was left in shadow, endlessly teasing him for what was so close yet still out of sight.

Back arched, her breasts peaked in the dark room while her left arm supported herself, her fingers gripping at the edge as if it were a lifeline while her other hand disappeared between her legs. The image of herself like this had her pausing. It was the most erotic thing she'd ever seen, aside from a shirtless and sweaty Damien, and she could hardly believe it was herself.

Focused on keeping her eyes open, Liana let her hand release the chair and slide up her body once more. She did not feel her own softs hand but Damien's calloused fingers teasing her heated skin.

Liana had to remind herself to keep her heavy lidded eyes open as pleasure threatened to overtake her. She lifted her leg onto the edge of the chair. She needed more. She needed to feel Damien's hips settled between her own. Feel the weight of him pressing into her flesh. Needed the caress of his fangs against her neck, not just her nails. She burned for his lips on hers, on every part of her body. She arched even more, her heel digging into the chair, the other planted on the floor as her hips rocked on the edge of the seat.

She was so close, the thought of Damien pleasuring himself to this memory nearly pushing her over the edge. Gripping the seat again lest she tumble out of the chair, her eyes focused on the spot where her arm disappeared behind her thigh. There was no mistaking the frantic movements. Breath ragged, hips jerking uncontrollably, she imagined Damien's hand making similar motions as he stroked himself. It was imagining him in front of her now, of him watching her do this, egging her on while touching himself that sent her over the edge. Entire body clenching as she cried out, her toes curling with the pleasure that electrified her body. It was so hard to keep her eyes open, but she did so for him, capturing every moment of her pleasure.

Breathing heavily, she slumped back in the chair. It took a moment for the high to wear off and realize what she'd done.

Thoroughly embarrassed after she'd already committed to everything, a blush stole over her cheeks. She didn't want Damien to see her shame though. Grinning to cover it, she strode toward the mirror confidently and said, "Goodnight."

That was where she ended the memory. Liana hoped he watched it tonight.

A sinister smile lifted her lips. Although she'd been embarrassed after the fact, she knew how erotic the act had been. So private and directed for his pleasure only, it had been the perfect gift. And tomorrow, they'd both finally sate the tension that had been building between them since the beginning.

Chapter Fifteen

Despite her fatigue, Liana couldn't sleep. She'd tossed and turned without getting any closer to dreaming. Something pulled at her to stay awake, told her to move. Her magic writhed beneath her skin, just as riled. Which is why she found herself wrapped in a thick cloak and boots while walking toward the temple, to where her magic directed her to go.

It was not Liana's first time seeing the temple yet it still awed her. She attended worship the past two weeks with Damien and the rest of the residents at Sancta Valles Castle, a completely different experience than what she was used to. They had it right though in that all breeds worshiped together. Their prayers to the gods and goddesses were slightly different but held the same meaning. It was the way all of the kingdom should follow, to be united as they claimed.

Walking up the marble staircase, she stared up at the arch of the gods' Sentinels. Standing on either side, the Sentinels' arms created the arch while their watchful eyes welcomed all inside. They stood as tall as three stories, their bodies wrapped in armor while each held a spear in their outer hands.

Her magic urged her forward, the heavy iron doors still open. Damien said they were only ever closed during the winter to keep out the cold but were never locked so anyone could access the temple when needed. Only two guards lingered at the base of the stairs to allow privacy to any worshiper.

The antechamber was not very large, a simple rectangular room that held closets to either side which were used to store cloaks and the like during worship days. Another archway led into the main temple, the border of the arch filled with symbols and emblems of the gods and goddesses.

Entering into the main temple, the colossal structure stretched out before her. Lit with a soft glow from many orbs of mage light and the ethereal glow from the moon shining in through stained glass windows, she walked down the center aisle which was lined by great round columns and endless pews. Her steps were slow and silent on the marble while she took her time admiring the vaulted ceiling and the intricate paintings crafted there. They depicted countless scenes from the *Book of Worship*, giving life to the histories of their gods once more.

Liana climbed the stairs of the dais, her magic pulling her deeper into the temple. The alcove at the back of the dais held shrines to their two most worshiped deities, Jupiter and Juno, the king and queen to the gods. To the left was a grand statue of Jupiter standing as tall as the ceiling and looking over all his people. To the right stood Juno, which is where her magic pulled her.

Under the gentle cast of mage light, the mother and protector of all, Juno, stood valiantly with a shield resting against her leg, a diadem upon her head, and her arm held aloft with an offering. In that hand she gripped a chalice with the symbol of unity; three circles overlapped, the central piece of them all contained a tree - the symbol of life. A replica of that chalice could be found in any temple and was used for ceremonies and worship days to remind all that they were meant to be one united people under the deities.

Liana kneeled on the cushioned bench and bowed her head, her magic instantly calming. "I pray to you, Goddess Juno. I pray for your guidance and wisdom as I embark on this new path in my life."

Tilting her head back, she looked up at the imposing figure. "I am so scared, Juno," she admitted on a whispered breath. "I've been trying so hard to stay strong, to play my role correctly. But, I'm haunted day and night by my past."

She slid off her knees and onto the bench, leaning against the wall and resting her arm upon the ledge so that she could lay her head down. Smoothing her fingers over the cool marble, Liana worried over her future with Damien. She worried that she wouldn't be strong enough to support him in his role or take on her responsibilities as queen. There was so much to know and so many moving parts all the time. One misstep and something could go seriously wrong for them all.

"In that cell, he broke the innocent child I'd been. He tainted the wondrous magic inside me. I think, worst of all, he made me doubt myself." Brushing a tear away, she couldn't bring herself to look upon the infallible deity above her. She had so many doubts and questions. "Why am I so scared? Why can I not be brave like Damien or his parents? Why do I have this incredible magic? It cannot be for what the prophecy claims because I do not want it to be true. I don't want that responsibility. How am I supposed to unite the kingdom?"

Silence filled the air around her, not even a cricket offered a song that she could cling to as a sign that the goddess listened.

"Maybe you could tell me who gave our ancestors that prophecy to begin with. Was it another deity? Or was it just some hopeful fool as Damien suggested?" If it didn't come from a deity, she'd feel less pressured to fulfill it, even though she could acknowledge that Triaedian did need something to steer it in a different direction. With a heavy sigh she closed her eyes. "It does not matter, I suppose. It was written and now people believe it to be true. Quite unfair though that they expect me to live up to such an impossible task."

Lifting her feet onto the bench, she curled into a ball with her head still resting at the feet of Juno. "Watch over me, Goddess Juno," she whispered, her eyes finally getting heavy with sleep.

As she drifted off, she felt a warmth envelope her and could have sworn she heard a woman speak, the words lost to her now.

Although she was soothed into sleep, her dreams were filled with terror. Flashes of her time in that cell, of an arrow protruding from Charlotte's chest, of Damien ripping the head off the mercenary's shoulders. They all tormented her.

She jerked awake, the remnants of someone screaming her name following her into the waking world. Jolting upright, Liana erected a shield and glanced around frantically. She found herself in the temple still while night still reigned outside the windows.

Hand on her chest, she took heavy breaths to calm her racing heart. Magic swirled and twitched with irritation beneath her skin ready to lash out at any threat. There was nothing though, just her own mind tormenting her.

Heavy footsteps alerted her to someone's presence. A groan nearly escaped her when she saw Luciano already halfway down the long aisle. He wore plain clothes as Damien often did, half of his salt and pepper hair pulled back.

The vampire strode right up to the wall beside her and leaned against it.

"I've been watching you since you left the castle. Someone could have attacked you at any moment, especially when you were asleep," he stated without any heat behind his words.

She shrugged. "It was a good thing that you watched me then." In truth, she had thought to bring a guard but purposefully gave them the slip to come here alone. She considered Luciano might be following like he'd been doing, although she'd hoped he had given that up by now.

They sat in silence for a moment, the air around her calming once more as the remnants of her dream faded. She didn't sleep for long based on the moon still lingering outside.

"Damien used to sit in that very spot every night after his transition." Luciano nodded to the bench she claimed. "He never said a word, just sat there for hours staring up at the goddess."

"Why?"

He shrugged. "Why do you sit there now?"

She looked up at the statue, a sense of peace filling her while her magic remained calm. There was no good way to explain to this hard man that she had a feeling to come here, that she was guided by her magic to do so. He probably wouldn't appreciate that explanation or would tell her that she shouldn't have blindly followed because it could have been a trap.

"Why are you here?" she asked, curling her arms around her legs.

He paused, glancing around the temple, his head cocking a bit to the side. "Privacy shield, if you would," he said expectantly.

With a heavy sigh, she did as commanded.

"I heard you earlier." Her stomach dropped at his admission. She'd said a lot earlier, the least of which being she was scared all the time. "After your moment in the carriage the other day, Damien told me what happened when you were a child. It makes more sense why you seem so skittish at certain times."

She waited, not sure if she was meant to respond to that or how. He took a few steps then sat on the other end of the bench, staring at the statue of Jupiter opposite them.

"You are good for Damien, everyone can see that. You calm his vampiric side like no one else. I've never seen him so happy before either."

Liana didn't dare move for fear it would end whatever was happening. Or perhaps she was dreaming because the Luciano she'd known was not prone to such candor.

"My grandson was born into a title he had no control over. He is the tenth vampire king of Triaedian and has a destiny to fulfill. He never believed in it because he didn't want to, just as you don't want to be the Savior." She flinched at the name, then readjusted so that her feet were flat on the floor once more. "You're both so alike. Both tormented by your gifts. Both hopeful fools."

She frowned. "I do not think that describes either of us." Damien may have difficulties with his vampire and she with her magic, but neither of them were hopeful fools.

"It does. Despite everything you've been through, you still hope for a better future. Despite what you know of mage males, you still hope that things will change, hope that you will not have to suffer their patriarchy. Damien, despite all he has seen of this world and of the people he rules, still hopes that the kingdom will unite."

While she didn't completely agree with him, she decided it wasn't worth arguing over. "You sound as though you don't believe it is possible to unite Triaedian," she pointed out instead.

He shook his head, his eyes still on Jupiter. "Under the right conditions, under the right rule, and with centuries of change, I think it is possible."

"Then why reprimand us for being these supposed hopeful fools if you believe it too?"

He finally faced her, dark brown eyes holding her gaze. "Because I am realistic about it. I know what it will take to make that prophecy a reality. It will take the two of you to stop hoping for something better to come along and to seize your destinies. You and Damien must become the king and queen of that prophecy. Neither of you can hide from it any longer. Claim the magic you were blessed with and fix this kingdom."

She scoffed, leaning back against the wall. "You make it sound so simple when there is nothing simple about this."

"What is so complicated?" he challenged.

"Everything." She stood to pace, her magic and anger swelling. "I've barely begun to understand the responsibilities as queen, the rebels are still out there threatening us, and I have absolutely no idea how to unite a kingdom."

"And?" he prompted.

She snapped her body toward him. "And, what?"

"You left a key problem off your list." He sat back, crossing his arms over his chest.

Throwing her hands up in exasperation, she asked, "What did I forget? As if that list weren't enough."

"You are tortured by your past and not in control of your magic."

She froze, her magic instantly coming to her defense. He raised a brow as if to say, I told you so. Beyond the point of denial, she reclaimed her seat once more, glaring across the temple at Jupiter. "Maybe. What would you recommend I do about any of that? I practice daily with Master Kinley for my magic. I have excellent control in that regard."

"What does it feel like when it acts without your control?" he asked calmly. The only reason she answered the infuriating vampire was because he didn't sound judgemental for once.

She shrugged. "It feels like a person, as if someone else is acting through me. It reacts to my emotions, to my surroundings, without my direction. Sometimes..." she paused, glancing at him with uncertainty. Doubt creeped in as she thought that she likely shouldn't be telling this vampire any of this. He kept his usually stern face blank. He'd already called her out though, and she knew he wouldn't let this drop. "Sometimes it feels like it has its own emotions too, it gets angry or sad. When Damien is near, it feels happy and content."

"Have you spoken to anyone about this? Kinley perhaps?"

She shook her head. "My magic is already far different from everyone else. I didn't want to add more to that."

"I doubt he would know anything anyway. Perhaps we could find answers elsewhere. The other mage kingdoms might have more knowledge but they are still stuck in their archaic patriarchy as well. It would not be safe for them to learn of your power."

Liana chewed at her lip. "We definitely don't need another enemy on our doorstep," she agreed. "What of that book? Did it have anything else of value in there aside from this damn prophecy?"

His eyes narrowed on her for the disrespect of the book. "*The Book of Kings* is a cherished text specifically created by the original founders of Triaedian for every king to follow. We all add our experiences and knowledge to help guide our successors."

"Yes, well, did it say anything more about the Savior? Or maybe why my magic is so different?"

He scrubbed a hand over his thick beard which was also speckled with gray. "It does not."

"Great. So I am no better off than when we started this conversation."

Again, he frowned at her. "You are so like Damien it is annoying," he grumbled.

"What, honest?"

"Vexing," he corrected. Shaking his head, he looked toward Jupiter again, deep in thought. "I could try to obtain some ancient texts from the other kingdoms. Perhaps they would have more discreet knowledge."

"Obtain how?"

"The usual way, of course. Now," He rushed on before she could ask more questions, "Back to my point about your past. You are going to have to deal with that before it becomes more of a problem."

Crossing her arms, she refused to let the memories consume her. "You seem to be full of answers tonight. How am I supposed to do that?"

"You may think that I am a cold, unfeeling bastard, but I am not." She raised a brow in disbelief which he chose to ignore. "I have been through many of my own traumas and helped many soldiers through theirs. It comes with the burden of such a long life and living in the world we do."

Her arms relaxed. The things he must have seen in his seven hundred years. The burden of his family's deaths. She may not have liked him all that much but she could sympathize with all he'd been through.

"The best thing to get over this is time, a luxury you do not have. Aside from that, we work through it." That sounded like the last thing she wanted to do. "Have you told anyone what happened, the full explanation?"

She shook her head. In a quiet voice she added, "I don't want to remember."

"Listen, I'm no expert in all of this, but the only thing that helped me was talking about it. I confided in my mate, gods rest her soul. If you would feel more comfortable with Damien, you should to talk to him. Otherwise, I'll be here as well."

Her eyes narrowed on him. "*You* are willing to help me?"

Luciano let a bit of annoyance poke through his facade. "Have I not made myself clear enough? You and Damien are the future of this kingdom. I will do whatever it takes to make that prophecy come true and protect my family."

Not quite convinced that he wanted to listen, she thought about going to Damien. She thought about telling him what happened from the very beginning but then saw his vampire lashing out at anyone or anything in his war path.

"What will talking do?" she questioned, doubt heavy in her tone.

A heavy sigh left the old vampire. "For me, it allows me to distance myself from it all. When I think about a traumatic event, I replay it in my mind exactly as I recall it. It feels like I'm reliving it with all the same emotions over again. When I talked about it, I clearly remembered everything but it was as if I became a bystander looking in. The emotions became less intense and easier to work through. It allowed me to finally see that event in the past and not a current threat."

She didn't think talking would help anything, it would only infuriate Damien and make her relive something she didn't want to relive. If she told Phillipa, the poor woman would likely pass on the spot from emotional suffering. She'd never confide in her family and put them at risk for knowing what she'd done.

Liana eyed the vampire beside her once more. Perhaps he wasn't the worst person she could talk to. "If you're truly offering, then I suppose I could attempt it."

He settled back on the bench and gestured with his hand for her to start. "No judgment, no commentary, unless you'd like some. Otherwise, I will simply listen."

Nodding, she took several deep breaths, her hands gripping the edge of the bench as she pulled up the memories of her past which lingered so close to the surface. The moment she started speaking, the entire story fell out of her. She told him every detail she could remember down to the little mouse that kept her company one night.

Some tears fell. Mostly though, she focused on describing everything, on getting her story out. It didn't take very long but by the end of it, she felt less raw than she imagined.

Sitting back, her head rested on the ledge of Juno's shrine. "I suppose I do feel a bit lighter after all that."

"Do you want to talk about it anymore?" he asked, having kept quiet that entire time.

She shrugged. "What else is there to say? I could ask why he did it, or what drove him to do such a thing to a child, but he's gone. It would all just be speculation now, nor would it help ease my pain."

He blew out a heavy breath. "If you want to hear my perspective on it, I would say that he was a separatist and misinterpreted the prophecy for his own gain. He was a greedy and sick man."

Liana nodded in agreement. "Do you think his son is the same?"

"Uncertain as of now. He is being closely watched though."

"I hope he is not. I will not allow my sister to marry him if that is the case."

"Perhaps she would help in our investigation of him. She could be the inside informant

that we lack at the moment."

Liana lifted her head, her eyes weighing down with fatigue. "You want to put my sister in harm's way to use her as a spy?"

Luciano raised an expectant brow. "You will be crowned tomorrow, Liana. You must start thinking like a monarch which includes using all avenues of knowledge acquisition."

She snorted. "If that's what you'd like to call it." Standing, she bit back a yawn. "I'm off to bed. Are you going to follow me or stay here?"

He stood, gesturing for her to lead the way. As they walked, he stayed one step behind her. "I assure you that anything said here tonight will go with me to my grave," he declared.

"I appreciate that. And thank you for listening." It grated on her nerves to thank him for anything after how rude he'd been to her for the past few weeks but the vampire did try to help her in his own way. He only grunted in response.

"Yes, well, as I said, I've dealt with torture victims before."

As sad as that was, she found herself hiding a smirk because the vampire couldn't just accept her thanks for his kind gesture.

They walked in silence back to her room where he barged in to check that everything was secure before bidding her goodnight.

"Luciano," she called before he could escape. He paused in the doorway. "I'll deny ever saying this but, you're not as horrible as I first thought you were."

His lips twitched with amusement. "Just as I will never admit that you are more capable than I first thought." With a wink, he slipped out the door.

Laughing to herself, she made her way to bed, finally ready to sleep. It had been an unexpected night, but a productive and pleasant one. Now, she'd just have to make it through the wedding and coronation tomorrow.

Chapter Sixteen

Liana's wedding was a day she refused to ever be happy about in the past. Now though, she was certainly happy if not overly nervous about being the center of attention for an entire day.

After a calm and private breakfast in her room, Liana soaked in the tub for a bit before her family arrived with an army of maids. As they were all primped and primed, food and drinks were served, keeping them nourished for the long ceremonies ahead.

Phillipa completed Liana's intricately braided updo with the aid of another maid. Before they started applying the cheek and lip rouge, she took a moment to eat from the tray of food. Charlotte joined her at the table, their mother and Eva gossiping like proper high society women.

"How are you?" Charlotte asked. They had not spoken much since their disagreement in the garden a few weeks ago.

"I am well. How are you?"

"Fine." She picked at a bundle of grapes. "I need to apologize, Liana. When I lost my temper in the garden... Frederick and I had an argument earlier and I was upset. I should not have said those things. I am so happy for you and the King. You deserve to be happy."

Liana placed her hand over her sister's. "You also deserve to be happy, Charlotte." She smiled in return.

"I am, truly. Today is about you though. How excited are you?"

Liana wanted to press the matter but let it go for now, her sister clearly did not want to discuss it. When they could have a moment alone, she would pull the truth from her.

"I've never been so happy in my life," she admitted. And truly she was. Never did she think that she would be happy on her wedding day. From the time she knew she'd be forced to marry Liana could only think of how miserable she would be. The wedding day was never something she looked forward to because that would symbolize the official end of her life. She'd be forced to become a proper high-society female and bow down to her husband. She'd be expected to bear many children and raise them like obedient mage.

Not today though. Today she was content, hopeful even. This was the marriage she didn't dare dream of. One where she loved the man she married. A man that cherished her, listened to her, and saw her as an equal. Liana felt all those things from Damien. He may be a cocky bastard sometimes, but he was also kind and gentle with her. Truly, she'd found her happy ending. Or rather, a happy beginning, because this was not the end for her, but the start of a new life where she did not have to hide anymore. Damien encouraged her to use her magic, to learn all that she could and she loved him all the more for it.

After the maids finished with the final touches to her face and before she could dress, Master Kinley performed the mage ceremony to ensure that the female is still pure. It was a simple spell and over in a minute. All Liana had to do was sit in a chair, her family around her while Master Kinley performed the magic. It found her still pure, which was quite the relief to her considering just how close they'd come to crossing the line.

When she was finally dressed, all the pieces in place, she stared at herself in the mirror, awed by the stunning gown. The dress, designed to her specifications, was a celebration of her love for Damien. Constructed of the finest, emerald silk, embellishments of gold thread wove elegant designs along the bodice and along the base of the skirts. The sleeves tapered into points at her elbow, matching the V-neck cut of her neckline. Around her neck sat a matching strip of silk that went halfway up her neck, while the gold design along the edges worked perfectly to match Damien's necklace. It sat near the base of her neck along the emerald fabric, the gold chains dangling.

He didn't know she'd chosen to wear the ceremonial neckpiece of the vampires and loved that she could surprise him with it. She loved both the necklace and the cloth, loved what it represented… that she was now Damien's alone to cherish.

Lady Monroe did not hold back her tears as she hiccupped and said, "You are stunning, my girl." For the first time, Liana felt that her mother spoke truthfully, as sad as that also made her to think. She always tried to forgive her mother for the hurtful things she'd said to her considering the pressure there was for Lady Monroe to marry her daughters off to rich husbands. Even now though, she found it difficult to offer a genuine smile given the past. In a time when a young girl needed love and guidance, all Lady Monroe offered were harsh criticisms and strict rules.

Liana smiled nonetheless, looking at her mother's tear-stained face. Her sisters stood beside her in beautiful gowns that were specially created for the wedding as well. Charlotte wore her typical navy to flatter her pale complexion and wheat blonde hair while Hannah stunned in a gown of purple. Eva looked regal in a work of art drafted from deep maroon fabric that very nearly detracted from Liana's dress.

"Damien is a lucky man to have you, Liana," Eva said with a genuine smile. Her heart skipped a beat at the approval in the High Lady's words. As much as she loved Damien, she felt wholly inadequate for the position of queen and often, unworthy of Damien. She kept up with him the best she could, but the confident, intelligent, and sly male was her superior; there was no denying it despite the bravado she fronted. He was also almost a century older than her with far more experience which likely contributed to her feelings of inadequacy.

A knock sounded at the door, thankfully drawing everyone's attention away from her for a moment. It allowed her to take a deep breath to calm her rising nerves and doubts.

"It is time. Are you ladies ready?" Lord Monroe called from outside to the door.

Lady Monroe rushed to the door and pulled her husband inside. "Come, look at our stunning daughter."

Lord Monroe's steps faltered as Liana turned to face him. His eyes widened before glossing over with tears. He cleared his throat, blinking rapidly. A decorative wooden chest hid beneath his right arm. She recognized it from his office because she'd broken into it countless times to borrow the books inside. He set it down on a chair before he took her hand to kiss the back of it. "You are beautiful, Liana."

"Thank you, Papa," she responded, her own tears threatening to fall. Unlike her mother, and so unlike other mage males, her father had supported her to the best of his ability. He indulged her oddities, even praised her for them. He could never bring himself to teach her magic though which had always been a great divide between them.

"The temple is overflowing with people. The entire road toward the temple is lined with spectators just to get a glimpse at you," Lord Monroe informed her. Liana gulped. That was not what she needed to hear. "High Lady," he said to Evangeline, "The King is ready and waiting by the carriage for you with your husband and Master Kinley." Evangeline nodded her head as thank you then left. Lord Monroe turned back to Liana. "He wanted me to inform you that you must keep a shield up at all times on the ride to the temple."

Liana nodded. "I will."

"Very good. Now, we must all be on our way. Ladies, if you will give me a moment alone with my daughter," Lord Monroe said, with a polite wave to the door. "Guards are waiting to escort you to the carriages." Lady Monroe gave her husband a rare kiss full of affection while tears threatened to drip down her face before they all left the room.

Lord Monroe clasped her hands in his own. "I am so proud of you, Liana. You have grown into a brave woman, and you deserve every happiness." Liana blinked away the tears that threatened to fall and ruin her expertly done makeup.

"I've brought you a gift." He grabbed the chest and opened it toward her. Liana gazed at the familiar books inside. "I will never be able to apologize enough for not allowing you access to these, or that I did not heed your pleas to learn magic. I am so sorry, my daughter. Please, take these. They are our family's spellbooks passed through the generations."

Liana caressed the thick tomes, joy and sadness filling her at the same time. No matter that she already memorized every spell in most of those books, she cherished the books for what they meant, that her father finally acknowledged her.

"I knew you were powerful, Liana. I knew you were stronger than even me, yet I did not allow you to learn what you were born into. I don't expect your forgiveness. Please, take these and know that I support you."

Liana took the chest to set it down before pulling him into a hug. "You have no idea how much this means to me, Papa," she said with a sniffle. He patted her back lightly.

"I'm sorry I didn't come to this on my own, that others had to make me realize you deserved this."

"Stop. Please, stop. You are forgiven. Do not think on it any longer." She pulled back, and he handed her a handkerchief. Offering a watery grin, he held out his arm to her.

"Shall we?" Liana patted at her face hoping things weren't too ruined before placing her hand in the crook of his elbow. This would be a new start for them all, not just her and Damien.

***

Liana rode in a carriage with her father and mother while her siblings piled into a carriage behind them. Liana kept shields around both carriages as they rode along the road to the temple which was a short drive away. Temporary wooden partitions were placed along the path to keep the crowds off the road and to keep them from reaching the carriages. She couldn't help but notice all the guards at every point. It looked as though Damien sequestered his entire army for this event. There had even been a guard every few feet inside the castle as they made their way to the carriage. Since the gates were open and so many people flocked to witness this historic event, Damien did not take any chances with security. Especially with the separatists and the threat looming over her head from that letter.

Liana sat forward in the carriage on the bench by herself. The horses walked along the drive allowing her to wave and smile at everyone as they passed just as Eva coached her to do. It was so loud, the crowd so large she could hardly believe it. People shouted and waved for attention, throwing bouquets of flowers and bundles of fabrics as offerings. Liana let them fall into the carriage harmlessly while keeping up her shield.

Once they arrived at the temple, guards flanked her as they escorted her inside where she entered through a side door into the antechamber. Her heart raced with excitement making the temple a blur around her. When the doors finally shut behind her family, Liana breathed a sigh of relief, the noise of the crowd cutting off.

"That was overwhelming," she complained. Two hands slid into her own. She smiled at each of her sisters gratefully and squeezed.

"They were all shouting your name," Hannah gushed. "How special that they all know who you are."

Charlotte snorted. "She is going to be the Queen, Hannah. Of course, they know her name."

"I know. It is just exciting, that is all."

Liana gave her younger sister a grateful smile. "It is exciting, isn't it?" she offered to which the girl smiled again. "Shall I do the same at your wedding one day? I will shout your name from the pews as you walk down the aisle."

Hannah giggled. "You'll be queen, you can't do such things."

Liana chuckled. "I will be queen which means I can do whatever I please," she said with a waggle of her brows. Hannah laughed again and it was just what she needed to calm down a bit.

Lord Monroe returned through the door that led into the main temple. "They are about to begin. Are you ready, Liana?" She gulped but nodded. She was beyond ready to marry Damien, it was the massive crowd of people waiting beyond those doors that she was not ready for.

Two guards stood by the double doors and opened them slightly to signal that she was ready. Across the temple, identical doors did the same. A blast of noise assaulted her, the temple beyond full of people and deafening chatter. When the first strings of the orchestra filled the temple however, the noise instantly quieted. Lord Monroe stood a step in front of her and to her right while her mother stood directly beside her. It was customary for the mage father to lead his daughter to the altar like leading a cow to slaughter. In vampire culture, the pair walked freely toward each other, their parents following behind as they met in the aisle then walked the rest of the way together.

Liana compromised and allowed her father to walk her halfway, then she'd take Damien's arm. For now, she slid her arm through her mother's and a hand into the crook of her father's elbow. As the music hit a certain note, the guards fully opened the doors. Her father took a step forward, her shield secured around everyone, even her siblings trailing behind her, and Liana followed.

She kept her gaze on the floor, nerves wracking her body with sudden fears of tripping filling her mind. So focused on her steps and avoiding the stares and gasps that followed her appearance, she forgot that she could see Damien now. Slowly, she lifted her gaze.

Her feet stumbled as her heart skipped a beat.

There he was. The vampire king that chose her out of everyone else.

Across the temple, striding toward her with confident steps along the carpeted aisle, he looked like a god incarnate. Everything else fell away as her legs guided her without thought toward him.

Forget the gods, this temple was built for him. Built for the vampire that stared at her as if she were the only thing giving him life. His eyes didn't once leave her own.

It was no surprise to find him dressed in black. The trousers were sleek and tucked into polished, knee-high boots. The coat he wore was magnificent; thin gold trim lined the structured fabric that fell to his thighs with the tall collar enhancing his height and framing that long, tanned neck. The vest beneath shone a bright yellow-gold with gleaming gold buttons. A white collared shirt peaked out beneath it all, highlighting his darker skin and perfectly trimmed beard. He kept it short just as Liana preferred but was not quite the style while his thick hair was secured back with two small braids starting from each temple.

The crown atop his head was familiar although he didn't wear it often. To see him now, in all his kingly glory, she would have felt inadequate if it weren't for the intensity with which he beckoned her forward. She couldn't resist him if she tried.

They finally met in the center of the temple, the pews filled near to overflowing. Lord Monroe took Liana's hand from his arm and held it toward Damien. Staring into those eyes, she eagerly waited as Damien's hand reached for hers. As soon as their skin touched, a sigh of relief escaped her. A sigh because finally she was back in his arms. When she stepped toward him, her arm fell away from her mother, the last piece of her following her into this new life with Damien. He would be her new family. He would be the one to hold her at night, to comfort her and support her. He would be her new home. There was no fear or nervousness in this moment. There was only her and him, and there was no doubt in her mind that she wanted this man with every part of her soul.

She let those thoughts shine in her eyes as he stared down at her. His eyes grew darker, his hand holding hers a bit too tightly. "You are magnificent, my love," he said for her ears only.

"I know," she quipped with a wink which had him grinning.

A low growl started in his chest. "That wink... that grin..." he breathed, his voice so low. "I am going to punish you for the torture you made me endure with your wedding present."

Liana erected another shield around themselves to hide their words. Her smile dropped.

"You did not like it?" she asked as her cheeks heated with shame and regret.

He growled, pulling her into his body, his eyes dark with lust. "I loved every torturous second of it."

Her breath hitched, her mind going blank. Someone stepped up beside them, putting a hand on Damien's shoulder.

Ramone suggested, "Perhaps we could move this along."

Damien shifted her hand to the crook of his arm before they turned and walked down the center of the temple to where the priest waited on the dais. Liana kept glancing up at Damien, unable to keep her eyes off him for very long. He caught her and smirked, bringing his other hand over to rest on hers.

They passed a line of guards who stood at the bottom of the stairs before Liana lifted the front of her long gown while Damien assisted. Their families sat in the front row on either side of the aisle and as the couple reached the top of the dais, the music slowly drifted out.

Not willing to part with Damien, she grabbed his hand as they faced each other. Damien smiled indulgently and grasped her other hand. They were not supposed to, but Liana had a knack for ignoring society standards.

The priest droned on beside them, giving the usual speech that Liana had already heard a few times before during rehearsals. Now though, the only thing she heard was the sound of her own heart beating furiously while she stared at the beautiful man before her.

Standing in front of the entire elite of Triaedian, Liana couldn't help but wonder how she ended up there.

None of this would be happening if she hadn't caught his eye in the ballroom that first night. Nor would it have continued unless he found her in that little alcove behind the statues. Then she recalled everything after and how perfectly everything turned. Recalled how he manipulated her into this engagement, but she refused to just be a pawn and fought him with her intelligence and wit to earn some respect. How he teased and tempted her with every caress. How he held her so lovingly. How he supported her every dream and protected her with an entire army.

She couldn't hold back how much she loved him, how much her magic loved him. She had to tell him, but she didn't want others to hear what was only meant for him.

Flaring her magic, she entered his mind like she would when taking memories but instead of taking, she gave. She said into his mind, *"I love you."* His entire body jerked which he quickly covered with clearing his throat, eyes narrowing on hers. She chuckled.

"Can you hear me?" he asked back. She nodded. *"I was not aware mage could speak between minds."*

"They cannot," she answered plainly. As far as Liana was aware, there was no spell that allowed that. Her magic was different though, as everyone liked to point out. She could do things no one else could. So why not let herself speak into his mind. As of yet, she hadn't reached a limit on what her magic was capable of. Her only limit being her own lack of knowledge on what was possible.

"You truly are magnificent, Liana."

"And..." she prompted, needing to hear the words.

"And I'm honored to be your husband."

"And?" She said again.

That damn brow rose. *"And you will make a wonderful queen."*

Liana frowned. *"You are being purposefully obtuse."* She wanted him to say it back, to confirm that she was not the only one lost in the other.

"I am?" He feigned innocence. *"About what?"*

"And now we..." the priest began onto the next prayer. There were still three more prayers to go considering the priest had to preside over the wedding as if it were both mage and vampire.

"I could look at you like this for the rest of eternity," he told her, a soft caress coming through the connection as if he actually stroked her hair. *"But the memory of you in front of that mirror, of your hands touching yourself... When I die, that will be my afterlife, seeing you like that on an endless loop."*

Her body heated even as she frowned. *"Do not speak of death on this day, or ever for that matter. The only way you are allowed to die is if I do it myself or we go together."*

He laughed, which had the priest pausing for a moment. They both ignored him.

"May I request that if you ever feel the need to kill me, please strangle me with these naughty hands. I shall die happily knowing that they also gave you such pleasure."

Her cheeks were as red as the stain on her lips. *"You are perverse."*

"Oh, if you only knew all the things I want to do to your luscious body, you'd run from me now."

She began to regret initiating this connection considering he had her melting on the altar in front of the entire kingdom without a second thought. Reassuring that her shield blocked their scents as well, she cleared her throat. *"I am glad you enjoyed your gift."* His resounding laugh echoed in her head.

"Enjoyed? No, I damn near died the moment I realized what you'd given me. Tell me, temptress, did you imagine me losing control while I relived your naughty memory?"

She was sure the priest knew something was going on between them now. He kept glancing back and forth between them. And when she broke out into a sweat, he paused.

"Are you well, my Lady?"

"Fine. Just hurry, please," she demanded, squeezing Damien's hands to keep her wobbly legs from giving out. Damien chuckled at her torture, and she launched back into his mind to get revenge.

"At first, I imagined it was you, that your fingers caressed me. Just like I'd done nearly every night since you'd been so close." His eyes narrowed on hers, his lips

parting as fangs slid out. She did her best to hide her smirk. *"The longer I dragged it out, the more I wished you were there, watching me. I imagined you standing before me so that you could see everything I hid from the mirror. Only when I imagined you losing control and taking me completely did I find my release."*

They both breathed a bit too heavily, but it was Damien that looked ready to haul her out of the temple.

"As soon as this marriage is official, I am dragging you back to the castle," he growled into her mind.

"What about the coronation?" She didn't give a damn about the coronation. She would willingly go with him.

He cursed. *"After that, if you insist."*

"And the ball afterward? Are you going to deny me my own wedding ball?"

He took a deep breath and closed his eyes briefly. When he opened them, they were clearer. *"My mighty temptress, you tease me so mercilessly. In the house of the gods no less."*

She smirked for real this time. *"I was bored."*

"Take pity on me, temptress, or the entire kingdom and the priest will see just how badly I need you."

Liana couldn't stop herself, she cracked a laugh, slapping a hand over her mouth as her shoulders shook. Damien smiled broadly while the priest stopped his blessings.

"I think we are blessed enough, Priest," Damien said to the man before pulling her hand back into his. "I stand before you, Liana Monroe, before our families, the kingdom of Triaedian, and the gods and ask that you find me worthy of being your husband. Will you do me the honor of becoming my bride?"

Liana still smiled as she nodded. "I do."

"And I, Damien Ashwood, take you as my wife. May the gods bless our union," he said before pulling her into a kiss. There were gasps, quickly followed by a deafening cheer.

Their king was married.

Chapter Seventeen

Liana could hardly breathe as Damien held her against him. His lips were desperate against hers, the temple falling away as he held her. With her magic still connected to his mind, she said again, *"I love you."*

"And, I love you, Liana, my wife." Something snapped inside her chest, her heart bursting with joy. Magic rushed through her body like fire racing along oil. This didn't burn though. It was a comforting warmth like falling into Damien's arms. His lips gentled on her own then the fire burned through her and down the connection.

Damien growled and held her tighter. She felt him, felt every inch of his body as her magic flowed into him. It searched every crevice, leaving a trace of itself along the way until it found his mind once more and curled up like a sleeping cat. When she tried pulling her magic away, it came but some stayed behind, especially the part in his mind. Pulling harder, it reared back and swiped at her.

Damien pressed his forehead to hers as they caught their breath. "What is that?" he questioned.

Panicking that he also felt it, she examined it closer. The magic didn't react to her prodding exploration, the feel of it protective in nature, almost as if it were a shield. There was more to it though, far more. The magic felt like a separate entity from her own, yet still her. She pulled on it again, the power flaring with protective energy and refusing to budge.

A voice whispered in her mind just as panic started to overwhelm her.

Mine, it said.

Liana gasped, understanding dawning. Her magic claimed him. It left its mark on him to warn all others away and to protect him. "I'm sorry, I didn't mean to," she responded quickly. "It was my magic, I didn't know what it was doing."

"What did it do?" he growled, his arms like iron bands around her.

She gulped. "Please don't be mad at me. You know I can't control it sometimes." She was near to tears with the fear that he might hate her. He buried his face in her neck.

"I am not mad. I feel powerful. I feel that I could kill everyone in this room for daring to even look at you. They are not worthy, no soul is worthy to see you." The priest yelped and stepped back a few feet. Liana guarded their words again, the shield having slipped.

"I think it marked you." Damien froze. "My magic marked you. You're mine."

He growled, his breath a heady huff against her neck that had her shivering. "You're mine and if I could mark you the way I plan to later, I would have to kill everyone for witnessing it."

She gulped, her mouth suddenly dry. "Let us not do that then." She pulled back, his arms reluctantly loosening. A gasp escaped her as she saw him, and she realized then that the entire room was silent. His eyes widened too.

"You're glowing," they said in unison. They each glanced down at their hands. Damien glowed with that same otherworldly light as she did on rare occasions.

"The gods have truly blessed this union!" the priest exclaimed before dropping to his knees and bowing until his head touched the ground.

"Praise the gods!" Ramone shouted then kneeled before his son and new wife. Evangeline mimicked him, quickly followed by Liana's entire family. Then the prayer rang out around the temple like a cacophony of music as their subjects began to bow within the pews.

Liana could only stare at the temple of people that thought them blessed by the gods. Damien took her hand and squeezed.

"Rise!" he commanded. To the priest he demanded, "Get her the crown and hurry this coronation along." The priest waved the altar boy over, her crown resting on a pillow of lush purple velvet. He picked up the crown which matched Damien's gold. Except hers was far daintier but still elaborately beautiful.

Liana kneeled before the priest as he picked up the crown. She recited the proper words back to him, pledging her life and soul to the safety and prosperity of Triaedian. There was a bit more she recited from sheer will, her mind too distracted by her elated magic and the bond she'd inadvertently created between her and Damien. He still held her hand, both of them still glowing.

The priest intoned one last prayer before bequeathing the crown to Liana. The gold band, a close replica of the diadem Juno was always depicted wearing, settled around her head. The front of her crown had two points of elegant filigree lining either side of the middle before it came to a final point at the top. It sat heavily upon her head as she turned to face her people.

The priest intoned, "I present, Queen Liana Ashwood." Shivers ran down her spine, the weight of something far heavier than everyone's stares pressing on her. Damien bowed his head to her, kissing her hand then the crowd once again bowed.

Damien led her off the dais and down the aisle once more, the people clapping reservedly while spelled orbs of light burst along the aisle in celebration. Their families followed until they were shut inside the antechamber again. Liana shielded the room as she gasped for air.

"What was that?" Eva snapped.

Damien ignored his mother, his fingers cupped beneath Liana's chin. "Are you alright?" She nodded curtly, still trying to adjust to the weight of the crown and seeing Damien glow like a firefly.

"We rehearsed this three times!" Eva raved. "And you two stand up there like giggling children and shirk all the normal customs."

"Mother, please," Damien commented, his voice low yet stern.

"You didn't even perform the coronation correctly."

"It was enough to be legally binding. Liana is the Queen, no matter the ceremony," Damien assured. Her past fears and inadequacies barreled into her with the force of an arrow through the chest. She'd done this. She screwed everything up. Her magic ruined everything. Just like always, she was not strong enough to control it.

Tears threatened to fall once more. She was sick of it though. She was sick of feeling weak and emotional. Sick of always being the problem. This was supposed to be a special day and she couldn't even get through this happy occasion without her oddities ruining it.

Liana pulled away from Damien and stalked to the doors. "We must head to the castle. The rest of the kingdom is waiting." Her voice was strong even as her heart threatened to crumble. The crowd outside was so loud that she could hear them clearly through the doors.

"There is nothing to be upset over, Liana," Damien said, joining her.

"I'm not upset," she lied coolly, staring at the doors.

"I'll be upset for you then," Eva declared. "That farce of a ceremony will not satisfy the heads of the council. They will demand another ceremony, or at worst, not accept Liana as queen."

Liana's shoulders tensed. She'd royally screwed things up. Keeping her spine straight and chin up, she stared at the door. What could she do now? There was no going back in there to do things over again. She wouldn't suffer the humiliation of that, nor would she make Damien suffer through it either.

"She said the sacred vows. That is all that is necessary, the rest is fluff," Damien defended.

"You know how much value they place on the ceremonies, Son. Your mother has a point. We will be lucky if the council accepts her claim to the crown without any arguments," Ramone added.

Liana's hands fisted, nails digging into her skin, the pain a welcome distraction. When would she learn? When would she finally gain control of herself, of her magic? Her body began to shake as anger and shame threatened to drown her. Even as she begged for control, magic leaked from her hands.

She had been so happy just minutes ago. Standing before Damien, their teasing and professions of love. It had been perfect. Then her magic acted out at the worst possible time, just as Luciano predicted.

Damien appeared before her, his hands resting on her shoulders. She jerked out of his touch, pacing away.

"Perhaps we could arrange another ceremony tonight, with just the council. Then she can perform the entire coronation," Eva suggested. Liana crossed her arms.

"Mother, drop it," Damien declared, his voice low and commanding. He stepped toward Liana, not giving her room to escape again. "You said the vows. They are legally bound to accept that. You are queen, Liana."

She nodded, avoiding his stare. "Excellent. Now, let us go before the crowds start a riot." Damien didn't loosen his hold.

"Don't do this, Liana," he warned.

"Do what? I'm starving and the people are waiting." He finally let her go when she shimmied out of his hold and headed for the doors again.

"I'm not leaving until you talk to me. I will not spend the rest of our wedding day with you upset," he declared to her back.

"I am not upset." The lie burned her tongue, especially in the temple of the gods.

"Fine. Then we will all suffer in this sweltering room until your temper tantrum is over."

Liana's entire body stiffened, her arms falling to her sides as magic dripped from her fingers. Slowly, she looked at him. If she had a mirror, she knew her eyes would be glowing with fury. He didn't flinch under her stare.

"Excuse me?" she questioned, her tone lethal.

Damien simply crossed his arms, his stance relaxed. "Go ahead. We are waiting." Is that what he thought of her? That she was some emotional child? "Do it now or lash out at everyone for the rest of the evening while you try to bury your feelings."

Liana glanced at her family. They stood huddled in a group, uncertain of what to do. Her father looked to Damien with anger while her mother stared at her with disappointment. Charlotte eyed her with pity and she didn't dare look at the others.

Staring at the doors again, she refused the tears. No more crying. "Open the doors," she commanded the guards, her voice thick.

"Don't move," Damien countered. Nails cutting her skin, she choked back the tears. She may be Queen of Triaedian, but he was still the King and held more power. Her words were powerful, but his were absolute.

He stood before her again. She stared at his chest, her heart aching. "You are cruel." Gone was the love she felt for him, buried beneath piles of anguish and shame.

"Perhaps. But you are hurting and refuse to deal with it." The gold of his vest kept her gaze as she thought over his words. She was hurting. Who wouldn't when they constantly disappointed everyone around them? When they continuously did the wrong thing and had no control of the power within.

"We are a partnership, Liana. Let me help you carry your burdens and help you work through them. Talk to me," he prompted. What was there to say that he already didn't know? He apparently already thought of her as a petty child and knew her magic had a mind of its own. He sighed at her silence. "You were hurt in the past, Liana and dealt with it by hiding yourself away from the world, by hiding your emotions from yourself. Even Phillipa hid your memories from you." She flinched at the reminder, not wanting to recall why her maid did such a thing. "As your husband, I'm asking you to stop hiding. Let me help you."

Liana wanted to cry at the tenderness in his words. She took his hands. "Your grandfather said you and I were so similar, but you and he are both annoying. You both push me to talk when I don't want to."

Luciano huffed from some dark corner in the room, having snuck in at some point. "You're welcome," he declared clearly.

They both ignored him and she erected a silencing shield just for the two of them. "I'm sorry I ruined everything. I didn't mean for any of that to happen. The ceremony... I was prepared to complete it correctly, but..." But then she saw him and knew she needed to tell him how much she loved him, and things got out of control from there. "I'm sorry."

He tapped her chin so that she looked into his icy blue eyes. "That was the most perfect wedding ceremony I could have ever dreamed for, my love. Do not be sorry. Do not regret a single moment of it."

"But the coronation..." He pressed a finger to her lips.

"Is valid no matter what anyone claims. You said the vows. You are the Queen." She dropped her head again.

"I'm sorry I couldn't keep my magic under control again."

He growled and pushed her chin up once more. "If you bow your head in shame one more time, I will punish you in the most pleasurable way."

Her brows furrowed. "Pleasurable punishment? I'm not sure..."

He interrupted her again. "With me kneeling between your bare thighs and...." Stopping his words, she halted his naughty lips by slapping a hand over them. Her face flushed with lust and embarrassment.

"Threatening me with such punishment will not entice me to behave."

Grinning beneath her fingers, he nipped at her skin before she could pull away. "Before I torture myself further, let us resolve this issue. You are perfect, my little mage, and there is not a single thing I would change about you. Do not apologize again and please, enjoy our wedding day."

More than anything she wanted to do that. Wanted to forget everyone and everything while they ate, drank, and danced the day away. "There is still the matter that your skin is glowing. That I am still glowing."

Hands resting on his hips, he nodded. "I felt whatever you did during our kiss. I felt your magic in every part of me. It felt wonderful actually. Like sinking into a hot spring. Then it settled like a weight in my mind. Still, I feel it there."

"When I tried to take it away, it revolted as if it had a mind of its own."

His furrowed brows had her wishing she hadn't said anything. He scrubbed a hand over his jaw. "It doesn't feel malicious. It feels like you. In all honesty, I feel safe."

She eyed him warily. "Are you lying to me?"

"Not at all. Whatever this is, it gives me a sense of comfort, of safety and love."

"So, you're not mad that I essentially marked you with magic unknowingly?"

He chuckled, pulling her into his arms once more. Liana rested her head on his chest. "I love that you marked me. Knowing you claimed me so permanently sends my male ego soaring and all I've wanted to do since is bite my claiming mark into this sweet, tender flesh." Fingers brushed over her neck along the fabric and necklace making her shiver. "I'm going to finally claim this body and when I'm buried inside you, I will bite you right here for everyone to see that you are mine."

Breathless, she buried her face in his chest. "It always leads back to sex with you."

"Since I met you, that's all I've thought about."

She sighed, wanting that as soon as possible. But there was still a feast and a ball to attend. This was progress though. This is what she needed, a firm hand that wouldn't let her wallow.

"You hurt me a lot before," she admitted in a whisper, looking up so that he could see in her eyes everything she felt. He stilled. "When you mocked me about a temper tantrum. I felt ashamed, especially with everyone here. You made me feel like a spoiled child."

"Perhaps it was cruel of me to do so. Perhaps I could have found a gentler way to confront you. In the moment though, I was angry. All I wanted was for you to be ecstatic with me instead of shutting me out and degrading yourself." He cupped her face. "That ends now. It will take time, but I will not let you hurt any longer. You're all mine now, and I will do everything in my power to make you happy."

She sank into his hold, wrapping her arms around his waist. "I don't deserve you."

His eyes darkened. "That is equally deserving of pleasurable punishment."

"Calm, vampire. Our families are still in this room, and we should get moving." When she tried to pull back, he grasped her around her back.

"Say it again. Tell me with these lips," he demanded, his eyes even darker than before. Despite the random request she knew exactly what he meant.

She raised her hand to his stubbly cheek and said, "I love you, Damien." His chest rumbled as if he were a cat purring.

"I love you, Liana," he declared, then kissed her until her toes curled. Only then did they break apart and face their families. They still had a long night ahead of them.

Chapter Eighteen

The newlyweds rode in the carriage back to the castle, the people going wild as they passed. She wasn't surprised to find Asher and Owen leading their carriage, acting as guards instead of family. She hadn't seen them at the ceremony, not that she saw much aside from Damien and the priest. The glow between them dimmed but remained visible and still unexplained. Perhaps they were blessed by the gods and that is why they glowed, although Liana didn't quite believe it. She thought it was the magic that she accidentally marked him with.

They were ushered to a room she'd never seen before, which was not that surprising considering how large the castle was and how little she had explored it. The grand suite was completed with bookcases and plenty of seating and even a piano. She took a seat beside Damien and was served a glass of wine. Asher and Owen claimed seats beside them.

"What are we doing here?" she wondered.

"Waiting until our guests move from the temple to the ballroom."

"And we couldn't have spent this time in the bedroom?"

He smirked devilishly. "Definitely not. Once I get you alone, I'm not letting you go for at least a week." Her thighs clenched at the promise in his voice.

"We can clearly still hear you," Asher commented before chugging the wine from his goblet.

Liana chuckled even as she blushed.

"What happened on the dais? Are you alright, Damien?" Owen questioned, his eyes wary as he looked between the couple.

"I am quite well, Cousin. Liana marked me with her magic, just as I shall soon mark her as a vampire does."

Asher whistled. "That is some mark. Is the glow permanent? Because that would make for some rather terrible sleuthing."

Liana scoffed. "What kind of sleuthing does a king require that others cannot do for him?" The males exchanged secretive grins but didn't answer. "Fine, don't tell me. As for the glowing, I have no idea."

Damien brushed his thumb over her palm. "It's alright, Liana. I'm sure it will dissipate. It is already fading with every moment. Don't think on it any longer."

She was about to reply, to tell him that it was all she thought about when their families entered. Damien's relatives took drinks from servants before scattering about the large room. Luciano lifted his glass toward them with a nod before chugging the liquid down and slinking off to a dark corner.

Liana couldn't quite believe last night happened in the temple with Luciano simply because he didn't seem like the type to care about her feelings. He said it was all for the kingdom though, that she had to be strong for Triaedian and for Damien. Still, it left her feeling far more comfortable with his presence even if she didn't trust him as wholeheartedly as Damien did.

Others trickled in after that, including Carlisle's fiancé, Master Ranville, and Lord Dietrich accompanied by their chosen Monroe sibling, and settled around the room. Her father was the last to enter and she realized why. Accompanying him was an older man nearly identical to her father. He aged a lot since she'd last seen him but retained that pompous air about him. Behind him trailed his wife and son who also had a young lady on his arm. There was one more gentleman that stood to the back that she couldn't quite see.

"Your Majesty, Queen Liana," her father said with a twinkle in his eye toward Liana, "Allow me to introduce my brother, Master Monroe, and his family, Lady Grace Monroe, Lord Trevor and his bride Lady Iris."

Damien stood to greet them properly. "A pleasure to meet you all. We are glad that you came all this way to witness our union."

"Your invitation was an honor we could not refuse, Your Majesty," Master Monroe said with a slight bow of his head.

Liana slowly rose from her seat, forcing a pleasant expression on her face. Her uncle had never been a kind man to her. A purebred mage male through and through, he found Liana's impropriety offensive and disobedient. There was a reason she had not seen him in years even though her father traveled to Sapphire Cove every summer with the rest of her siblings to visit. Liana always stayed home with Phillipa even though she loved visiting the ocean.

"Uncle, Auntie, Trevor," she said to each with a nod of her head. "A pleasure to meet you, Lady Iris." The petite, mousy woman curtsied.

"You've grown," her uncle pointed out uselessly.

"That is typically what happens to a child," she remarked with a sickly-sweet smile.

He huffed. "Still have that foul mouth, I see."

Damien tensed beside her. She squeezed his hand and spoke into his mind, *"Leave it."*

Lady Grace Monroe interjected in the awkward silence. "You've grown into such a beautiful young woman, Liana. We've missed you on the coast."

"I've missed you, Auntie." The woman had a heart of gold which was one of the regrets she held about not visiting Sapphire Cove. It was just another example of how atrocious mage society was that this poor woman had to endure a life shackled to the brute beside her.

"Who are you, Sir?" Owen asked, glaring at the man in back. He stood taller than her uncle and cousin with a mass of blonde curls falling to his shoulders. An expertly tailored suit framed his long, lean frame making him look as handsome and elite as any royal.

"Sorry to crash the wedding, but I had to see my little Ana." Green eyes sparkled as a smirk filled his lips, one dimple imprinting his right cheek, looking so very familiar.

Liana gasped. "Elias?" she asked incredulously before launching at him. Amused by her reaction, he laughed and caught her with open arms.

"I'm surprised you remembered me," he teased.

"Elias, it is so good to see you." She reached a hand up to cup his face. "You're so grown up, I hardly recognized you."

"I could say the same to you, still cute as a button but I am pleased to see you're not covered in dirt."

She huffed a laugh giving his cheek a gentle tap. "Always so cheeky." She always romped around as a child, getting into things she shouldn't which would often leave her dirty and her dresses tattered.

He grinned back at her, that dimple on full display. "Wouldn't want to disappoint."

An arm circled her waist and pulled her away from him.

"Who are you?" Damien demanded. Elias's eyes dropped to the possessive arm around her waist then to Damien and back to her. His eyes narrowed in anger before he covered it with a smile again.

"Scholar Elias Baker, Your Majesty. I'm an old friend of Queen Liana."

"You were not invited," Damien responded.

"I was not, much to my dismay." He reached into his pocket and held his palm out. Liana gasped once more, while Damien tensed in anticipation. She grabbed the stone from his hand which she'd carved their initials into many years ago.

"Considering I was promised a friend forever, I expected an invitation."

"I can't believe you kept this for so long!" A song started playing on the piano and she noticed her sisters had taken to playing while the others settled around the room, studiously ignoring them.

"Of course, I did. You made me a promise." She had. Then she did a poor job of keeping it. Elias was Wesley's age and had been the son of a baker in Sapphire Cove. Every time the Monroe's visited, they played together every day despite the age difference. He was the only mage boy she knew that didn't mind roughing it with a girl. She performed so much magic with him and taught him all of it.

The rock in her hand was from her last summer there. She carved their initials and sealed it with a magical promise, that they would be friends forever.

"You must think me a terrible friend," she conceded. He shrugged, looking away for a moment to hide the sudden flash of anger in his eyes.

"It took a while, but I finally pried it out of Charlotte why you didn't return. She told me what happened. I don't blame you for not coming back, but I expected a letter at least."

She shook her head even as Damien tensed behind her.

"*What happened?*" he asked in her mind.

"*It is a long story. We can discuss it later.*"

"*Tell me now,*" he demanded.

Ignoring him for a moment, she said aloud, "I'm sorry, Elias. I should have written. Can you forgive me?"

He hummed for a moment, debating. "For you, I think I could manage it."

She rolled her eyes. With a wave of her hand, she summoned another seat so he could sit beside her. "Sit, you must tell me everything."

A servant brought him wine which he gladly accepted. Damien released his hold around her waist only to shackle their hands together as they reclaimed their seats. More servants entered with trays of bite-sized food to serve everyone, and she took the opportunity to tell him why she never returned to visit her family in Sapphire Cove.

"My uncle never liked me. He thought I was ill-mannered and disobedient. One summer, I returned home late for supper. It wouldn't have been so bad if my clothes weren't torn to shreds and covered in dirt from playing and experimenting with magic all day with Elias and a few other kids. Uncle scolded me, tried to teach me a lesson. He slapped me when I talked back and tried to lock me in the pantry for the night. I didn't realize why then, but I panicked and destroyed the door, along with everything in the pantry."

It made sense to her now why she'd reacted so violently. At only thirteen years old, she had already been captured by Master Ranville, although she didn't remember at the time.

Damien's hand tightened on her own as he ignored the offered food. Liana dug in eagerly.

"He and Father got in a huge fight about it and when I said I'd never return, Father didn't question it. I stayed home with Phillipa every summer after that."

"I see why you've been so jaded toward men," Damien offered.

Liana chuckled. *"You've changed my views a bit."* She gave him a wink knowing it would tease him before turning her attention to Elias. "When did you become a scholar? I thought you'd take over your parent's bakery," she questioned.

"Well, I have you to thank for that actually."

"Me? What did I do?"

"I used all that magic you taught me and provided services to the community at a reduced price than what your uncle and the other mage charged. Between that and my parent's savings, I paid for a position in the mage school and earned my way to the top. I'm set to start Master training in one month."

"Gods! Are you serious?"

He chuckled at her disbelief. "I am. Unfortunately for me, your uncle is my instructor. However, that will not stop me now. And I never would have made it without you."

She reached for his hand and squeezed. "You would have. You're intelligent and powerful. You would have made it."

"I wouldn't, just like the rest of the lower class that never get the chance to become Masters. But thank you for the confidence." Her heart dropped hearing those words because they were so brutally honest. There were so few Masters in Triaedian because, not only was it very difficult magic but, the elite mage prided themselves on being better than the average mage and made it nearly impossible for any to succeed without money or influence. "Now, tell me about you. This," he said waving toward the king, "is far more interesting."

She groaned. "It's really not. I accidentally hit him with a love spell and now he won't leave me alone."

Elias barked out a surprised laugh. "I don't doubt that at all, little Ana." The smile plastered to her face couldn't have gotten any wider until he used her old nickname, then it felt as if her face would split in two.

"*Is that what you've done to me, Wife? Cast a spell over me?*" Damien whispered in her mind. Over her shoulder, she grinned at him.

"*Definitely,*" she responded secretly back into his mind. He pulled her hand into his lap and stroked his fingers over the pulse at her wrist. Her gaze heated at the intimate touch, and he smirked, knowing exactly what he was doing to her. When she looked back to Elias, his gaze was on their hands, his countenance shifted to worry.

"Are you happy, Liana?" he asked softly.

Her brows furrowed. "Yes, Elias. Why…"

"I remember everything you told me," he interrupted as he inspected Damien again, fearless of the king before him. "Does he treat you well? Are you allowed to use your magic?"

Liana's gaze softened. "Elias, you are too good a friend." She patted his arm. "Don't worry though, I am happy with Damien. He is not like the mage males."

Elias did not look convinced.

"I love him, Elias. He is good to me." He nodded, hiding his face in his wine glass as he drank deeply.

Damien finally spoke to the man, leaning around Liana. "Would you rather interrogate me directly? Because I'm sure that could be arranged," he growled.

"There will be no fighting," she declared.

"I didn't say there would be a fight." She gave him a droll look. Damien was possessive to a fault, there would most certainly be a fight.

"I'll accept that offer," Elias declared to which Liana gaped.

"Damien would kill you in an instant."

"That confident in my talents, are you?" Elias jested.

She huffed. "I know you're trying to help me in some misguided attempt at protecting me from him, but that is not necessary. Damien is mine. I chose him. There is no hate or disrespect between us."

He nodded. "I believe you. It is just hard to reconcile the girl you once were to who you are now... with him."

Her head tilted sympathetically. "We have not seen each other in five years, Elias. We are both different."

"Be grateful that I do not throw you out of this castle myself for questioning me. If it weren't for Liana, you'd be escorted out in pieces."

Elias nodded. "Apologies, Your Highness. I'd do it again though. For Liana, I would do it again despite your threats."

"As I said, for that reason alone, you are still breathing."

"That is enough, gentlemen," Liana interjected. They sat back, tempers cooling.

Elias leaned over and whispered, "Is Charlotte still single?"

Liana grinned, her anger melting away. "You still fancy her, don't you?"

"Most certainly."

"She's engaged actually, to Master Ranville."

"Your uncle said as much. I'd hoped it wasn't true." He eyed her with that dimple in full force. "Would you want to help me break them up? I'm in the market to snatch up my dream girl."

Liana's fingers sparked with magic at the hint of mischief. "You have no idea how happy I'd be to help with that."

"Quite the show you two put on, Your Highnesses," Lord Dietrich commented, pulling everyone's attention back on them. "It will be the talk of the kingdom for months."

"We shall reconvene on this later," Elias promised in a whisper.

"Definitely," she reciprocated. In the back of her mind, she'd always known that Charlotte did not like Master Ranville. Then at the garden the other day, the way she snapped at Liana for being happy, she knew there was something wrong there. She thought of Ranville's father, of his violent tendencies, of how he kidnapped a child and wondered if the son was like the father. Besides, Elias was a good man. A selfless and kind man that would make her far happier. As long as she could look past his middle-class status, which was sure to change now that he would become a Master in a few years.

The only thing he didn't have now was a renowned lineage in the eyes of the mage. Liana didn't count that for anything compared to happiness though. And the mage lineages were all full of pompous asses.

"Perhaps it will give them something else to focus on aside from these separatists," Ramone groused.

"Doubtful. And considering the level of security around here, you know that as well, Your Highness," Master Ranville pointed out.

"The separatists remain a very real threat. Despite this joyous occasion, I have not let my guard down. But that does not mean I will let it ruin our day. No more talk of them," Damien declared. Liana thought of the threatening letter which she knew had to have come from the separatists. There was no doubt in her mind despite their lack of movement since she annihilated their numbers by the lake.

"Where shall you go on your honeymoon?" Eva asked to change the subject.

Liana was not aware that they would go anywhere. She assumed they would stay here given the threat.

"That's a surprise. You know that, Mother," Damien chided. The woman simply smirked. She knew exactly what she was doing.

"You've planned a honeymoon?" He nodded. "We don't need to go. I thought we had no plans, and I am pleased with staying here."

"But I am not. You deserve time away, Liana. Time to relax, just me and you." She flared her magic carefully, needing to speak to him privately and spoke into his mind once more.

"I'm sure we can have just as much sex here as we can anywhere else. All I want is you."

"Gods, woman. And you say all I think about is sex." He shifted, crossing one ankle over his knee. *"You are getting a honeymoon, Wife."*

She sighed. *"If I have to work on my emotions, you have to work on your demandingness."*

"Is it really so terrible that I want to steal you away for a week so we can be alone and away from all this?"

"And when shall you depart, Your Highness? I could offer concealed passage out of the city," Master Ranville offered.

"That is a generous offer, however, our plans are already set to leave tomorrow night with Master Kinley's aid."

"Very well. If you change plans, my offer stands."

Damien nodded while Liana responded to his earlier question. *"Well now you're making me feel guilty."* She sighed again. *"Thank you for your thoughtfulness. I would greatly enjoy a week alone with you... with endless sex."* He accidentally inhaled the wine he sipped and started choking. Liana rolled her lips to hide her smile even as she thumped his back.

"Oh dear, are you alright, Husband?" He coughed a few more times, glaring over his shoulder at her.

"Quite alright, Wife. Just swallowed wrong."

"Hmm, well, if you can manage the rest of your drink *alone,*" she stressed, "then I'd like to join my sisters." She sashayed away knowing precisely what she was doing.

"You play a dangerous game, Wife." She was surprised the connection worked even when they weren't touching but didn't let it startle her.

"Who said the game ever ended, Husband?"

"Devious temptress."

"Wicked vampire." His grin filled her mind, and she swore she even felt the caress of his fangs.

This man was everything she'd ever dreamed of and more.

Chapter Nineteen

As expected, Liana and Damien made their grand entrance into the ball-room. There was polite clapping, all those invited of high-society were full of class beyond the cheers and shouts the commoners offered. They sat upon the dais, their food served to them before everyone else. A small orchestra played soft music while the people ate and chatted. Then the greetings started in which Liana plastered a smile to her face and thanked everyone that offered their well wishes.

"This is torturous."

"You find most courtly things torturous," Damien replied into her mind.

"So do you," she retorted.

"Less so with you by my side."

She glanced at him out of the corner of her eye. *"Silver-tongued fox."*

He smirked and winked. *"That is better than, wicked vampire."*

"Better than, Husband?"

He growled, soft and low, the courtier before them jerking back from their bow. "Thank you, Scholar Samdon," he said to cover her lack of attention before replying to her. *"No, not better."*

"Better than, my love?"

His body remained relaxed on his throne even as his hand gripped the armrest. *"Not better than that."* Damien gave a polite response to the couple in front of them. "Thank you, Mr. and Mrs. Whitt. May the gods bless your new union as well." At least he kept up with his kingly duties. Liana completely shirked her own, having too much fun teasing her husband.

"So, you like being called, wicked vampire or silver-tongued fox. And you really like being called, husband or my love. What about, my first and only lover?"

His eyes slid to hers. *"Are you sure you're not a sadist, my love? You find too much joy in torturing me."*

She laughed aloud, the latest courtiers eyeing her oddly. Damien took care of them. *"Perhaps. But then what does that make you considering you love me torturing you?"*

"A hopeless fool in love with an evil temptress?" Smothering her laugh, she looked to the next guest.

It took much longer to finish the greetings. By the time they were done, she was hungry again. Luckily Phillipa stayed near and brought her some snacks from the buffet table. She and Damien watched as the dancing began. She observed for a while, even picking out Charlotte dancing with Elias. She hoped it would work in their favor considering Elias always had a crush on Charlotte and her sister only shunned him because of his lack of title. He was about to be a Master mage though, and perhaps they could be happy together.

The only thing standing in their way was Charlotte's stubbornness and current engagement to another man. It would be difficult to break her engagement to Ranville but not impossible. Especially not when her sister was the queen.

"Are we allowed to dance?" she questioned after many songs had passed.

"Of course. I was waiting for you to finish," he said, glancing at her empty plate. Standing, she dropped the plate into her seat and held out her hand eagerly. The moment his fingers brushed her own, she felt her magic pulse in response, happiness radiating from it.

They stayed near the dais, joining the crowd of dancers halfway through. When the song ended, the orchestra stopped, and everyone left the dancefloor. Liana frowned, questioning what was happening. It wasn't long before the music started again.

Damien held his hand out to her and bowed slightly at the waist. "My wife, may I have this dance?"

Sliding her hand into his, she fell into his body and the rhythm of the dance. Staring into his eyes, she forgot the ballroom of people watching, forgot that she was now their queen. Right now she was doing something she loved with someone she loved even more. She let him guide her around the dancefloor, the song chosen specifically for a solo couple. There were no exchanges of partners for this dance. There was only her and him caught in an embrace that never faltered as their feet graced the floor.

His graceful movements paled in comparison to hers. She was made for dancing and loved every second of it. One song bled into another without their steps faltering. After the third song, he slowed then swayed, holding her close.

"You are magnificent, my love. Truly, you are a gift from the gods." Her already heated cheeks flushed.

"And you are a silver-tongued fox." He smirked before pulling her into a kiss. It was languid but full of heat. He dragged her back to the dais where they reclined on their thrones, his hand still threaded through hers as they were served more wine.

"*This is where I first saw you,*" he said into her mind. "*I sat here, looking out over the crowd, bored as usual, when my eyes landed on a beautiful mage. Your luscious, brown waves were piled atop your head while a pearl necklace wrapped around your tantalizing throat. Even from here those dazzling green eyes entranced me.*"

His fingers caressed the pulse at her wrist, her heart pounding thunderously. "*The moment I saw you I wanted to taste you. I watched you all night until I saw you escape the ballroom and knew I couldn't resist. The moment I was near enough to scent you without interference, I knew I was in trouble. Just your scent alone was enough to drive me wild with need. And then you opened your mouth, and I was defeated by your honesty and wit. There was no one else I could ever love as much as you.*"

Liana stared at his profile, eyes brimming with tears. He turned to her then, his face open and honest. *"I waited a long time for you, Liana, and you are more than I ever dared to want."* He kissed her knuckles and a tear fell.

There were no teasing words when she responded this time, no nicknames.

"I've been terrified of marriage since I understood what it would mean for me... a cage. A shackle to a man that would control me however he pleased. I fought you in the beginning because I didn't want to be your pawn. I didn't want to be your personal mage even if it meant I was able to learn more magic. But you stole my heart by treating me like your equal, by confronting all my fears and proving me wrong. I never even believed a man like you existed, let alone that I would get to call you mine."

He smiled, kissing her knuckles again. *"I'm glad we found each other."*

She nodded, blinking back more tears. "Dance with me, Husband," she said aloud. He followed and this time they fell into the crowd, and everyone kept dancing. She danced for countless songs, Damien never faltering or asking to sit down. He was grace incarnate as she followed his every move. Even when their partners changed, she watched him. Every move he made was effortless and confident. He was a man that knew how to use his body as a weapon and a tool of seduction. He was sin and pleasure, and he was all hers.

"I think it is time we leave," Liana gasped as they came back together. Damien didn't need to be told twice. He lifted her out of the throng of dancers and set her back on her feet as they walked toward the tables where their families sat.

They were nearly there, Liana breathless from their dancing, when a glass shattered nearby. No one paid it much attention, the music too loud and everyone too drunk. That was until a second glass broke and fire blazed out of the corner of her eye. The room gasped as a whole. Damien shoved her behind him as their thrones caught fire, the flames raging upward on the wall in seconds, obviously created by magic.

Liana shoved Damien aside and took a few steps closer, her arm raised as her magic tangled with the flames. Once she had a feel for the magic, she swiped her hand and the flames disappeared. Everyone stood silent, staring up at the words that were burned into the stone wall.

'You were warned'

Damien's hands clamped on her shoulders right as the entire world shattered around her. Screams filled her ears as some of the glass windows shattered. Damien shielded her with his body even though she'd had a shield around them from the moment her magic sensed danger. She peaked out to see bodies pouring in through the windows.

She reacted, or more like her magic reacted. Magic erupted from her, shields of power sealing the windows so that no more assailants could get through. Damien shoved her into his father's arms before racing off to help apprehend the attackers, Luciano right beside him. Liana didn't need the protection but allowed Ramone to stand guard at her back while she focused on keeping her shields up as countless mage tried to blast them down from the outside.

The patrons stared back and forth between her and the action on the other side of the ballroom, awed by her power. There would be no keeping it a secret anymore. To hell with it though. She now understood why she'd been terrified to reveal her power. She wasn't a child anymore though and her magic saved the lives of everyone in this room. It would have been wrong to hide and not help. Damien would protect her. His family would as well, most of all, Luciano.

Surprisingly though, the attack ended quickly on her shield and those trapped inside were apprehended easily. Damien returned to her side shortly after.

"You can drop the shield, my soldiers have the area secured."

Liana did, grabbing Damien's hand for comfort. Ramone stayed at her back and pointed out, "That seemed rather staged."

Damien nodded at his father. "It was a very small contingent of men. They weren't sent to do any damage except to rile everyone."

"How did they get through all the guards?" Liana worried.

"Master Kinley is checking on that." She nodded then looked back at the damning wall.

You were warned. It was a message. A message to her. They'd warned her to not marry the king, threatened that she'd suffer a fate worse than death. A cage flashed in her mind and set her body to trembling.

Damien pulled her into a hug. "They came for me. That message is for me."

"Hush. I won't let anyone near you," he promised, his voice lethal. Hands clutched at his front as she tried to force the terror from her veins.

"I can't... I won't survive another cage." Magic sparked from her fingers as her breathing sped up. A voice screamed in her mind, "Why did the gods send you?" She flinched as she felt the phantom kick to her ribs and whimpered. Damien held her tighter.

"Liana, stop. You are safe. You are in the castle with me." His voice was distant in this dark place inside her mind. "Liana, please. Hear my voice," he whispered into her ear, his hot breath caressing her skin. "Feel my arms around you, listen to my voice. You are safe. You are safe," he repeated like an order for her to believe him.

Forcing her mind back to last night, she remembered what Luciano told her. That it was all in the past. Her memories couldn't hurt her now. Especially not now when she was far more adept and had an overprotective husband. She wrapped her arms around him and squeezed, that voice and the pain that followed fading to the back of her mind. "Thank you," she breathed, her heart calming.

"Will you escort the Monroe family to some rooms?" Damien asked his father. "I do not want them leaving tonight with these events and I want a host of guards outside their rooms."

"Of course," Ramone agreed.

"Hold on to me. I'll get us out of here quickly." Liana nodded and locked her arms around his neck as he lifted her, massive dress and all. Damien ran out of the ballroom with vampiric speed. He stopped in his bedroom. Their bedroom now. Setting her down on the bed, he rifled through one of the wardrobes and pulled out a sleeping gown. Neither of them said anything as he helped her out of the gown and into the thin fabric for sleep. In the blink of an eye, he changed into his own sleep attire which were loose pants and pulled her into bed.

Liana sighed heavily, her head resting in the crook of his shoulder, the side of her face on his bare chest. One arm rested over his abdomen, a leg between his. She fell asleep instantly, the events of the day and previous night crashing into her brutally. It was not the night either of them planned for.

Chapter Twenty

Liana woke the next morning in an unfamiliar room without any knowledge of how she got there, and with Damien beneath her. The room they were in was far smaller than theirs in the castle. It was big enough for only the bed, a small hearth, one wooden chair and a table with a basin of water. The walls were made of a solid facade of white stone. Wooden shutters over the two small windows were weathered by age and the bright sun beating down on them.

She lifted her head from his chest. Their bed was rather small as well. The only reason they fit was because she lay nearly on top of him. His eyes popped open with her movement, alert and ready. When he found her awake, his body relaxed again.

"How are you feeling?" he asked, his voice rough with sleep.

She shrugged. "Considering I woke up in an unfamiliar room with a man in my bed, I'm not so bad."

He grinned. "You forget that I am your husband. We are allowed to sleep together."

"True. How do you explain the unfamiliar room then?"

His brows furrowed in concern. "I wanted to get you away from the city for a while, to have a carefree honeymoon. I snuck you out in the middle of the night to bring you here. Nobody knows where we are." A crash of pots and pans rang through the house followed by manly cursing. Damien looked to the ceiling and sighed, begging for patience. "No one except Asher and Owen. They are our only guards for the next week and Master Kinley protected us all with anti-tracking charms." He lifted their left wrists, both clad in braided leather bands which she could feel were full of magic.

"And where did you sneak me off to?" she questioned, linking their hands together and resting her chin back on his chest.

"Sevilla. It's a province north of the city known for their vineyards. This cottage sits on the land I own."

"I've never been to a vineyard."

His other hand lazily traced up and down her back. "Then I shall give you a tour when you wish and provide a tasting from some of our barrels."

"I'm intrigued." She was more than content to stay there and forget everything that happened last night until more crashing and cursing reached their ears.

"Will you stop that? You'll wake them," Owen scolded.

"Stop yelling. You're going to wake them."

"We are awake, you buffoons. These walls are made of paper," he said in a normal voice which their vampiric hearing had no trouble picking up on.

"Yes, and don't you forget that when you get up to your newlywed business," Asher shouted back. "We don't need to hear any of that."

"Piss off!" Damien shouted back while her cheeks flamed. Asher laughed, followed by another clatter of pans. There had been no newlywed business yet and considering how much they yearned for each other, that was a tragic miracle.

The scent of fire reached them followed by shouts. "Liana, a bit of magical help out here please!" Asher called.

Groaning, she rolled out of bed and padded toward the door. Before she could leave, Damien pulled his shirt over her head as added coverage to her thin sleeping gown.

When she entered the kitchen, flames consumed the stove licking their way up the back wall. With a simple wave of her hand, the flames died out. She flung the windows open and pushed the smoke out. Hands on her hips, she glared at Asher. Pointing to a chair, she bit out, "Sit."

Wisely, he sat. Grumbling under her breath about worthless men, she summoned parchment and a quill to jot a quick note to Phillipa, then sent it off. "Now, sit here quietly and try not burn the place down again. I will have breakfast here shortly."

Damien snickered as he followed her back to their bedroom. By the time they were both appropriately dressed, Liana in a simple gown she usually wore to garden in and Damien in a simple shirt and trousers, Phillipa responded. She took the note back to the kitchen where Owen and Asher appeared to be having a staring contest. She snapped her fingers in front of Asher's face which had him blinking.

He cursed, glaring at her which she only laughed at. "That was for waking me up this morning." He didn't truly wake her but she found utter enjoyment in teasing him.

Phillipa left a detailed note on everything that was prepared. The maid knew how her magic worked and what was required. One by one, she summoned the dishes Phillipa described. A small feast for breakfast was served, and a basket set aside for a picnic Liana planned for later. The men gaped between her and the food.

Damien inspected the serving dishes. "These are from the castle. How did you..." He trailed off, his voice full of wonder.

Liana found plates in the cupboard and passed them out. "I can summon anything as long as I know its exact location and a description of it. I had Phillipa ask the chef for a meal."

"We are far from the castle. How far away can you summon?" Damien questioned to which she shrugged.

"As far as Sapphire Cove to the capital. That's the farthest I've traveled before."

Asher's mouth gaped. "That's on opposite sides of the kingdom." She shrugged again while shoveling food into her mouth. "Incredible."

"What do you all have planned for today?" she wondered, quickly changing the topic.

"Nothing. This time is yours. We shall do whatever you please," Damien answered.

"I'd like a tour of the vineyard, otherwise, I'm not sure."

"Then that is what we shall do."

After breakfast, Damien walked her around the vineyard while their guards stayed at the house. They were only a shout away and would reach them in seconds if needed. As it were, Liana needed this privacy with Damien, needed him all to herself without prying eyes or ears. Without worry of an impending attack.

All day, they walked through the rows of grapes as he explained the process of wine making and the difficulties of farming grapes. He brought her to the winery where barrels and barrels of wine waited. There were a few workers around, but they didn't pay them any mind as Damien took her to the sampling room. She tasted the variety of wines available and chose her favorite to bring with them on a picnic.

He briefly showed her the plot of empty land where a third of the grapes were burned. She vaguely remembered Ranville mentioning it during one of their many courting events over a month ago then again, when his grandmother asked about it. Apparently arson, but no suspects.

Once they picked a secluded spot among the grapes, she summoned the basket Phillipa also prepared. Reclined on the blanket, they snacked on the dried meats and cheeses with bread and wine.

Pleasantly relaxed, Liana reclined, resting her head in Damien's lap. A breeze rustled through the vines enhancing the sweet scent of the grapes. There wasn't much shade offered from the brilliant sun so she summoned an umbrella which planted in the ground behind them.

"Now this is perfect."

Damien hummed in agreement, his fingers brushing through her hair lazily. They stayed like that for a while, Liana nearly falling asleep until Damien shifted so he could lay down as well. With one hand behind his head, he held her close as she shifted so that she lay flush against him, her head on his chest.

"I cannot remember the last time I was this relaxed," he admitted. Now she could only hum in response and fell asleep. She woke much later, the sun near to setting.

"I'm sorry, I did not mean to fall asleep on you like that."

He smiled. "Nothing to be sorry for, my love. I was quite content to rest here as well."

"Is there more to the tour or was that all?"

"That was all."

Resting her chin on his chest, she stared up at him. She simply watched him, hardly able to believe this vampire, this king, was all hers.

"Why do you stare at me so intently?" he asked softly. There were so many reasons why she did. Because he is everything she ever dreamed of having. Because he is so gentle and loving. Because he is also fierce and powerful, and protective. Mostly though, because she loved him.

Pushing up, she brought their lips together. He accepted her eagerly, his lips slow and soft on her own. Content to stay that way, she kissed him tenderly, slowly. His hand caressed up and down her back, the other still behind his head. She could have stayed that way for hours if that churning heat between her legs didn't pulse stronger with every breath.

Her thigh rubbed along his, her hips pressing into his. She deepened the kiss which had his other hand delving into her hair as he rolled onto his side. His mouth claimed hers, teeth nipping her lips and tongue teasing her own. This vampire knew exactly how to drive her insane with just a kiss.

Fingers grappling with his shirt, she found the edge and slipped them beneath, meeting hard muscle. His abdomen contracted as if her touch burned then he growled and pulled her closer. Sliding her hands higher, the hard planes of his torso rose and fell with each breath as she revealed the muscular, tanned skin beneath. She broke their kiss, shoving his shirt upward. He yanked it off before reclaiming her mouth, pressing her into the ground fully with his body. She loved feeling the weight of him above her.

He ripped his mouth away. "Are you ready for this? Stop me now because I don't think I'll have the strength if we continue."

"I'm ready," she declared, pulling him back to her mouth. He shifted her skirts up her thighs and settled his hips between hers, the friction exactly what she needed. Leaving her lips, he trailed kisses down to her neck where he nipped at the sensitive skin. A moan rumbled from her chest practically begging for him to do it again. His hands slipped to the ties on the front of her gown then he pulled her to a seated position. Before she could blink, he pulled it all over her head, leaving her bare to his gaze.

It took every ounce of willpower to not hide beneath that heated gaze. He had seen her naked in her memory but that was different. She hadn't been in front of him, and the candlelight hid a lot. He tugged her slippers off then paused, his eyes drinking in the sight of her body exposed in the golden light of the setting sun.

"So beautiful," he said before falling on her again. His lips were frantic as they tasted her once more. One hand slid down her body, cupping her breast for a moment before sliding down her abdomen. Her breath hitched and halted as she anticipated the touch.

"Gods, I cannot wait to claim all of you," he growled. Instead of plunging into the heat begging for his touch, he bit down on the swell of her breast. Back arching off the ground, her fingers dug into his dark hair. A slick swipe of his tongue soothed the spot.

"Damien, please." She wasn't sure what she begged for, but as long as he kept his lips on her, she didn't care.

"I'm going to bite you here very soon," he moved to her other breast to engulf the tip and bit without breaking the skin. When he sucked hard, she couldn't help the surprised moan that escaped her. "And I'm going to suck down your delicious blood."

"Yes. Do it," she panted, her eyes closed and head lolling to the side already boneless.

He chuckled darkly. "Not yet." Lips trailed down her belly, her heart pounding out of her chest. "Eyes open, love. Watch me as I kneel before you and show you just how much I love you." Leaning up on her elbows, her eyes snapped open to hold his glacial gaze that melted her on the spot. He brushed his fingers along her inner thighs then pushed them open even more as he lowered himself to the blanket. Hot breath brushed her sensitive skin and she groaned, forcing herself to keep her eyes open.

She was a mess of moans, watching him slowly torture her with his fingers and mouth.

She couldn't see, couldn't speak. She could only breathe as he caressed and pleasured her body expertly until he pushed her over the edge of ecstasy.

A ghost of a smile titled her lips while she lay there panting, boneless and sated. There was a rustling of clothes then Damien's weight pressed into her again. Hovering over her, he brushed her mussed hair off her face.

"You are stunning, my love. A true temptress sent to torture me." She huffed a laugh, her eyes peaked open. Seeing him there, leaning over her with such love in his eyes and the setting sun making his silhouette stand out in stark relief, she couldn't help but smile.

He sat back, his glorious body on full display, a subtle orange glow lit him and the vines around them as the sun had minutes left until it fully set. He was the first man she'd ever seen this way... naked and ready to devour her. She followed him up and reached for him, curious. Gently, her fingers slid over the hard length of him. He hissed through his teeth, and she looked to him for guidance.

"Is this alright?" She circled him at the base where a dark patch of hair met with the rest of his body then dragged her fingertips along the underside of him.

Hands fisted at his side, he mumbled through clenched teeth, "If by alright, you mean the purest form of torture I've ever experienced, then yes, it is alright."

Her brows furrowed. "Does that mean you don't like it? Show me what you do like?"

"I will... someday." He gently removed her hand and pushed her back to the ground. "Right now, I need to be inside you with my fangs buried in your neck." She gulped, a rush of heat pooling between her legs. His weight settled like a balm over her and Liana completely relaxed into his touch.

When his hips drove forward then pulled back her mouth parted in silent pleasure, hands fisted in the blanket. If this was pain, she'd beg for it over and over again. He slid forward only to pull back again. A moan dragged out of her for the length of him that retreated.

"You okay?" he panted above her, his chest heaving worse than hers.

"Gods, yes. Please, keep going." She pulled him down for a kiss then wrapped her legs around his waist, his hips sinking flush against her own.

"Okay?" he grunted.

"Yes." They lay there, their bodies connected in the most primal way, the connection between them flaring, that magic inside Damien reconnecting with her. She was now wholly Damien's.

"*Do you feel that,*" she whispered between their minds, the moment too intimate for even spoken words. He dropped his forehead to hers, eyes closed. Her voice was lighter than air, a phantom of sound between them as she said, "I am yours." His breath hitched. "Heart, body and soul I am yours."

His lips sealed over hers as he pulled back and thrusted completely into her. He lost himself inside her just as she lost herself to him. They were a tangle of limbs and mouths, his body finally filling that ache inside her so completely. Their skin began to glow as magic sparked from her fingers harmlessly into his hair... onto his back when she scored her nails along his shoulders... against the firm muscles of his backside while she begged for more.

"You're mine," he growled, his fangs heavy in his mouth, his sharp features even sharper as he let himself slip into his vampiric side. Liana arched her neck for him, a silent plea for those fangs to sink into her flesh. A plea for him to end the torture of fantasizing about this moment for months.

He kissed the sensitive spot then struck. There was no pain as the deadly points pierced her skin, there was only pleasure. And when he sucked down his first mouthful, her jaw dropped in a silent scream as she combusted around him. His hips slammed against hers erratically until he broke away from her neck, roaring into the night as he thrust once more.

Liana clung to him; her body spent. His tongue sealed over his bite, making her shiver delightfully. He rolled, pulling her on top so that she draped over his body. Only their heavy breathing filled the night air.

There were no words.

That was not simply sex. It had been something far more. A melding of their bodies, of their souls.

Slowly, their breathing returned to a normal pace as she rested her hands on his chest and her chin upon her hands. His eyes were closed, his lips swollen like hers surely were.

With a grunt, he lifted his sprawled arms to hold her. "Are we both alive?" he asked. Out of everything he could have said, he chose that. And that was why she loved him so much. Laughing, she couldn't stop, her entire body shaking with it.

He rolled them to their sides and cocooned her with his body. "We should return to the house," he said reluctantly.

"No, I like it out here. In fact, I want to sleep under the stars tonight."

"It's too dangerous. Someone could ambush us."

"You hid us away in a very private place and snuck out of the city. Besides, I'll keep a shield around us. We'll be fine." She summoned the pillows and blanket from their bed at the house and snuggled into his chest.

He sighed, readjusting his pillow. "Fine. Are you hungry?"

"No."

"Are you tired?" His voice softened as he combed his fingers through her hair.

"Not at all. Talk to me."

"About what?"

"Anything. Tell me about your childhood."

"There is not much to tell. I was raised in the castle."

"Come on, I've told you practically every detail of my life. Give me something."

"You didn't tell me about Elias," he groused.

She rolled her eyes. "Elias is an old friend I shamefully let drift out of my life. He doesn't like me in that way either. He's always had an eye for my sister."

"He certainly had no trouble standing up for you the other day."

"Are you really going to act the jealous fool when I am lying naked in your arms?" Damien looked down, eyes roving over her body as if to double check that she truly was still naked then grinned and pulled her close. "Point made, Wife. How about I tell you of the little I remember from my childhood that didn't involve my extensive education. But first, answer me something."

Too sated for their witty banter, she simply asked, "What?"

"Do you remember the night we met?"

Her eyes drifted softly closed as she smiled dreamily. "Explicitly." It had been a magical yet terrifying moment for her. Feared she'd been caught for her magic but enraptured by the king's charm.

"What happened to the spell you wrote into your skin? I see no marks on your skin now."

Magic rose to her palms, a triggered response that she hadn't yet mastered. Shoving her magic down, Liana whispered a revealing spell. All the spells she'd ever written into her skin appeared, moving like liquid across her body.

Damien peeled the blanket off her shoulders to expose more of the words.

"This is incredible," he breathed, fingertips tracing down her back to follow the spells. "What are these? I don't recognize them."

She squeezed her arms tighter around his waist and buried her face in his chest not wanting to tell him yet another odd thing about her. "My own spells."

Damien stilled. His words were soft and hesitant when he asked, "You created all these spells yourself?"

"Please don't tell anyone. I know a Master Mage is supposed to be the only one capable of creating new spells but so can I and I do not want anything else to make me different from everyone."

He blew out a heavy breath and pulled the blanket back up to cover them both. "Oh, Liana, my love, you are extraordinary. This is nothing to hide from. In fact, you should celebrate it. Gods, you should shove it right down the mage's throats that you are stronger than them."

"There is a large enough target on my back. I'm not going to make it larger," she countered.

He finally reclined, keeping one hand behind his head and the other locked around her. "Valid point. We will keep this a secret." His fingers stroked softly along her back, lulling her nerves to calm once more.

"There is nothing in your kings-only book about me, about my power, is there?"

He blew out a heavy sigh. "Nothing. I combed through it again after our discussion with Luciano the other day."

"Perhaps one day we will find an answer. Luciano offered to search the other kingdoms for any helpful information. Discreetly, and most likely illegally of course."

He chuckled. "That sounds like my grandfather."

"Did he tell you about the other night in the temple?"

He tensed beneath her. "No. What happened?"

"Nothing bad. I couldn't sleep the night before the wedding and felt drawn to the temple. He followed me there and convinced me that talking about what happened in that cell would help me."

"And, did it?" His fingers resumed their soothing slide over her arm.

"As much as I hate to admit he was right about anything, I think it may have helped a bit. I told him everything. I purposefully remembered and analyzed what happened which I think helped me feel less threatened now if that makes any sense."

"It does, and you are incredible, Liana. I love you more than I could ever explain."

She hid her smile in his chest, her arm wrapped over his waist. "I love you. Now, enough about me, tell me everything about your childhood."

His stories lulled her into sleep, his voice smooth and soothing.

They woke once during the night to thoroughly devour each other again. Then a second time with the rising of the sun.

When they finally returned to the house in the morning, she filled the old basin with warm water which was only large enough for one to bathe in. Damien let her bathe first then she summoned fresh water while she went to the kitchen to make a decent meal before Asher tried again.

It was a simple meal of eggs and warmed meat with bread considering that was all they had in the cupboard. She and Damien were eating when Asher and Owen joined them. Asher sat across from her at the small dinette, his eyes instantly homing in on the mark on her neck. She'd left her hair down for simplicity's sake but Damien's mark was clearly visible.

"Gods. That is quite the claiming mark."

Liana's hand went to the sore spot. "Is there something wrong?" she worried.

Damien kicked Asher under the table. "There is nothing wrong. I just put the mark in a bit higher spot than most do."

"Why?"

"Because you're mine," he explained simply.

She rolled her eyes, mumbling, "Territorial males." Asher gave her a sympathetic chuckle. "Where is it normally placed?"

"The inner thigh," Asher supplied quickly.

Eyes wide, she looked at Damien. "How many claiming marks do you need?"

Owen snorted, trying to hide his laughter while Asher laughed outright. The picture of male satisfaction, Damien lazed in his chair with a smirk.

"Only one claiming mark. The others were just for fun," he explained with a wink. He had bitten each time they had sex, each in a different spot. She certainly hadn't complained at the time. Cheeks flaming, she shoved bread into her mouth. "Only the spot on your neck will scar like a claiming mark, this others will dissipate."

Quick to change topics, she wondered, "What is there to do today?"

"Truthfully, there is not much else to do around here except drink wine. There is a lake nearby if you'd like to row."

Not having much luck any time they went on the boats, she did not go for that option. They instead spent the afternoon playing cards, the males schooling her in the art of bluffing and betting.

Over the next week, their days were spent mostly alone either in the house or wandering the property. They spent some time with his cousins, but this was their honeymoon and the males made themselves scarce. One afternoon they finally dragged her to the lake so they could swim while she read on the dock. Otherwise, she basked in the time she had with Damien. They spent most of their time naked in their bedroom, or the bathing chamber, or sometimes the kitchen when his cousins were purposefully out of the house. During their walks, he'd often find a convenient tree to shove her up against or a boulder to lean her over. Liana welcomed it all.

She couldn't get enough of him after that first taste. Nor could he. Not only were they senseless with lust, they exchanged blood with every climax. He bit into whatever inch of skin he wanted, and she'd slice open his wrist to drink down that unnaturally sweet liquid. It would make her live nearly as long as him if she drank from him consistently, but it also made her feel stronger, faster even, although Damien said that wouldn't happen.

It was a sad day when they had to return to the castle. She'd loved living in isolation without responsibilities. There'd be no escaping what awaited them at home though. So much was left unresolved.

Chapter Twenty-one

It was early morning when they arrived back at the castle. Under the first rays of the sun, they snuck back into the city without any fanfare, which is how the males preferred it considering it was less of a chance for anyone to plot an attack.

She and Damien bathed quickly after their travels, and while Damien went to dress, Phillipa aided her to don a gown fit for a queen. A whole new wardrobe had been created for her now that she was queen, and unfortunately, she had to wear them. The gowns were beautiful but far more extravagant and heavier than she was used to. Moving felt like a chore and there would be no chance of moving quickly in them.

Nevertheless, she wore the gown and joined Damien in his study where Ramone, Eva, Luciano, Asher and Owen already waited. It crossed her mind to ask why Luciano was present and none of his other grandparents but decided not to question the ancient vampire.

Damien stood, meeting her halfway, kissing the back of her hand. "You look lovely, my queen."

She blushed even as she shifted under the suffocating weight of the gown. "What have I missed?" she asked, eager to get started.

"Not much," Ramone interjected. "We were just explaining that the ballroom has been fully restored after the attack."

As she sat in the winged-back chair Damien led her to, she didn't miss the pointed glances at her neck from his parents then back to him.

"Really, Damien? Could you have been more territorial?" Eva drawled.

Liana internally cursed the gods, questioning if it were the gods' sole purpose to make her constantly embarrassed. Because they were succeeding.

He grinned. "No, I think that is about the most territorial spot I could place my mark."

Eva pursed her lips. "The other mage will not approve."

"We are married, Mother, the mark does not change that, nor do I care what they approve or disapprove of."

"They are already on edge about the marriage, you did not have to flaunt it in their faces by placing a vampiric mark on a mage female."

Damien glowered at his mother, then Ramone interceded. "He has a point, Eva. They are married, even if that mark wasn't visible, it would still be on her somewhere."

"Am I the only one to see sense around here? This is like dangling meat in front of a hound. The mage council..."

Liana interrupted, her voice rising over the former queen. "What sense does it make to hide a mark my husband gave me when it would be something to be prideful over if I were a vampire as well?" Eva narrowed her eyes on her but she wouldn't back down. No one else would speak about her as if she were an object to fight over. This was her life, one she'd fought to make everything she'd ever dreamed of. This would be her first stand among many to come, because she knew there would be plenty more.

"What sense does it make to hide a mark that symbolizes our union? The first publicized union between a vampire and a mage. Are we not citizens of Triaedian? Are we not a kingdom of unity and equality? If they have a problem with my mark, I'm sure there are others more worthy of the position to uphold the morals and ideals of this kingdom."

Eva didn't move a muscle, not even to blink in response.

"Well said, my queen," Damien said slyly then suggested lascivious acts privately between their minds. Oh, he was happy with her alright, and insatiable. "Now, on to more pressing matters," he said, moving on as if he hadn't just teased her into a frenzy. She made sure to keep a tight shield around herself because of that. "What else did you discover about the attack on our wedding?"

Luciano answered, "The few rebels that were apprehended could only confirm that they were there only as a ruse. They were instructed to kill if they had a chance but mainly to cause chaos."

"How spiteful," Asher added.

Damien gave a quick nod. "How did they get in?"

"Appears a few of the soldiers let them in. Master Kinley did a bit of mind work on them to find the truth. They were separatists and let them through the east gate." His father handed him a list of names. "They are waiting in the dungeons, although we've gotten all the answers we could from them." Damien slipped the list into his pocket.

"Their families, have you interrogated them?"

"Yes, with the help from the mage council, Master Ranville and Lord Monroe supplied us with truth serum and mind spells. Master Kinley already has his students and Castors creating more because we will no doubt need plenty of it. Those families were not involved or aware of their treason."

Liana admired the exchange of information how succinct and efficient they were. It was clear that they had done this many times before.

"How much of the truth serum do we have now?" Damien questioned.

"None that I know of," Ramone answered. "Why, what are you thinking?"

Damien rubbed at the stubble along his jaw as he glanced at her then to Asher and Owen. "I want all the guards that are placed inside the castle and at the gates to be questioned. I need their loyalty assured."

"That is not wise, son," Ramone cautioned.

"Perhaps, but I will not have this castle breached again."

"If you force your army to submit to interrogation of that manner, they will lose faith in you."

Lips pursed and jaw clenching, Damien paused. "I know, but there are traitors in our midst."

"Damien, think for a moment. Put aside your fear…"

"I am not fearful," he ground out.

"You are. You know better than this. An idea such as this never would have passed your lips before you met Liana," Ramone pointed out. Liana looked back and forth between them, all of this new to her. It rankled her nerves to hear that Damien worried himself so much over her safety when they'd already discussed it. She could protect herself.

Damien ran his fingers through his hair which hung loosely again now that they were back in the castle. "What am I to do then? Let traitorous guards into our home?"

No one answered. Liana looked at everyone, their faces blank while Damien stood to pace. "I'll have a select guard monitoring our halls and escorting Liana. They will voluntarily submit to questioning if they want the position and a pay raise."

"I have my magic and a shield. I don't need guards," Liana interjected.

"That is not a variable I am willing to accept. It relies too heavily on your constant vigilance. You'd need to have a shield up at all times."

"Then I will have a shield up," she declared. She did most days anyway.

"No. I can't… I can't risk it. They could break through your shield like that mercenary did a few months ago on your balcony."

Liana raised a brow. She'd forgotten that happened considering everything else that had been a whirlwind since meeting Damien. That mercenary had been able to get through her shield to stab her, but that wouldn't happen again. She'd been training with Master Kinley and he'd taught her so many defensive spells that no one would be able to get close to her again.

"You will have a guarded escort wherever you go."

"There will be nothing left at risk, Damien. I will keep a shield up at all times. Even further, I could create a talisman that I could wear that would hold the shield for me. I'd much rather do that than be followed around at all hours of the day. Aside from all of that, Master Kinley is training me well. I know so much more defensive magic now."

"I've already decided. You will have four guards at all times. Mother, Father, pick a guard you trust. Owen, Asher, look out for each other. Until the separatists are dealt with, everyone must be on guard." He didn't bother directing his grandfather, Luciano, the vampire far older and wiser at keeping himself safe.

Liana dug her fingers into the armrest as she breathed deeply to keep from overreacting. It was impossible for her to ignore his blatant disregard for her abilities and to stay calm about it. Even below the anger though there was hurt because he didn't trust her enough to protect herself.

"Damien, I do not agree with this decision," she started, keeping her voice even. "I will compromise with one guard like your parents."

He reclaimed his seat beside her without even looking at her. "This is not a situation I am willing to compromise on."

"Well, it is not a situation I am inclined to agree with," she countered. His eyes were like ice when he glanced at her.

"Four guards, end of discussion."

Regrettably, her fingers sparked with magic, the anger inside her reaching critical levels. She heaved breath, willing herself to calm. It was a struggle to not just yell and demand he leave her be. "You are making me very angry, Damien."

"Yes, well, at least you will be alive to be angry at me." He stood, circling around to his desk before sitting again. Another breath filled her lungs then released slowly as she fought the urge to blast him with magic. She looked to Luciano for help.

"Damien, you cannot assign the Queen four guards. You will look paranoid and as if you are not in control of the situation. Liana has proven herself in training, give her one guard and trust that she will protect herself as well." Luciano's words were reasonable yet Damien growled at him.

"Perhaps we can come back to this discussion later," Ramone suggested. "There is something more important you must know."

"What?" Damien snapped.

"There have been a series of murders in the city over the past month. "

"And why am I just now hearing about them?" Damien interjected.

Eva scoffed. "Calm yourself, Son, and do not speak to your father that way. You know very well that the city councils are meant to deal with these matters until it becomes a problem for the crown."

Damien stood and paced to the window behind his desk, his arms crossed and body going still.

Ramone cleared his throat. "The murders started out small. It was one person here and there. What has become the problem is that the victims are clearly murdered by another species. Or at least, staged to look that way."

"Staged? What do you mean?" Liana questioned.

"Well, for example, there have been two separate mage murdered by blood loss with only vampire fang marks. Shifters were found killed by a mage spell. And a vampire mauled by an animal," Ramone explained.

"Is it the rebels?" Flashes of the warning on the ballroom wall bombarded her mind.

"Nothing confirmed, but it is suspicious."

"Why though? Who were the victims? Were they people of title with an opposing agenda?" Liana could only think of her father at that moment. She'd been personally threatened by the rebels and if people were now being murdered for their beliefs, or their connections, she'd find a way to protect him.

"This is how it started last time," Damien whispered, still facing the window. He turned then and leaned his hands on his desk, brows furrowed. "They are trying to incite fear. They are turning our people against one another."

Ramone nodded. "I believe so. The victims were commoners not of noble blood or status. The investigations so far have revealed no motives other than a crime of prejudice."

"What do we do?" Liana asked. "How could they still be so active? I thought that day by the lake their numbers were significantly diminished." Her explosive power that day should have been enough to deter further action, at least, she naively hoped so.

"You rendered their numbers unconscious in the forest that day, but you also knocked out my army, and not for very long. We could only kill so many of them before they began to wake with our diminished numbers," Damien explained.

Liana stared down at her twisting hands. She'd saved everyone that day but also hindered them. Thoughts and ideas raced through her head but she couldn't see a way that could have prevented their own army from falling as well. She didn't know a spell, or if one even existed. How would the spell even know who was on their side or not?

"I could work with Master Kinley on a spell that would not affect our army for the future," she suggested.

"That would be wise, Liana," Eva offered.

She gave a quick nod of thanks then turned to Damien. "I am much faster than anyone else at brewing potions. I could get you a batch of truth serum in half the time to use for interrogations. I've even developed a serum that allows the drinker to eavesdrop up to one block away."

Damien straightened once more, resting one hand on the sword at his hip. "We are vampires, we already hear much farther than that. And, as of yet, we don't have anyone to interrogate." He snatched his crown off his desk but didn't put it on as he strode toward the doors. "Asher, Owen, we're going to the councils to see what they've got on these investigations so far."

Liana rushed after him. "I'm going with you."

Damien halted with his hand on the doorknob. "You are not."

Liana glanced at Eva for help but the woman simply stared back. Walking closer, she argued, "I am the most powerful mage in the kingdom. I can help."

He finally faced her and took her face in his hands. "Shield please," he demanded and she immediately erected an opaque shield to hide their conversation. "I know, love. I know you could probably figure all of this out much faster than me, but I cannot let that happen right now. The only thing I can focus on is your safety. The bond is too fresh and all I want to do is lock you away with me in our bedroom and not come out for a year."

His thumb stroked over her cheek repeatedly. "I might be willing to entertain that idea, as long as you never leave either."

Smirking, he pressed a chaste kiss to her lips. "In my fantasies, absolutely yes. But, I am king, and I need to know you are safe so I can focus on keeping this kingdom from destruction."

"When you explain it that way, I suppose I don't have much of an option." He didn't seem to hear the sarcasm in her tone or chose to ignore it.

He pulled her into an embrace, burying his nose in her neck, his lips so close to his claiming mark. "You mean everything to me, Liana. Please, indulge me for now. Stay in the castle, stick close to your guards, and always have a shield up."

"For now, my king. For now, I will agree to one guard and I will not leave the castle without telling you first. And, of course, I will always have a shield up."

He sighed and pulled back. "Sasha shall be your one guard then. She will not be happy to be back on guard duty but I'll give her new throwing daggers to smooth things over."

"I don't want to anger anyone, Damien," Liana replied quickly. "Someone else will be fine."

He smirked, some private humor playing across his face. "Sasha is the only person I trust you with. She is my best soldier and she will do what is necessary, don't you worry about her."

"Fine, but you must also take caution with yourself. I worry about you too."

His smile grew. "I adore that you care. I'm a hundred year old vampire though, I am well trained with enhanced senses on top of that."

Liana frowned. "You are not immortal though, cocky vampire. Return safely home to me or I will have the gods torture you in the afterlife until I join you to do it myself."

A chuckle escaped him while he stepped back and gave a mocking bow. Liana let the shield drop. "Whatever you decree, my queen," he teased. He glanced to where Asher now reclined on the sofa beside Eva. "Let's go." He winked playfully at Liana before leading his cousins out.

Ramone walked up behind her, his arm settled over her shoulders in a comforting gesture. "Do not despair, Liana. I was much the same when I first mated Eva. It is in a vampire's nature to be overly protective of their mate."

"When does that instinct go away?"

Eva laughed outright while Ramone gave her a smug smile. "I'll let you know if it ever happens."

Liana groaned, dropping her face into her hands. Eva stepped in front of her, pulling gently on her wrists. "Remember our discussion in the hall when you first moved to the castle?" Liana nodded. "This is who Damien is. This is how vampires are. Some resistance keeps them in line but, accept his protectiveness and you will be far happier in the end." She leaned in and whispered, "You just have to know how to work it to your advantage."

"How?" she wondered, whispering as well although Ramone and Luciano could hear them perfectly.

"Now that is a discussion for another time," Eva answered conspiratorially.

Ramone leaned in, "I'd like to be privy to that discussion as well."

Despite the seriousness of everything they faced, Liana found herself laughing. The rebels were still out there, that threat lingering always, yet she had to remember to not live in fear. Damien and his family helped her do that.

"If you knew all my secrets, Husband, I would not have nearly as much fun with you."

Ramone darted around Liana and grabbed his wife in a loving embrace. "You may do whatever you please with me, my love."

Blushing, Liana quietly made her exit, Luciano on her heels.

She could do this. She could be queen and a vampire's wife. At least she would try.

Chapter Twenty-two

Back in their quarters, Liana fussed over her dress, unable to tolerate the heavy gown made for her. Hardly able to move or breathe under the structured fabric she rang for Phillipa to help her out of it.

"Please find whichever seamstress is making my clothes and ask for lighter dresses. I can hardly breathe in that thing."

"I can imagine. I can hardly lift it. I'll have her alter these to be lighter and request that she make some of the thinner gowns you prefer. I'm sure she'll be able to make them look gaudy enough to please the courtiers."

"Is there anything in my wardrobe that doesn't weigh more than me?" Liana flung the uncomfortable heels off her feet too. "Any slippers without heels? And a much smaller crown if possible." She followed Phillipa into the room dedicated to her wardrobe which was larger than her bedroom at her parent's home.

Phillipa laid the gown over a green velvet bench and went to the rack of gowns without full skirts. They were tea gowns and much more reasonable. Liana set her crown atop the discarded gown and ventured over to Phillipa, picking a navy, satin gown with silver thread detailing and silver slippers.

"Thank you," Liana said while Phillipa tied the last of the bodice together at her back.

"You are very welcome, my dear. Now, what else do you have planned for the day?" The maid set a smaller, silver tiara with sapphires upon her head for the finishing touch.

"A bit of exploring." She truly wanted to see the mage training rooms Master Kinley mentioned during their training weeks ago. She just never found the time to indulge in her explorations. When they walked out of the King's Suite, Sasha stood outside the doors, on guard.

The blonde haired beauty bowed at the waist quickly. "Your Majesty."

"Hello, Sasha. A pleasure to see you again. How have you been?"

"Well, Your Majesty, thank you."

"Excellent. Good to hear," she rambled. "Well, I was interested in seeing the mage training rooms. Do you know where they might be?"

"I do, Your Majesty. Please, follow me."

Sasha led her and Phillipa through the castle to the first floor in the east wing. They stopped before a set of arched wooden doors and knocked. It took a few moments for someone to open it, a lock clicking right before they did. A man with a mess of dirty blonde curls and dark brown eyes stuck his head out the barely cracked door.

"What do you want?" the man groused. Sasha turned her body slightly to reveal Liana standing behind her.

"Queen Liana wished for a tour of the mage training rooms."

The man's eyes widened in surprise as he caught sight of her. The door fell open and he bowed his tall frame deeply. "Forgive me, Your Majesty, I did not see you there. Of course, you are welcome to see the mage training rooms. I'd be honored to give you a tour."

Liana grimaced at the man's bowed head, giving Sasha an uncomfortable look. The guard gave her a nod of encouragement which had Liana's spine straightening. "Rise, Sir," she stated. "What is your name?"

"Rafael, Your Majesty."

"A pleasure to meet you, Rafael. I would very much like a tour if you have the time."

"It would be my honor, Your Majesty. Right this way."

Liana felt the barrier of magic as they passed through the archway - a spell placed for security to keep any unwelcome guests out. Rafael shut the doors behind them while Liana stared in awe at the grand room.

Pillars of gray stone supported the arched ceilings while the far side held a striking arrangement of windows to let in the brilliant sun. Lining the walls of the room stood endless bookshelves full of not only leather-bound tomes but every supply a mage could ever need; beakers, jars, herbs, plants, and endless amounts of items. In neat rows down the center of the room were long work benches, each with a mage stationed at them. Some had students as they gathered around the teacher that demonstrated the lesson.

"This is our workroom, Your Majesty. This is where we make all the potions and salves. We have every ingredient available among the shelves on the perimeter of the room, along with spellbooks. As you can see, we have many mage working to create various items."

They walked to the right as Liana began to explore the shelves. There were far too many things to discover as her eyes roved over the bountiful supplies.

"How do you keep all these materials stocked?" she wondered in awe. Many items were difficult to come by for the more advanced spells and potions.

"His Majesty makes it a point to keep us well stocked. He spares no expense for our stores which we are incredibly grateful for."

"That is very generous of him," she commented. Considering he was a vampire, it was generous, and more so, surprising.

"Yes, the entire Ashwood line of royals has always been generous to the mage, Your Majesty. They understand that we can only appropriately provide for them and protect them if we have the supplies to do so." She nodded her understanding. It shouldn't have been such a surprise to her. The mage were part of the army, and these supplies were their weapons. The ingredients were equivalent to swords and arrows, except they were turned into deadly potions and explosives.

"What is your role in the army, Rafael?" she questioned, needing to learn more about the hierarchy of mage within the army.

"I am a Castor, just as every other mage in this room is, Your Majesty."

Embarrassed by her lack of knowledge, she tried not to let it show as she asked, "What are Castors?"

"We are the potion makers. We also imbue the soldier's weapons with magic."

"What kind of magic?"

"Mostly we spell them to last without much care. We cast spells to keep the blade of a sword from never dulling or rusting, shields from ever denting and so forth," he explained. Stopping at a workbench, he introduced another Castor. "Your Majesty, this is Castor Milton." The dark-skinned man with gray peppering his temples bowed his head. "He is working on this barrel of new swords to protect them from aging."

"Would you mind if I observed for a moment, Castor Milton?" Liana asked, eager to see what spell he used.

"Not at all, Your Majesty." His deep voice was soft and kind which put her slightly more at ease. He pulled a plain sword from the barrel and laid it upon his workbench. Gripping the hilt in one hand and the blade in the other, he recited the spell for her to hear. It was a simple spell, one she remembered from her father's books. The man said another spell then another which all aimed to keep the blade sharp and useful for decades.

"Is there not a spell that combines all those elements?" she questioned. To say each spell on all those blades would be time consuming and draining for the mage.

"Master Kinley has been working on such a spell for years. It is a difficult task to create new spells which is why only the Masters know how, Your Majesty."

Liana didn't correct Castor Milton because for most mage, the man was correct. For her though, creating spells was all too easy. She'd come up with something later to give to Master Kinley.

"Of course, Castor Milton," she said with a polite smile. "Thank you for your time." Rafael led them onward around the room. "What other ranks are there among the mage?" she asked.

"It is only Castors and Combat Mage, Your Majesty."

She'd have to research more about the ranks of mage within the army rather than continue to ask questions and seem like an ignorant queen. Still, her plans remained. Female mage would still be recruited if they chose to be soldiers, no matter what rank they ascended to. No position would be off-limits.

They walked along the perimeter, some mage stopping to bow as they worked or searched for an ingredient. For the most part, they all went about their business. She noticed a group of five younger male mage gathered around an older gentleman with graying hair at his work bench.

"And for this last step, we cut the sage. Now, be particular in how you cut it, boys. It is important that you get it right or your entire batch of truth serum will be ruined." Liana paused to watch. Truth serum was her specialty after fiddling with it for years, using her siblings as test subjects. "We cut one leaf at a time to ensure precision." The mage folded one leaf along the stem then put the point of his blade to the stem and sliced along the leaf. He started at the base and continued at an angle to the very tip. He held up the perfectly sliced leaf, the scent of fresh sage filling the air. It reminded her of endless days in her father's workroom as she secretly concocted potions while he was away on council business.

"Once you add the leaves, it will take one full day for them to steep and complete the potion. When the pale liquid turns clear, your potion is complete." The man moved to toss the leaves in and Liana couldn't help herself.

"Excuse me," she said, halting him as she hurried to the table. More than a few people turned to see what the commotion was about. "Excuse me, Sir, but the potion will be done sooner if you muddle the leaves into a paste."

His thick, dark brows furrowed. "Your Majesty, what are you doing here?" he questioned bluntly, too surprised to hold his tongue.

"Taking a tour," she responded, then reached for the mortar and pestle nearby. "If I may, Sir, I must show you that the serum can be completed much quicker if you muddle the leaves and add a few more." She didn't wait for his reply as she grabbed the cut leaves, along with fresh ones, and dumped them in the mortar.

"That is not correct, Your Majesty. The cuts have to be precise. That is the only way for the serum to be effective."

"No, that is what your old texts say. This is far better." After a quick grind, the leaves formed a paste which she scraped into the green liquid bubbling in an iron pot beside the workbench. After three stirs, the liquid went clear followed by stunned gasps. "See, faster and more potent if you wish to test it out."

The old man gaped at her then the pot. "Where did you learn this?"

"I like to tinker with potions and spells. I discovered it years ago."

He had no words. Neither did the open-mouthed students behind him.

"Impressive, Your Majesty. That will certainly save us time in the future. We shall change all the records to account for your innovation," Rafael explained deftly before nudging her along. "If you would follow me, the combat training room is through that archway."

Liana nodded to the group in farewell before joining Rafael. Sasha followed closely while the hairs on the back of Liana's neck rose. They were all staring, she knew they were. Perhaps she shouldn't have corrected the steps of the potion, but it was such an easy solution to cut the time down exponentially. There were plenty more tricks she learned over the years, most simply because she was a child at the time and didn't follow directions carefully or didn't know how to do something. Her potions usually came out perfectly, if not stronger. Some didn't end so well, but those were rare occasions.

Perhaps she'd compose her own potion book one day with the improved instructions. Gods, she could even continue to tinker now that she had access to unlimited supplies and didn't have to hide her interest.

"Rafael, is there an unclaimed workbench here?" she asked, excited by the prospect of having her own space where she didn't have to hide or sneak around in.

"There are a few at the back." They were already walking that way and came upon four empty workbenches. Liana ran her hand over the smooth stone surface. A shaft of sunlight lit the gray rock, her magic tittering beneath her skin at the prospect of more freedom and use. Liana smiled at the delight of her magic and thought the bench would make a fantastic space for her.

"I'd like to claim this bench if I may," she said, standing before it, feeling the rightness of it settle into her bones. This is what she'd always wanted. To have the freedom to practice magic as she pleased. Damien promised her that she could, that he would provide her the best education a mage could find. This is where she would expand her knowledge of potions while Master Kinley continued her combat lessons.

"Your Majesty, that might not be the best thing. I'm sure you would be more comfortable in a private workroom where you would have your own supplies and quiet to focus," Rafael advised, his voice shaking.

"No, I'd prefer to work here." She loved the environment of the grand room, the feel of genuine wonder and thirst for knowledge that permeated the air. They were all mage here, all simply exploring their crafts while in pursuit of defending their home. She wanted to work with everyone, wanted to listen to their teachings and observe with the other students. This was everything she ever wanted.

"Your Majesty, with all due respect, I do not think it wise for you to work here."

Liana gripped the edge of the stone to keep calm. "Why is that? Because I am a female and we are forbidden to practice magic?"

Rafael shifted from foot to foot, eyes seeking out the others to help him. No one interfered in their conversation if they bothered paying attention at all. "Well, yes, partly…"

"I believe the Queen has made herself clear, Castor," Sasha interrupted, stepping closer to the mage, her hand going to the pommel of her sword. Rafael's face blanched. "This is her bench, and you will make it known that no one else is to touch it."

Rafael nodded, then bowed his head slightly toward Liana. "Of course, Your Majesty. We would be honored to have you in our company."

"There is no need to lie to me," Liana declared, exasperated.

"You are dismissed. I will show Queen Liana to the training room," Sasha commanded. The man hurried away, not bothering to look back. "This way," Sasha directed, gesturing toward the archway at the far back corner of the room.

As they walked, Liana whispered to her guard, "He was absolutely terrified of you."

Sasha's lips twitched but she refrained from smirking. "He is one of the smarter mage I know. Smart enough to know that he should be afraid of me."

Liana gulped. "Why is that?"

"The only reason you have one guard is because I am the guard."

Liana waited for further explanation. "You are saying that you are far better than the other soldiers?" she surmised.

Sasha stopped in the archway to look at her. They were equal in height, standing shoulder to shoulder. "I do not brag, it is merely the truth that I am better. Uncle Luciano made sure of it."

That vampire had a hand in everything and everyone's lives in this castle it seemed. Nobody she'd heard of was worse off because of his intervention though, in fact, they were better off, his family especially. Still hating to admit the cantankerous vampire was useful at all, Liana could see how hard he worked to help others.

"I must say that I feel infinitely safer with you by my side then, Sasha." She bowed her head slightly. "And thank you for standing up for me. Not many have done that."

"Female mage deserve just as much as the males. I support you in that."

Liana gave her a half smile. "Thank you, but I meant me in particular. Not many have stood up for me and it is much appreciated."

Sasha blinked, her brows furrowing slightly. "You're welcome."

Liana turned toward the training room. It mirrored the potions room except there were no shelves lining the walls or workbenches. Wide open flooring with a column of stone pillars composed the room in which at least a hundred mage gathered. Some leaned against the walls while others were split into pairs, practicing on each other.

Magic buzzed in the air which had her own magic surging to the tips of her fingers, eager to be used. Amidst the pairs, instructors strolled through the room, observing and correcting when needed. Liana yearned to be out there. To be learning as well.

Some of the mage glanced her way but did not react which she was somewhat grateful for. The last thing she wanted was to bring attention to herself. Unfortunately, one of the instructors noticed her and approached. He was a taller male with his long brown hair tied back and kind hazel eyes.

"Your Majesty," he said with a bow. "What do we owe the honor of your presence?"

"Just taking a tour," Liana responded. "What is your name?"

"I am Docent Matthew, Your Majesty. A pleasure to meet you."

"Docent?" she questioned, making a note to immediately learn all ranking officials.

"It means I am a mid-level instructor to the other mage. Although I will be promoted to Mentor soon, which is the highest-level instructor aside from Master, of course."

She wanted to thank the man for his inconspicuous explanations of the rankings but offered him a smile instead. "Blessings on your promotion, Matthew."

"Thank you. How may I serve you, Your Majesty?"

"Oh, I do not require anything. I simply came to observe."

"Shall I fetch you a chair?"

"No, thank you. Don't worry about me. Carry on with your teachings."

He bowed his head. "A pleasure to meet you, Your Majesty."

As he returned to his students, Liana slinked along the wall just beyond the archway and stood out of the way with Sasha to her right. They watched in silence, the mage around them sneaking glances at them and whispering. Liana knew Sasha could hear them. She would have asked to know their gossip if the woman hadn't tensed with each new whisper. No doubt they were insulting her in some way. She was a female mage after all, she had no right to be here.

Liana kept her back straight and her eyes on the students because they were wrong. She had more right to be here than any of them. She deserved to be here, to learn magic. And she was queen now. She could do whatever she pleased. So, there she stood absorbing this new experience.

"My Queen," Master Kinley greeted once he spotted her. "May I help you with something? Are you ready to resume your lessons?"

"I am ready to resume lessons, Master Kinley, however, for now, I would simply like to observe. I am intrigued by how you teach others." She hadn't had a lesson since the day before the wedding. It had been a nice break, one that she was eager to put an end to.

"You are welcome here, of course, Your Majesty. Is there anything in particular that I may show you?"

"I do not wish to be a bother. I will observe from here."

Master Kinley bowed his head. "As you wish." He stalked off, rejoining the crowd.

She stayed hours in the training room. At first, she stayed in her spot, avoiding all attention. Then her curiosity got the best of her, and she slinked around the room, picking out the more talented mage, or the ones that needed the most correcting. She observed it all, eager to learn. It wasn't that she didn't know these spells because she did. She knew them all. They were basic defense spells she learned before she even had her first bleed. Her attention focused more on how the students performed and how the instructors taught.

After about half an hour, more mage sauntered into the training room. Master Kinley called for a change in training which had the less experienced mage filing out. The next group took their place, the stragglers lining the walls joining as well.

It became clear as soon as they started that they were far more advanced. They paired off and immediately started sparring with magic. Things became heated quickly with the pairs focused on out doing the other. Liana watched excitedly. She loved the competitiveness and the quick action because beneath it all there was a base of knowledge that fueled their actions. One day she would get to that level where she could fire off spells and react to an opponent.

Soon. It would be one day soon, she promised herself.

Chapter Twenty-three

Eager to return to the mage training rooms the next morning, Phillipa assisted in dressing Liana in a simple gown from her old wardrobe. She'd gushed about the mage to Damien last night when he joined her for supper in their private chambers. He encouraged her to return and start working on whatever she pleased.

Nearly bouncing out of her skin, she grabbed the blank notebook Phillipa retrieved for her and slid into the sturdier slippers she preferred over the fashionable ones with a lifted heel. Before she could race out the door, Sasha knocked and entered. After a slight bow, she announced,

"High Lady Evangeline to see you, Your Majesty."

Eva didn't wait for permission to enter as she brushed by the guard. She stopped in her

tracks, brows furrowing. "What in the gods are you wearing, child?"

Liana kept her chin held high at the obvious insult. "What brought you by this early, Eva?"

Lips pursed, Eva sauntered toward the dressing room. "You have morning tea with the councilman's wives this morning, or did you forget?" she asked, clearly already knowing the answer.

Liana had forgotten. She kissed Damien goodbye this morning knowing he would be sequestered in his monthly council meeting which would last for hours. He said they discussed business for about an hour before devolving into debauchery and games, often leading into a hunt through the forest by midday. Liana laughed at it all, finding it all rather on par with high society and completely forgot that she would be entertaining their wives. He didn't mention it either, not that he would. He rarely spoke of her duties as queen, whether that be because he thought she could handle it all or didn't want to upset her by reminding her of them, Liana didn't know.

Disappointment crashed into her, the joy and excitement of the mage training rooms dwindling.

"Phillipa, the canary gown for Liana," Eva directed.

Liana's eyes widened and she shook her head at her maid. She hated that gown. It made her look like a fluffy chick and washed out her color completely.

"Perhaps the powder blue, High Lady? The yellow does not mesh well with her complexion and makes her look rather ill."

Eva tutted but nodded. "Very well. The powder blue is quite stunning with her dark hair. I will take the yellow off your hands, dear."

While Phillipa fussed to get the new gown, Liana recited the names of all the wives in her head. There were six in total to match the six councilmen. Two of each species to keep things balanced with Damien being the ultimate power among them.

She removed her comfortable gown and stepped into the formal one Phillipa held out for her. The powder blue was quite pretty but it was the dainty lacy detailing with pearl accents that really took it over the top. It was truly a gown made to impress the high-society folk. Her feet squished into the silver slippers, adding another inch of height to her already tall frame.

"Phillipa, the pearl earrings as well. No necklace so that her claiming mark is more easily visible."

Liana lifted a brow at the high lady. "I thought the mark was too controversial from your perspective."

Eva stepped toward her, delicate hands landing on Liana's shoulders as she looked in the mirror at her. "It is, which is precisely why you must show it off."

The vampire smirked and gave her a wink before walking off. "I shall meet you in the courtyard. Let everyone else settle before you make your entrance, Your Majesty," she said with a hint of teasing.

Phillipa handed her the pearl earrings. "I do not understand that woman," she whispered.

Liana could only laugh. "I only understand that she is cunning and brilliant."

"I suppose any queen of Triaedian needs to be."

Liana sighed at her reflection. She hardly recognized herself these days but that was only superficial. She was still herself, only enhanced so that she may survive in this new world of court politics. "That they do."

When she finally made it down to the Queen's Courtyard, which was on the third level in the back of the castle, and was made stunning by the surrounding cliffs of the mountain. Being settled beneath the cliffs created a sense of privacy and distance from the city, and offered shelter from the rising sun. The grass and lush bushes still held the soft dew of the morning giving off a fresh, earthy scent and keeping it relatively cool. She'd been here only once before with Eva, but this would be her private space to entertain her guests, not that she planned on having many. There was a certain level of decorum expected of her though and she would host the courtiers and councilmen's wives when needed.

The seven women sat around one table, Eva already entertaining the ladies. They all stood when Liana arrived and gave respectful curtsies, including Eva.

She strode toward her seat, shoulders back and chin up. "Greetings, every-one," she said, just as instructed. When she sat in the iron chair, the other ladies followed. A servant poured tea into her cup and placed a plate of fruits, cheeses, and thinly sliced meat before her.

"Lady Emilia, I hear congratulations are in order for you. You had a grandson born just yesterday, correct?" Liana started, speaking to one of the shifters.

She gave a brief nod, a genuine smile tilting her lips. "Yes, our first grandchild. We are all thrilled. My son is eager to host the child's birth ceremony tonight."

Liana vaguely recalled the birth ceremony shifters took part in. On the first full moon of the child's life they would baptize them under the watchful and protective eye of the Goddess Luna.

"Do not let us keep you if there are preparations to be made," Liana offered genuinely.

"Appreciated, Queen Liana, however, all of the preparations are well in hand. I've come to catch up on all the latest court gossip and enjoy your husband's delicious wine." She smirked and sipped at said wine.

A streak of possessiveness had her spine stiffening. Her husband, Damien. All hers. The newness of it all still had her a bit giddy. She hid her proud smirk behind her glass.

"I heard you caused quite the stir in the mage training rooms yesterday, my Queen. Is that true?" Lady Georgina Kent questioned. The mage female radiated beauty in her golden gown. Delicate gold chains hung around her neck, complementing her dark skin while gold accents were braided into her black hair. The female was closer in age to Liana than any of the other ladies, while her husband, Lord Bastian Kent was almost two decades older than her. Not that their age difference surprised her considering the patriarchy of mage society.

That thought had her pausing and almost laughing aloud. The age gap between herself and Damien was far greater and nearly comical. Luckily for Liana though, Damien retained his youth while Lord Bastian aged without grace.

Quelling her judgment and hypocrisy, Liana kept her magic calm. "I did not mean to stir anything, Lady Kent. I went for a tour and helped with a potion. That was all." Quite peeved that they all heard about that in less than a day, she attempted to keep her annoyance off her face. There shouldn't be anything to gossip about in her opinion. Nor were her daily activities, although, now that she was queen, perhaps they were.

The young woman snorted a laugh. "Bastian couldn't stop raving about you last night after Master Kinley told him what you'd done. He told me they have barrels full of truth serum which took only half a day to make. That would have taken them weeks before you intervened."

Liana forced herself not to fidget. "I like to experiment with potions. It was a happy accident one day that I stumbled upon the alternative method," she explained humbly. In truth, it was no accident. She read the instructions and the theory behind the purpose of the precise cuts along the sage then created her own instructions. The purpose was to release as much of the essence held within the leaf which was done along the spines of it and not damaging the integrity of the plant. Liana hadn't understood why the integrity of the plant mattered and ground the leaves down, extracting more essence than before. The result had her and her siblings cackling for hours after she slipped the elixir into their mother's tea one morning.

"Is that because of your power? We've all heard what you did by the lake and saw what happened at the wedding ceremony," Georgina said, pushing for more.

"Oh my, that was quite the sight with the two of you up on the altar, glowing as if you were gods reincarnate," Lady Monet, the wife of one of the vampire lords chimed in.

Liana's magic lurched to attention, ready to protect her from danger. There were no threats today though, only harsh judgments. "I enjoy magic and potions because they are fascinating to me. In regard to my power, I am quite strong in comparison to many."

"How are you so powerful?" Georgina questioned. "Your uncle is a Master Mage, otherwise, your lineage is not known for being overtly strong."

Liana sipped her tea, taking a moment to let the probing question settle and to not react defensively. "I was born with my gifts, just like every other mage." She turned her attention to Lady Emilia once more even as Georgina opened her mouth to ask another question. "Would you mind me asking about the birth ceremony, Emilia? I only know what I've read and wondered if the account was accurate."

The fit, older female flushed under her attention and nodded eagerly. "The birth ceremony is vital in the connection of the child to its animal self. The

Goddess Luna solidifies the link between the pair so that they grow and mature together. When they are ready, the shift will be seamless."

"What would happen if the child weren't baptized?"

Her face fell as she shook her head. "They are prone to fits of rage and more likely to go feral. Their shifting will be hard to regulate, the body and the animal constantly fighting for dominance."

"How terrible," Liana exclaimed.

"Yes, quite so. My husband and I will baptize a few orphans every year just to avoid such a fate."

"Gods bless you, for doing so," Liana praised. "What happens to the orphans after that?"

"A family of the same animal shifter will take them into their own."

Surprised by that answer, Liana couldn't quite wrap her mind around that. "That is a very selfless thing to do."

Emilia shrugged. "We are shifters. We are a pack. We take care of each other."

The other breeds would not be so quick to adopt a child that wasn't theirs, or didn't know their origins. Mage would be the least likely considering they wouldn't want to taint their perfect lineage with unknown blood. She was unsure of the vampires. They were not easily conceived though, so she thought there weren't likely very many orphans.

"Have you all heard of the murders in the city?" Lady Monet chimed in, changing the topic.

Georgina gasped. "They've got me so scared. I told Bastian we are not going back to our home in the city until it's resolved. I feel much safer in the castle."

Liana held back a snort. The young woman probably told the truth, but Liana had also seen her drooling over Damien and the other guards during training.

"They've got the entire city scared," Lady Monet corrected.

"And distrustful," Lady Kinely, the wife of Master Kinley, interjected. "The breeds are separating themselves even more now."

"My son has been made aware. This will all be taken care of swiftly," Eva declared. "Now, someone please tell me they heard about the debacle at the end of season ball in Sapphire Cove," she said, expertly diverting the conversation which Liana was grateful for.

She'd have to talk with Damien about the situation and see if there was anything she could do to help. For now, she had to suffer through endless tea and gossip.

At some point they retired inside where half of them played a board game while the others practiced the latest dance steps. Liana practiced the dancing considering she hated the game they played and loved to dance.

When supper finally came, Liana couldn't have left the women fast enough. They all separated and went to change into more formal attire. Liana collapsed onto their bed while Phillipa scoured through her extensive wardrobe for a gown that was extravagant enough to impress the ladies but light enough for Liana to not suffocate.

Damien found her sprawled out, his own servant following on his heels. The vampire was silent as he went into Damien's separate wardrobe to prepare his dinner outfit. It had taken Liana a moment to get used to Matthew. The scrawny servant was always so quiet and startled her often. Now she knew when to expect him so his presence wasn't so alarming.

Damien climbed over her, straddling her body while she kept her eyes closed. He placed a gentle kiss upon her lips. "Is my wife alive?" he teased, knowing full well that she breathed and could hear her heart beating as it sped up with his nearness.

"Barely. That was the most draining day I've had in a while. I think I'd prefer spending an entire day with Luciano compared to that."

Damien chuckled, his body settling over hers, his weight a soothing balm to her wrecked nerves and she finally opened her eyes to look into his clear blue ones. His pupils were dilated and now that she paid attention, she could feel his heart beating faster than usual. A sheen of sweat lined his entire flushed body, his musky scent more powerful than usual.

"I think you two secretly get along, but neither of you is ever going to admit that," he teased.

"I have no idea what you're talking about," she denied facetiously. Raising her hand, she felt his forehead then plunged her magic into him. "Are you well? You seem feverish." Her magic connected instantly with that mark she left in him, a pulse of acceptance and awareness going through her before it inspected the rest of him. No illness to be found, which was good considering vampires did not get sick, from natural causes anyway. They could be poisoned with a very select few types of toxins.

"Quite well. We just got back from a hunt. I'm still a bit worked up."

She smirked at his explanation. "If that's the case, perhaps we should skip supper and work out some more of that energy."

His lips claimed hers without delay but he pulled away too soon. "Always a tempting offer, my little mage. Grandfather already warned me that if I didn't show up, he'd beat my ass, so we are going."

She frowned, sitting up as he climbed off the bed. "And what was it you said about me and him getting along, because I sincerely doubt that."

Laughing, he pulled off his tunic and looked over his shoulder at her. Her eyes were not focused on his, the expanse of tanned, muscular flesh too much to resist. "We have to go, Liana. They need to see us as a united front." He walked into the bathing chamber and she followed. "They also need to get to know you, to know how intelligent, cunning and powerful you are in your own right." He pulled off his boots and dropped his trousers, his complimentary words falling flat while she admired him.

"Fine, we shall go." He stepped into the tub and dunked his head under. "Would you like some help before I go?" she questioned, her voice low and sultry.

"Leave me be, temptress. I know your tactics." He kept his back to her, grabbing the bar of soap and dunking his head beneath the water once more.

Sauntering to her wardrobe, she let him be for now and let Phillipa help her change into a maroon gown with gold and black beading along the bodice. Not leaving him for too long, he was still bathing when she said into his mind, *"How is your bath? Lonely?"*

"Temptress," he growled back.

"I am only thinking of you, Husband. What kind of wife would I be if I didn't cater to your every need?"

"I swear the gods were punishing me for something when they gave me such a bold female to fall in love with."

She snorted a laugh. *"More like rewarded you."*

"Liana?" Phillipa questioned, snapping her fingers in front of Liana's face. The younger mage jolted. "What is wrong with you? You were staring off into nothing."

Damien ran through the archway with vampiric speed dressed in only a drying cloth while she was down to her thin chemise. He wrapped an arm around her waist and pulled her back into his body. His lips landed on her neck, right over her claiming mark. Her eyelids dropped, her body rushing with heat.

"Tell her to behave, Phillipa," he teased before rushing out again.

Catching her balance after his quick departure, she cleared her throat, well aware of the blush on her cheeks.

"Do I want to know?" the older female asked, holding the dress down for Liana to step into.

Liana erected a privacy shield. "You cannot tell anyone, Phillipa. Damien and I can speak to each other in our minds."

The maid's brows furrowed. Pulling the gown up, she moved around to Liana's back to start tying the laces. "Speak in each other's minds? How is that possible?"

Liana just shrugged. "How is anything I do possible?"

The woman conceded on that point. "What does it sound like?"

"It is a bit strange, especially the first time it happened. It sounds like our voices but not so much through our ears, but more like it was my own thought."

"Odd. Is that why you went all blank in the face just now?"

Giggling, she nodded. "Yeah. I'll have to be more careful with that in the future so no one suspects anything."

"Even if they did suspect something, I doubt it would be that. I'd never have even guessed at it."

It was just as well because no one needed to know they had a secret form of communication, much less that she was capable of performing such unique magic. Already, it was getting harder to keep her powerful magic a secret.

"Yes, well, let us pray that this night goes swiftly and without incident," Liana stated, sincerely hoping it would be a quiet evening with the councilors.

She should have known better than to ask the gods for such. She knew they would give her anything but a quiet evening.

Chapter Twenty-four

Damien rolled over in their bed, Liana groaning as he bumped into her and woke her.

Death coated her tongue while her head pounded with a ferociousness she hadn't felt since dancing on pub tables.

"What, in the name of the gods, happened last night?" she cursed, shoving him away because the stench of alcohol on him made her nauseous.

He groaned, hugging a pillow to his chest. "I'm never drinking with you again."

"Me? What did I do?" she whispered in outrage, her head throbbing with every word.

One icy blue eye peaked open. "Do you truly not remember?"

Liana blanked. She recalled their supper last night and after dinner drinks. There were a few infuriating moments where she had to stand up for herself, but nothing out of the ordinary. Then they all retired for the evening.

Something niggled at the back of her mind and she gasped as she recalled bits and pieces. "Asher!" she complained. "That scoundrel!"

Damien clamped a hand over his ear, wincing. Rolling over, he pulled the service bell to summon a servant. "I never imagined anyone could challenge my cousin for the title of worst drunkard until last night, my little mage."

"I swear, it was all his fault. He was egging me on and trying to embarrass me in front of your family." Asher had arrived with Owen after the councilors left for the evening, bringing with them an entire barrel's worth of wine bottles. The rest of his family trickled in, stating that most of them would be leaving tomorrow to return to their homes. Asher dubbed it a celebration, much to Liana's dismay, and proceeded to get everyone drunk. She loosened up after a few drinks, even joining Asher on the coffee table for a stumbling dance which left her falling into Armand's lap.

The entire night, she saw what it was truly like to party with vampires, at least, Damien's family anyway. They kept it somewhat reserved without any live blood donors around, although there was plenty of it in goblets throughout the night.

Damien kept himself somewhat controlled, along with Luciano, despite the many guards around the castle. At one point though, Liana teased him into drinking from her while her blood coursed with wine and magic. He fell right into the party after that. Games and dancing filled their time, music playing throughout the night with the spelled instruments Liana had going.

It had been the most free she'd felt in a long time. The most accepted too. His family accepted her into their lives without so much as an ill word spoken to her, excluding Luciano, of course. They spoke to her as if she were any other family member and encouraged her magic all night, hugging and praising her for what she did.

It became quite a blur by the early hours of the morning. She didn't even recall getting back to their room.

"Did you undress me?" she wondered.

He squinted his eyes open again. "I think so," he responded, uncertainty clouding his voice. She chuckled, immediately followed by a groan.

A knock sounded on their bedroom door. "Enter," Damien said. It must have been a vampire servant because it had barely been a whisper. "I need blood. And have breakfast sent to us this morning."

"Right away, Your Majesty. It is after noon, would you still like breakfast?"

Liana hid her laughing under the blanket. "I don't care. Just tell the cook we need something to sop up the alcohol."

The servant bowed then bolted. He returned quickly with a goblet of blood before leaving once more, shutting the door this time. Damien downed it in a few gulps.

"Give me a moment and I'll give you my blood. It won't do you any good right now," he explained. Knowing his blood was the best hangover cure, she grunted in agreement.

"I like your family," she whispered.

"They like you." Scooting over, she snuggled into his chest, his arm draping over her.

"You smell like wine."

He grunted. "So do you." Climbing out of bed, he lifted her too and carried her into the bathing chamber. Stepping into the tub, he sat down and let her drape over him, still dead to the world. Mustering up enough energy, she filled the tub with hot water while he poured scented oil into it. Sighing, she wrapped her arms around his waist and closed her eyes.

"You make me so happy," she admitted.

His fingers brushed up and down her spine. "You make me feel like the luckiest man alive."

Her magic thrummed happily, slithering out of her fingertips to envelop and caress Damien. "Honestly, Damien, I couldn't have ever imagined loving you this much or feeling so accepted by your family."

He hummed, his head resting back along the lip of the tub, his eyes closed while a little smirk played along his lips. "And I couldn't ever have imagined that magic could feel this good. It feels like your soft fingers are everywhere at once."

She let her magic go, let it worship this man that made them feel so loved. "Yes, well, at least you feel good. I don't think my cheeks will ever fade back to normal after what your family witnessed last night."

"We were all having a good time. It's nothing to be embarrassed about."

She sat up, the water sluicing down her front which had his eyes cracking open and tracking the droplets over her bare skin. "Really? It's normal then to goad you into chasing me around then biting me?"

He cracked a laugh and pulled her back down so that their chests were flush. "We are vampires. We live for the hunt." He silenced her with a kiss.

Neither of them were in any rush to get out of the bath, and when she finally tasted her hangover cure, her lips wrapped around his wrist, they definitely weren't leaving until they were both satisfied.

Eventually though, they had to dress and say their farewells to his family.

It was nearing late afternoon by the time they met his family in the drive, their carriages packed. Their farewells were far warmer than their greetings, Liana getting a hug from each family member.

Damien's aunt, Ophelia, was the last to go, holding onto Owen and Asher with death grips. "You two will come visit me soon. And bring a female with you too. I could use some grandbabies soon."

"Of course, Mother," Asher appeased with a cheesy grin.

Owen just grunted, but gave his mother a hug. The intimidating vampire gripped Asher's father by the shoulder. "Keep my mother safe and happy," he said, which sounded an awful lot like a warning to Liana's ears.

The male nodded, not affected in the slightest, likely used to it after all these years.

The last of the carriages faded down the mountainside and they turned to go inside. "Why am I not surprised to see you are still here?" Liana commented, finding Luciano behind them. The vampire didn't respond.

"Grandfather offered to stay indefinitely."

She eyed the man. "Your stay wouldn't have anything to do with a certain prophecy would it?"

"It does," he answered without hesitation. Liana rolled her eyes and kept walking. That damn prophecy was the most ridiculous thing she'd ever heard. There was no way she was some promised savior of Triaedian.

A guard bolted in front of them, his breathing heavy and his white tunic stained with blood. He immediately dropped to one knee and bowed his head. "Your Majesty, there has been an attack on the mage council."

Liana's heart dropped out of her chest, her magic surging into her fingertips. The mage council. Her father.

"What happened?" Damien demanded. He turned to Asher, "Get our gear, now."

The soldier remained bowed. "We were outside the council chambers when we heard the first screams. Someone had locked the door with magic though and we couldn't get in. By the time we made it through the windows on the opposite side of the building, the rogue vampire had already attacked several mage. The threat was neutralized and I came to you immediately."

Asher returned just in time, throwing swords to Owen and Damien. Her husband looped the scabbard around his waist and buckled it.

"Luciano, stay here with Liana. The rest of you, with me to the mage council building."

"I'm going with you," Liana demanded, tears building in her eyes as worry for her father threatened to overwhelm her.

"You are too close to the situation and I can't have you there, Liana. I will be too worried about you to focus. Just stay here and stay safe." He ran off, disappearing with his vampiric speed, the other three following after him.

She turned to Luciano. "Don't you dare tell me to stay here. You know I am more valuable there with my magic."

He nodded, unfolding his arms as he stepped toward her. "I know. Which is why I waited for him to get a head start. Let's go, my queen," he prompted before scooping her up and bolting after them.

It took only minutes before they stopped outside the council building. The king's soldiers guarding the doors bowed at the waist when they spotted her and Luciano. She paid them no mind as she shoved through the doors and hurried down the halls, following her magical connection to Damien that led her directly to him.

Mages gathered in the main council room, others darted in and out with determined purpose plastered on their faces, some scurried along with potions and bandages. Liana strode into the chamber, noting the overturned chairs and tables. A young male shoved his way out of a crowded group, blood staining his hands and clothes. He rushed past Liana without a glance, his eyes wide and terrified.

She shoved her way between two males to find a young boy bleeding out from a horrific wound on his neck. A male leaned over him wearing the green smocks of the healers, his hands working quickly to mix together potions while a spell held firm against the wound to keep any more blood from leaking out. Liana pushed to the boy's side, his face so ashen and young that it broke her heart. When he looked her way, his lids heavy, she gave him a tender smile.

"You'll be alright," she reassured. Ignoring the discontent of the males around her, she took his hand in her own and let her magic surge into the boy. There were no spells needed. Not with her magic as she'd finally come to accept. She didn't need the male's spells to do anything. She didn't need the male's at all. They only ever seemed to hold her back.

Her magic bounded through his body aiming for his neck where it began to heal him from the inside out. Silence descended as the small group watched in shock as the boy's skin began to grow and close once more, little sparks of gold knitted it all together. It took only seconds before his neck returned to normal, not even a scar left behind.

"Thank you, Your Majesty. Gods bless you," the healer said. He propped the boy up on his leg and forced a potion down his throat. "This will replenish your blood, boy," he told the lad. Sensing that he would live now, Liana went in search of others that might require help.

The moment she stepped outside the group a hand gripped her arm.

"Owen?" she questioned, the furious look on his face giving her pause.

"He told you to stay at the castle," he growled.

Despite her instincts screaming at her to back up from this angry vampire, she stood her ground. "And I am more valuable than any of you combined," she argued, not bothering to be humble. In this instance, her magic was far more valuable than their combat skills.

"This is bigger than you and your need to be included, this is a very real threat to us all."

"I do not feel the need to be included out of some misguided attempt to be close to him. I need to be included because I am queen now, and I have powerful magic. I am useful."

His brows slammed down further over his eyes. "He must give all of his focus to this matter, and he cannot do that while you are near."

Liana seriously fought the urge to roll her eyes. "You overestimate Damien's focus on me."

Owen stepped closer, his face so close now that she had to pull her head back to keep him in view. "And you under-estimate his obsession with you."

Liana paused, searching his face for a hint of an explanation. She knew he was overprotective, that his vampiric side drove him to the extreme need of protecting her at all costs, but this was different. She was different. She could protect herself and these were her people. Her magic could be the difference between life and death for someone.

"You have no idea what it means to be a vampire, and you don't understand anything he is dealing with now that he has marked you as his," Owen said under his breath, his eyes weary of everyone around them before falling to the claiming mark on her neck.

"Queen Liana!" Someone called her name, distracting her for the briefest moment which was long enough for Owen to disappear. "Come quick. It's your father," another healer in green urged and she forgot about Owen's implicating words.

The healer led her further into the chamber, beyond the front row of benches to the dais where the council of mages usually presided over the meetings. The ornate wooden table was flipped on its side, the chairs shoved out of the way. Two bodies were set next to each other on the floor and beyond any help. Their faces were covered with bloodied coats and for a heart stopping moment, she thought the worst, but the healer kept dragging her forward.

"Move! Move!" he yelled, shoving through the crowd.

Three bodies lay in the middle. She didn't look too long at the body on the left which was missing a head. Her gaze fell upon Master Ranville and her father instead. Both immobilized by magic, their wounds matched those of the boy. She knew what made those wounds and what creature lay beside them beheaded. A vampire attack on the mage council was exactly what Triaedian didn't need right now.

She dropped to her knees beside her father, a healer on his other side while Damien kneeled at his head, his wrist cut and bleeding into her father's mouth. Lord Monroe remained unconscious despite all those working on him, and she knew why. She felt the puddle of blood soaking through her skirts. Saw that his chest barely rose with a breath. If she were a vampire, she would have heard the dangerously weak beat of his heart.

"Liana, you shouldn't be here," Damien growled, his tone warning and sorrowful all at once.

Tears sprang to her eyes. She wouldn't lose her father. She could heal him.

Magic flared in her veins in an instant pouring directly into him. With everything she had, she prayed to the gods and goddesses to save her father. She prayed that her magic would be enough. That all this power would be good for something.

"Liana, he is too far gone," Damien said gently as he took his wrist away and wiped it on his trousers, his skin already healing.

She shook her head. She could save him.

When her magic fell on her father's wound it tugged and knitted flesh back together. It took far more effort and concentration on her end than it did with the boy, something she didn't want to ponder why. She coaxed her magic to keep going, urged it to continue healing despite the difficulty. She gave it more power. She gave everything she had to seal the torn flesh at his neck and the claw marks along his arms and torso.

Sweat slicked her skin by the time his wounds sealed, and she let her magic fall back into her body. Breathing heavily, she waited for him to open his eyes. When he didn't, she looked up to Damien. Grief seized her heart when she saw defeat there.

"No," she breathed, tears coming faster. The healer poured more potion down her father's throat, but most of it dribbled down his cheeks uselessly.

"He's lost too much blood, Liana. I'm sorry," Damien explained but she wouldn't hear it.

"Please, help me," she called to the goddesses like she had when Cassia was in danger. "Please! You have to help me." She shoved her magic back into her father's veins and called out to the deities for guidance. Someone helped her once before. They guided her on how to save Cassia and her daughter, they could guide her again.

She begged and pleaded, offering her magic at any cost.

"Please," she screamed aloud, her voice cracking. Bowing her head over his body, she felt his chest rise once then fall. She feared that would be the last breath he ever took, tears falling onto his blood-soaked shirt.

Silence fell over her, a warm embrace seeming to envelop her in the same moment. She blinked away her foggy vision to stare at the figure before her. The woman smiled gently at her, her naturally tanned skin glowing from within just as Liana once did. Her glow was dimmed so it didn't blind anyone while ebony locks were gathered in an intricate network of twists and braids woven with strands of gold thread which hung heavily over one shoulder. Wearing a simple sheath of white, the woman's eyes were the most stunning of all as they were a true molten gold.

"Who are you?" Liana asked, her voice soft and worried. Deep down though, she knew who this was. Knew that a goddess knelt before her.

The woman merely smiled and reached for Liana's hands. Her touch barely registered as she guided Liana's hands over her father's body.

"You do not need spells," the woman said, her voice whisper soft and effortlessly melodic. "You are power. You control it. Desire it and you shall achieve it," she guided. "To save your father though, it will come at a price," she warned.

Liana's tears fell faster. "I'll pay it. What is your price?"

The goddess offered a sad smile. "This will drain your magic for days, it will drain all of you for days, and it will only buy him a bit more time."

She choked on a sob. "How much longer? Why cannot he live?"

"You cannot cheat death, my daughter. You may give him months or years. I do not know. That is for the fates to decide."

She had no problem giving up her magic for a few days - and would likely be unconscious for days as well - if it meant getting any amount of time with her father back. Enough time for everyone to savor whatever time they had left and to say goodbyes.

"Fine. Do it. Help me, please."

A power so similar to her own flowed through the woman's hands into hers, the surge of it far greater than anything she'd felt before. Liana's eyes fell closed at the pure euphoric feeling of the goddess's power and followed with her own as she revived Lord Monroe, filling his body with blood once more.

Liana glanced around the others to confirm that this truly happened and was not a twisted fantasy; to confirm that she hadn't lost her mind. When she looked though, the room around them was frozen in time.

"Not frozen, just slowed," the woman said as if reading her thoughts.

The flow of magic stopped, and Liana knew without a doubt that her father lived. She looked back to the goddess, so many questions brewing beneath the surface.

"Why me?" she asked, desperation clawing at her throat. "Why am I this powerful? Why am I different?"

The woman smiled once more and lifted a hand to cup Liana's cheek. "You were destined to be the one. Be brave, daughter."

Liana's eyes widened at her words. They explained nothing, only confused her more.

Daughter? Did she mean daughter as in she was another of her children, just as all in the kingdom were her children? Surely, that was the only explanation. And what did she mean that Liana was destined to be the one? She could only think that it was that prophecy again. Perhaps it was the goddess that spoke it into existence, and if a goddess believed in it, who was Liana to disagree, despite her continued misgivings about the entire prophecy.

In the next second, the glowing woman was gone, and Liana flinched as the noise of the world crashed down upon her once more.

"Liana?" Damien questioned as she swayed over her father, the sudden loss of the goddess and the power required to heal her father from near death causing stars to cross her vision.

"I'm fine," she said through gritted teeth. Below her, Lord Monroe blinked his eyes open. Confusion furrowed his brow when he spotted Liana.

"What are you doing here?" he asked, sitting up quickly. The others gasped in surprise at his sudden recovery, not even realizing that she'd healed him in the brief moment of time where everything seemed to pause around her.

Murmurs started, drifting through the room quickly. Murmurs of a miracle, of god-like power.

"Did you heal him?" Damien asked in a whisper as he settled his arm around her back, pulling her in close and away from prying eyes.

She could only nod, her own shock at seeing the goddess too profound.

Her father leaned in close. "You healed me, Liana? How bad was it?"

She looked to the spot on his neck that had been torn apart moments ago yet was now as smooth and whole as ever. Red coated her fingers. Her father's blood. She had been so close to losing him. If the goddess had not helped her, he likely would be gone.

Damien's arm wrapped around her tighter when tears spilled over her lashes once more. "We did not think you would make it," he answered for her.

Lord Monroe placed a hand on her shoulder. "Thank you, Liana." He glanced around the ruined room and spotted Master Ranville beside them. "The last thing I want to do is draw more attention to you, Liana, but are you able to heal him as well?"

Liana could only shake her head as she felt the deep, gnawing emptiness deep in her chest where her magic usually resided. It was completely gone, as was her price.

"How is Master Ranville?" Lord Monroe asked of the healer.

"He is stable, my Lord. Just needs a bit of rest," the man responded, which was lucky for him because Liana had nothing left to give.

Liana shoved to her feet, Damien hovering and inevitably supporting her as her knees wavered with weakness.

"Are you well, wife?" he questioned, his hands gripping her so tight on her hips that it was painful.

"I will be once you take your claws out of me," she whispered angrily, the loss of her magic leaving her raw and terrified. His fingers loosened instantly.

"Perhaps it is best that you return home, Liana," Lord Monroe suggested as he eyed the room, their whispers growing louder.

"Why? So that I may hide after such a miraculous feat of magic? If I were male, you all would be applauding and praising me for the magic I performed here today, yet you are telling me to run and hide." Despite the male at her back supporting most of her weight, Liana kept her chin held high.

Her father leaned in close. "And I could not be prouder of you or more grateful for you saving my life. However, our people are not used to a powerful female yet and until that day comes, you must give them time to adjust. And that may be safer for you to do at the castle."

Liana didn't want to hide. Her magic didn't deserve to be something the people feared or distrusted. It was gifted by the goddess herself, or so she assumed.

Lord Monroe took her hand in his when he saw that she would not relent. "Truly, daughter, I am astounded and elated by your power, but you must give me time to make the others feel the same. We shall keep you updated on the situation once we know more, for now, please stay safe."

Her head spun precariously, the room tilting at an odd angle. "I want to know everything," she declared to her father before stepping out of Damien's hold. "Luciano," she called for the vampire and instantly grabbed his arm to support herself. "We are going back to the castle."

Without a word to Damien, she walked on wobbly legs toward the exit her hand gripped so tightly on Luciano's arm she was surprised the male didn't say anything. Feeling all eyes on her, she forced herself to walk straight until they were out of the council chambers. He led her off to the side where Liana collapsed against the wall, her breaths coming in quick pants as bile rose in the back of her throat.

"What is wrong?"

Liana swallowed down her nausea just as Damien appeared, kneeling beside Luciano. "I can feel you are ill, what's wrong?" he questioned, his hand cupping her cheek.

Liana shoved him off. "Leave me be. Luciano, take me home, please."

"Do not be angry with me. I left you behind because I am only ever concerned for your safety."

"I am weak and drained. I doubt I'll make it back to the castle before passing out. So let's leave this discussion for later," she declared. "Luciano, now please." Liana lifted her arms toward the vampire hoping he would take her side and just get her out of there.

He lifted Liana into her arms.

"We shall speak when I return," Damien said.

Liana would hold him to it.

Chapter Twenty-five

The moment Luciano set her down in bed, Liana rolled over and vomited onto the floor. The man moved quickly though and caught most in a wash basin before setting it outside on the balcony so the smell didn't linger.

A cold sweat wracked her body before the shivering started.

"Is this normal?" he asked.

Liana thought it had just been magic depletion again, but this felt different. She felt like she was dying. "I need Phillipa."

Luciano nodded and raced away only to return quickly with Phillipa in his arms. Her maid's eyes widened at all the blood soaked through her gown and Liana's pale face.

"Gods, what happened? Where are you hurt? We need a healer!"

"It's not her blood. She used magic to save many people and then she fell ill," Luciano explained.

Phillipa wiped a hand over Liana's sweaty brow. "What do you need?"

"I.. I don't... know." Her voice stuttered as her body shook. "I feel terrible."

"I will fetch a healer," Luciano declared.

Before he could run off, a blinding gold light filled the room then Liana felt the bed dip behind her.

"Not to worry," the goddess said, her voice stronger and more tangible than before. She gathered Liana into her arms and stroked a hand through her hair.

Beside the bed, Phillipa gasped and stumbled backward while Luciano went as rigid as a statue. "She is finally transitioning into what she was always meant to be," she stated, her words soft and prideful.

Calming power entered Liana's body, stilling the shivers and relieving the cold sweat. Liana sighed in relief.

"Who are you?" Luciano asked, his voice softer than she'd ever heard it before.

Liana looked up to the softly glowing woman, knowing in her bones that this woman holding her so gently with magic that felt so similar to her own was a goddess. "Juno," she whispered reverently.

Juno smiled brightly and nodded, her fingers still gently combing through Liana's hair.

Phillipa gasped and dropped to her knees, bowing her head all the way to the floor while Luciano dropped to one knee.

"Is the prophecy true then?" he questioned.

The goddess nodded which had Liana groaning.

"Great, now he will be a smug ass for the rest of eternity," Liana complained.

Juno laughed. "I spoke that prophecy to your grandfather, the first King of Triaedian, knowing that she would be needed in time."

Luciano bowed his head. "It is an honor to meet you, Goddess Juno. And an even greater honor to hear your truths." He glanced at Liana for a moment then back to the deity. "How may I be of service to you, to Liana?"

"Valiant warrior, you are doing all that is required. Protect her. Love her. Cherish her. And I will ask that you and your grandson guide her through what is to come."

He raised a questioning brow. "What is to come?"

"Liana gave all her magic to save her father today. When she goes to sleep soon, she will rest for days as she transitions into what she was always meant to be."

Phillipa finally climbed off the floor and took Liana's hand in her own. "What transition?"

"Her magic will come back with time. It will grow stronger, an extension of my own, and she will become immortal like her mate."

Phillipa gasped and praised the goddess.

"Do I really need *more* power?" Liana questioned. What magic she had already caused her great suffering.

"For what is to come, you will need it. For now, you must rest and when you wake, you will be reborn."

"What am I supposed to do? How do I save Triaedian?" Liana asked, sensing that the goddess would leave soon.

"Trust in yourself, Liana. You are exactly who you need to be." The deity disappeared, her comforting embrace and golden glow leaving the world feeling unusually gray and cold.

Phillipa cursed as she gathered Liana into her arms. "Child, you are amazing. The gods truly blessed you."

"The Goddess Juno blessed me," she corrected, her body beginning to shiver once more. "I do not feel well again," she complained, hunching over her stomach.

"Perhaps we should aid you into sleep until this transformation is complete," Luciano suggested. Liana nodded. Anything would be better than how she felt now.

"Someone please tell Damien about this. He will be worried when I don't wake."

"We will take care of everything, sweetheart. You just rest now."

Luciano ran out, presumably to get a sleeping potion. Despite the shocking news and being in the presence of a goddess, the lack of magic left Liana feeling empty more than anything else. None of it could stop thoughts of her father either which had her tearing up again. She only bought him some time, and there was no telling how much time.

Sleep would be a much needed reprieve from the grief filling her.

***

She woke slowly from sleep, not recalling any dreams if she had any. Her body felt well rested and languid, her mind sharp and ready for the day. Her magic pulsed happily in her chest, back with her once more.

Rolling onto her side, she stretched like a cat, bumping into Damien. He jolted out of sleep, his eyes wide and inspecting.

"How long was I out?" she questioned, remembering precisely what happened before she passed out.

"Five days," he answered, his voice gruff from sleep. Dawn peeked in through the windows highlighting his unshaven beard and the shadows beneath his eyes.

"You worried that whole time, didn't you?" she accused. "I told them to tell you what was happening..."

He cut her off, pulling her into his chest and kissing her. "Knowing what is happening and understanding are two very different things. Neither helped me worry any less. The first night, your heart stopped for at least a minute ten times. I had a vampire and the healers in here round the clock to keep an eye on you."

Her body shivered at the terror in his voice. She had no idea it would be so dramatic. "I'm sorry you had to sit through that. I didn't know. She said I would just sleep and be reborn."

He blew out a heavy breath.

"Can I go now?" Luciano questioned, surprising her. She glanced toward their bedroom door where he already stood with his hand on the doorknob.

"Yes. Thank you." Damien snuggled down into the bed once he was gone. "I had him listen to your heart so I could get some sleep."

"Oh Damien, I'm sorry." She could only imagine how much of a wreck she would have been if put in his position.

"Hush, now. It's over. Tell me, do you feel reborn?" he teased, shoving aside his own turmoil to comfort her.

"I feel refreshed and strong. I'm not sure about anything else. My magic is certainly back too."

"Good. We can practice later." His eyes drifted closed.

"Take my blood, Damien. You look like death." Holding her wrist to his mouth, he didn't bite, already asleep. She created two small punctures in her wrist with magic. He latched on out of instinct, his eyes popping open. "You can sleep after you drink." Thankfully, he drank his fill.

"You taste the same, just far more potent on the magic. It feels like tingling on my tongue."

"Is that a bad feeling?" she worried.

"No, just different. You're still my favorite blood source." He grinned, the skin lighter beneath his eyes already.

"How many titles are you going to give me? Blood source, temptress, vixen, little mage, wife, and queen. I doubt I can hold much more."

Laughing, he buried his nose in her neck. "I'll give you a thousand more, goddess."

"That is not going to be one of them. I'm not a goddess."

"She gifted you her power and immortality. Close enough."

Sighing, she ran her fingers through his thick hair and scratched along his scalp. "Goddess Juno. I cannot believe I met her. She spoke to me, even ran her fingers through my hair just like this."

He purred deep in his chest, his breath teasing her neck. "I'd never seen Grandfather so mystified. She was all he could talk about for hours. Phillipa couldn't even speak after they told me what happened."

She savored this moment with him in her arms as she remembered the warnings from Juno. "She said I only bought my father time, that death would come for him soon."

His arms tightened around her. "I am sorry, my love. We will be sure to leave him with extra guards and a healer."

She shook her head, tears forming in her eyes. "He cannot cheat death twice. That was part of the price. I had to go through this transition and he would only get a bit more time."

"Then we will be sure to spend as much time with him as possible."

A tear dripped down her cheek landing in his hair. "What of her other warnings? She said I had to be prepared for what is to come. What is coming?"

"I can take a guess and say the separatists."

Frowning at the obvious answer, she wondered what they were planning. "Was the attack on the mage council orchestrated by the separatists?"

"It appears so. Someone had to have locked my guards out and let the rogue vampire in. Such an outright attack on the mage by a vampire does not buy us any favors for unity among the breeds. It has further divided the people."

"Is it not obvious to them that it is just the work of the separatists? There is nothing to be afraid of otherwise."

"They believe what they want to believe. Some people spread lies while we try to spread the truth. It will always be that way with the crown versus the separatists."

She huffed, her nails digging a bit too hard into his scalp which had him nipping at the skin of her throat. "Sorry. I'm just so upset. How can they be so strong? Even if I didn't completely decimate their numbers that day at the lake, it should have weakened them significantly."

"They regrouped, recruited more. They are turning too many to their side with these attacks as of late too."

"What do we do to stop them?" What she really wanted to know was, how did she become the savior to stop all of this killing and separatist idiocy?

"We are doing our best to quell some of the terror and to find those responsible."

"I'll help. I don't know how yet, but I will help."

He kissed her neck. "My brave queen," he whispered.

"Seriously, Damien. I am going to help." He hummed, his head nodding the barest bit on her chest. "You rest, and I'll come up with a masterful plan to end them for good."

His chest rumbled with a weak laugh. Softening her fingers, she continued running them over his scalp.

It wasn't entirely a joke when she said she'd come up with a plan. It would be a very short and vague plan because she had no idea what she was doing but she'd figure something out.

There were a lot of things she had to figure out. First and foremost, what did she transition into? How had her magic changed and how could she use it all to her advantage? If she were to be this savior Juno expected her to be, she had a lot of work to do.

The next few months would be busy, she could already predict. Between training her magic, resuming combat training, trying to deal with the separatists and keeping up with her queenly responsibilities, she would be busy.

That wouldn't be terrible though. She'd have Damien by her side. She'd have his family to support her as well, even if she was making this up as she went along.

One thing was certain though, she felt more determined than ever to prove that she was worthy, that she was given this magic for a purpose and she wouldn't let anyone down.

Holding Damien, she let him rest, soaking in these last few peaceful moments before their lives would become infinitely more complicated. As she'd told him before though, with him by her side, she could do anything.

Afterword

Thank you for sticking through this lengthy journey with me.

Liana and Damien's story will come to a close in Improper Savior.

I promise to not make you wait so long for the third and final book.

Acknowledgments

Thank you to my family and friends for supporting me all the way. Thank you to my best friend and sister for listening to me rant and rave about life and my writing. Thank you for always making time for me.

Thank you to everyone that is following along with Liana and Damien. This second book has been a long time coming.